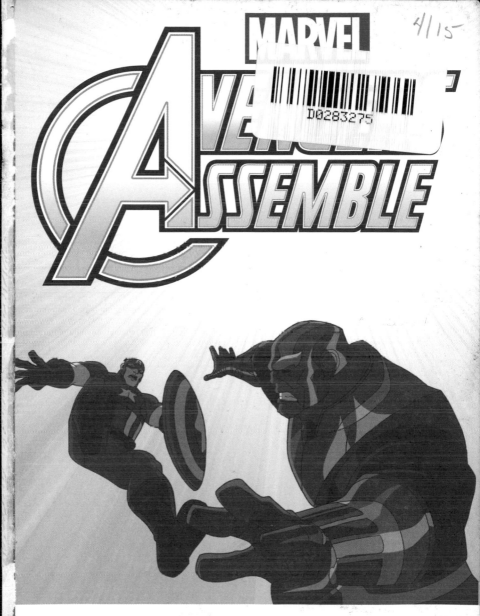

MARVEL UNIVERSE ALL-NEW AVENGERS ASSEMBLE VOL. 1. Contains material originally published in magazine form as MARVEL UNIVERSE AVENGERS ASSEMBLE SEASON TWO #1-4. First printing 2015. ISBN# 978-0-7851-9358-6. Published by MARVEL WORLDWIDE, INC., a subsidiary of MARVEL ENTERTAINMENT, LLC. OFFICE OF PUBLICATION: 135 West 50th Street, New York, NY 10020. Copyright © 2014 and 2015 Marvel Characters, Inc. All rights reserved. All characters featured in this issue and the distinctive names and likenesses thereof, and all related indicia are trademarks of Marvel Characters, Inc. No similarity between any of the names, characters, persons, and/or institutions in this magazine with those of any living or dead person or institution is intended, and any such similarity which may exist is purely coincidental. **Printed in the U.S.A.** ALAN FINE, EVP - Office of the President, Marvel Worldwide, Inc. and EVP & CMO Marvel Characters B.V.; DAN BUCKLEY, Publisher & President - Print, Animation & Digital Divisions; JOE QUESADA, Chief Creative Officer; TOM BREVOORT, SVP of Publishing; DAVID BOGART, SVP of Operations & Procurement, Publishing; C.B. CEBULSKI, SVP of Creator & Content Development; DAVID GABRIEL, SVP Print, Sales & Marketing; JIM O'KEEFE, VP of Operations & Logistics; DAN CARR, Executive Director of Publishing Technology; SUSAN CRESPI, Editorial Operations Manager; ALEX MORALES, Publishing Operations Manager; STAN LEE, Chairman Emeritus. For information regarding advertising in Marvel Comics or on Marvel.com, please contact Niza Disla, Director of Marvel Partnerships, at ndisla@marvel.com. For Marvel subscription inquiries, please call 800-217-9158. **Manufactured between 2/13/2015 and 3/23/2015 by SHERIDAN BOOKS, INC., CHELSEA, MI, USA.**

10 9 8 7 6 5 4 3 2 1

MARVEL

AVENGERS ASSEMBLE

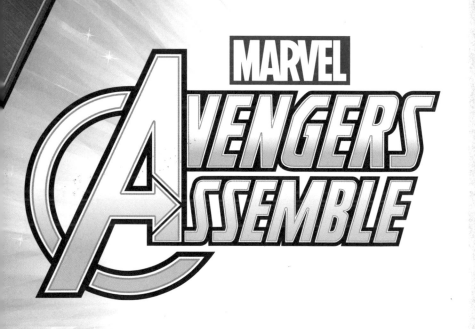

Based on the TV series written by
**KEVIN BURKE, CHRIS "DOC" WYATT,
MAN OF ACTION, JAY FAERBER &
TODD CASEY**

Directed by
TIM ELDRED & PAUL PIGNOTTI

Art by
MARVEL ANIMATION

Adapted by
JOE CARAMAGNA

Special Thanks to Jenny Whitlock & Product Factory

Editor
SEBASTIAN GIRNER

Consulting Editor
JON MOISAN

Senior Editor
MARK PANICCIA

Collection Editor
ALEX STARBUCK

Assistant Editor
SARAH BRUNSTAD

Editors, Special Projects
JENNIFER GRÜNWALD & MARK D. BEAZLEY

Senior Editor, Special Projects
JEFF YOUNGQUIST

SVP Print, Sales & Marketing
DAVID GABRIEL

Head of Marvel Television
JEPH LOEB

Book Designer
JOE FRONTIRRE

Editor In Chief
AXEL ALONSO

Chief Creative Officer
JOE QUESADA

Publisher
DAN BUCKLEY

Executive Producer
ALAN FINE

AVENGERS created by
STAN LEE & JACK KIRBY

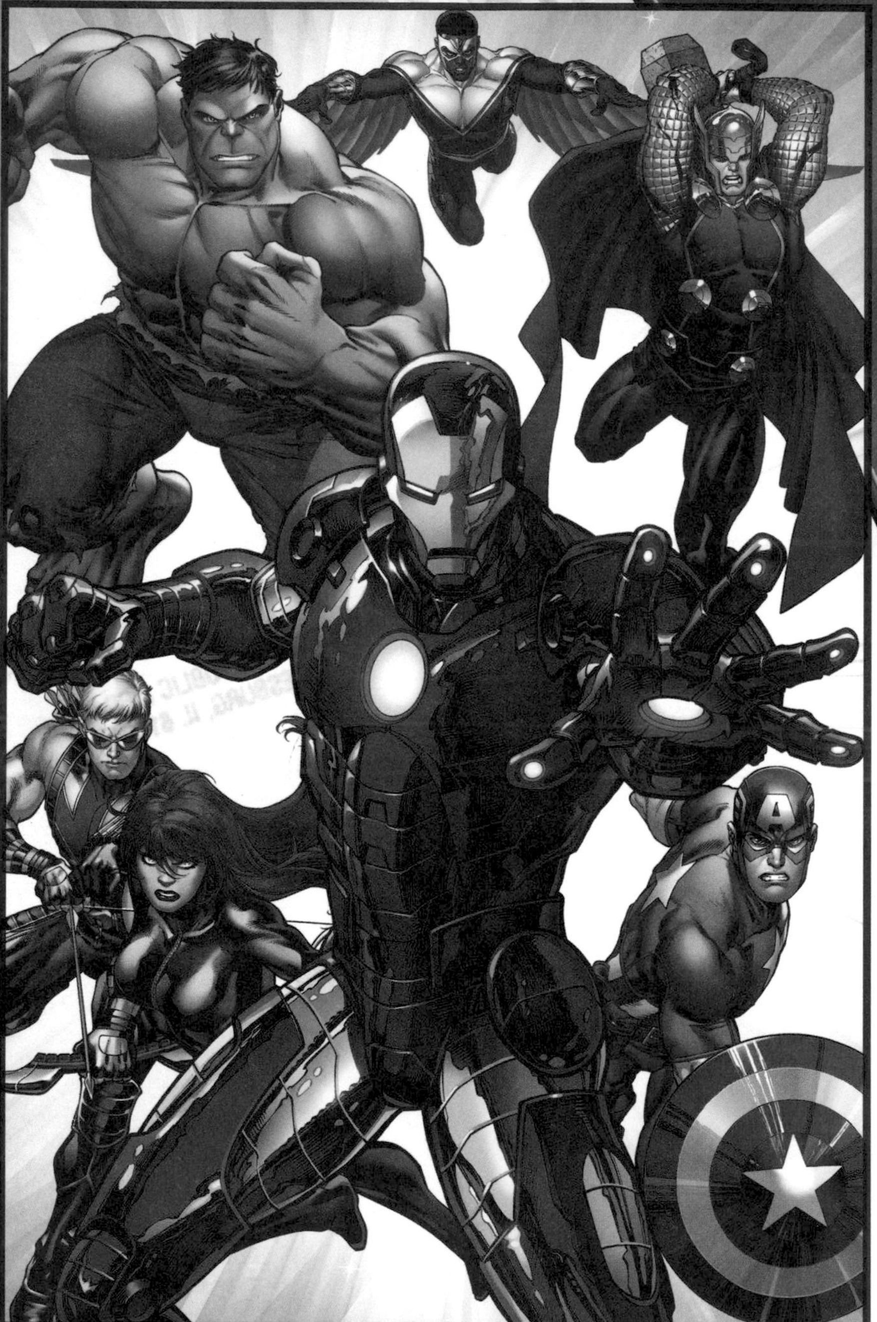

#1 BASED ON "THE ARSENAL"

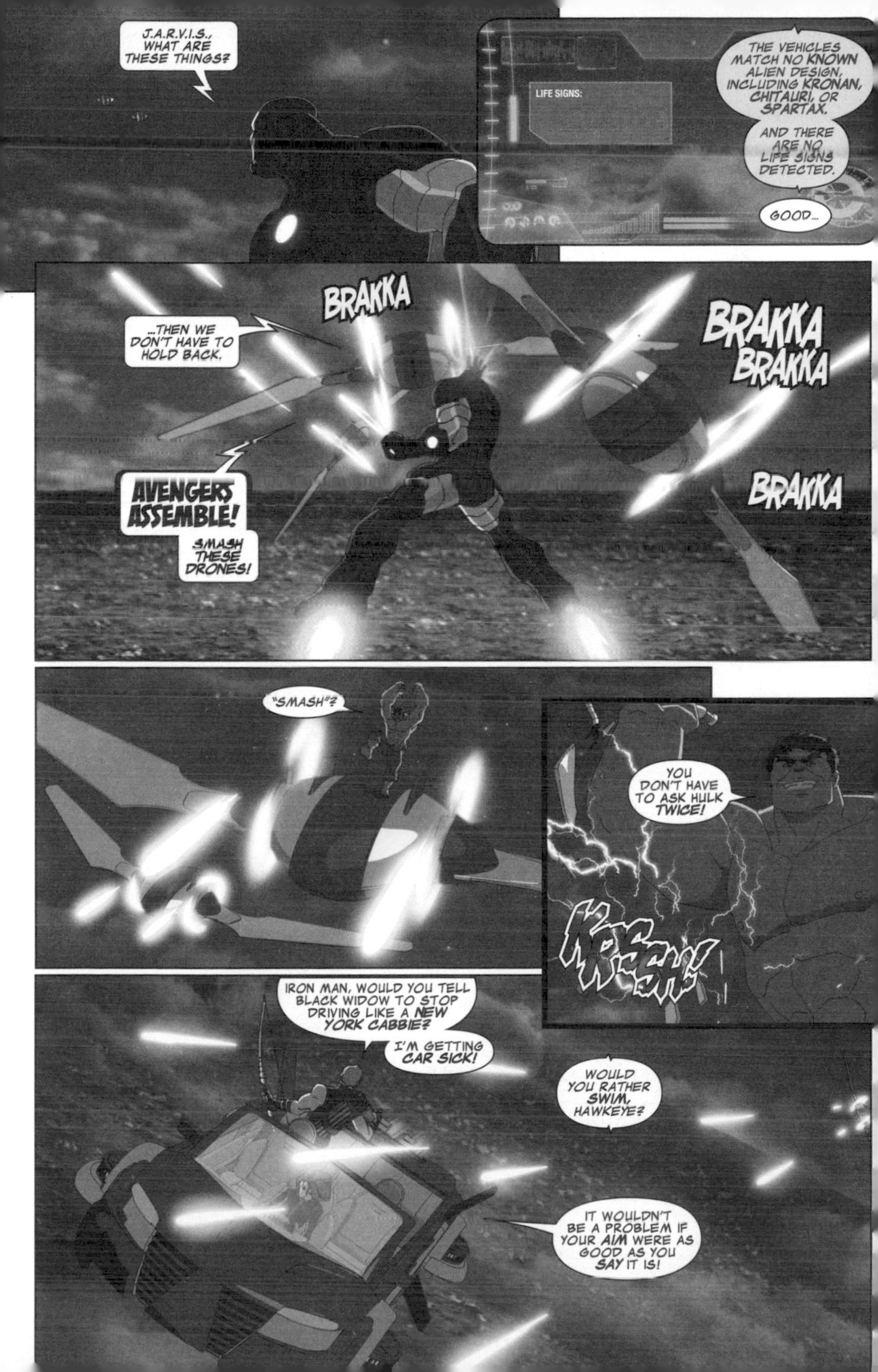
J.A.R.V.I.S., WHAT ARE THESE THINGS?
LIFE SIGNS:
THE VEHICLES MATCH NO KNOWN ALIEN DESIGN, INCLUDING KRONAN, CHITAURI, OR SPARTAX.
AND THERE ARE NO LIFE SIGNS DETECTED.
GOOD...
BRAKKA
...THEN WE DON'T HAVE TO HOLD BACK.
BRAKKA BRAKKA
BRAKKA
AVENGERS ASSEMBLE!
SMASH THESE DRONES!
"SMASH"?
YOU DON'T HAVE TO ASK HULK TWICE!
KRSSH!
IRON MAN, WOULD YOU TELL BLACK WIDOW TO STOP DRIVING LIKE A NEW YORK CABBIE?
I'M GETTING CAR SICK!
WOULD YOU RATHER SWIM, HAWKEYE?
IT WOULDN'T BE A PROBLEM IF YOUR AIM WERE AS GOOD AS YOU SAY IT IS!

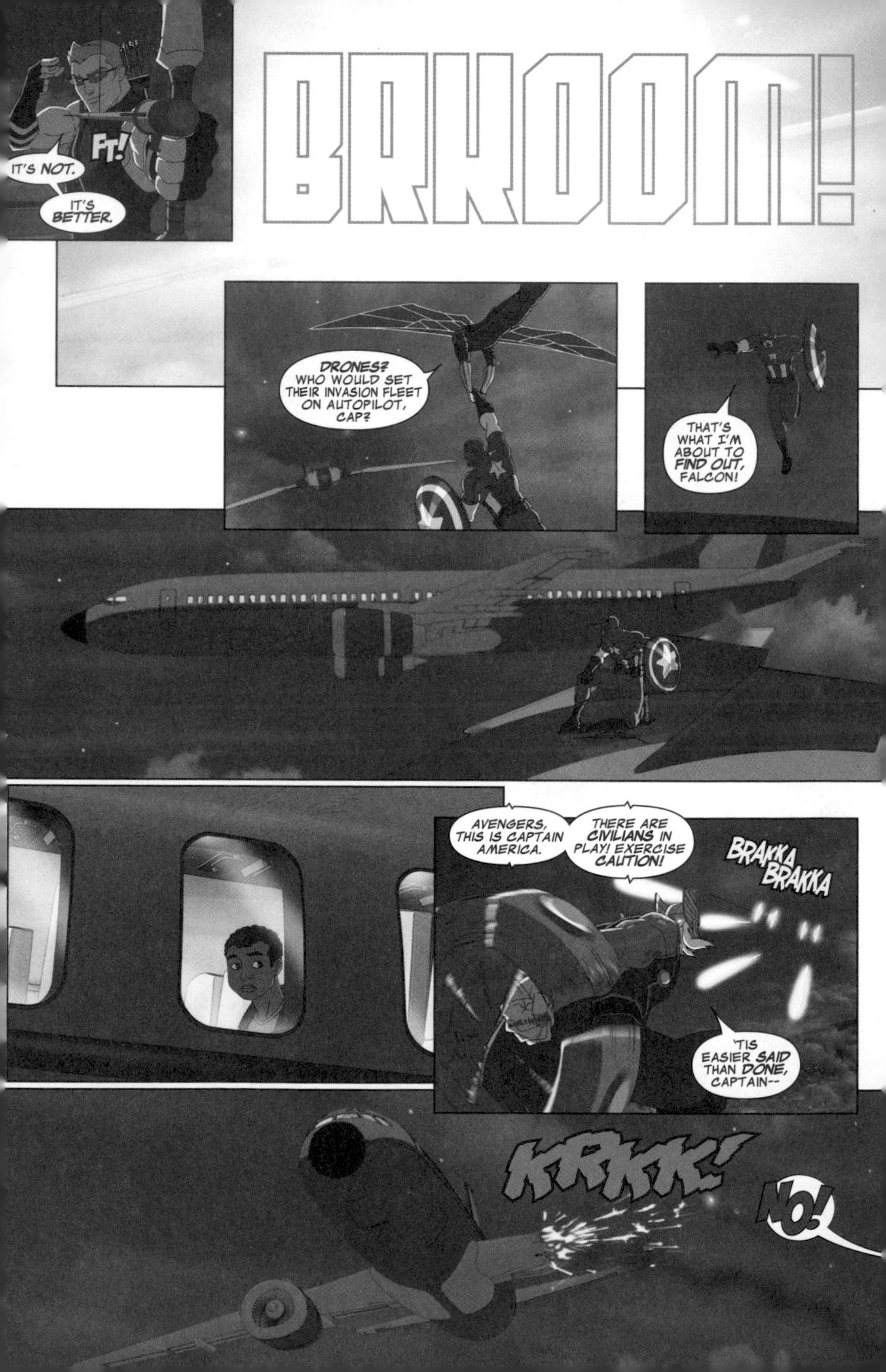
FT!
IT'S NOT.
IT'S BETTER.
BRKOOM!
DRONES? WHO WOULD SET THEIR INVASION FLEET ON AUTOPILOT, CAP?
THAT'S WHAT I'M ABOUT TO FIND OUT, FALCON!
AVENGERS, THIS IS CAPTAIN AMERICA.
THERE ARE CIVILIANS IN PLAY! EXERCISE CAUTION!
BRAKKA BRAKKA
'TIS EASIER SAID THAN DONE, CAPTAIN--
KRKK!
NO!

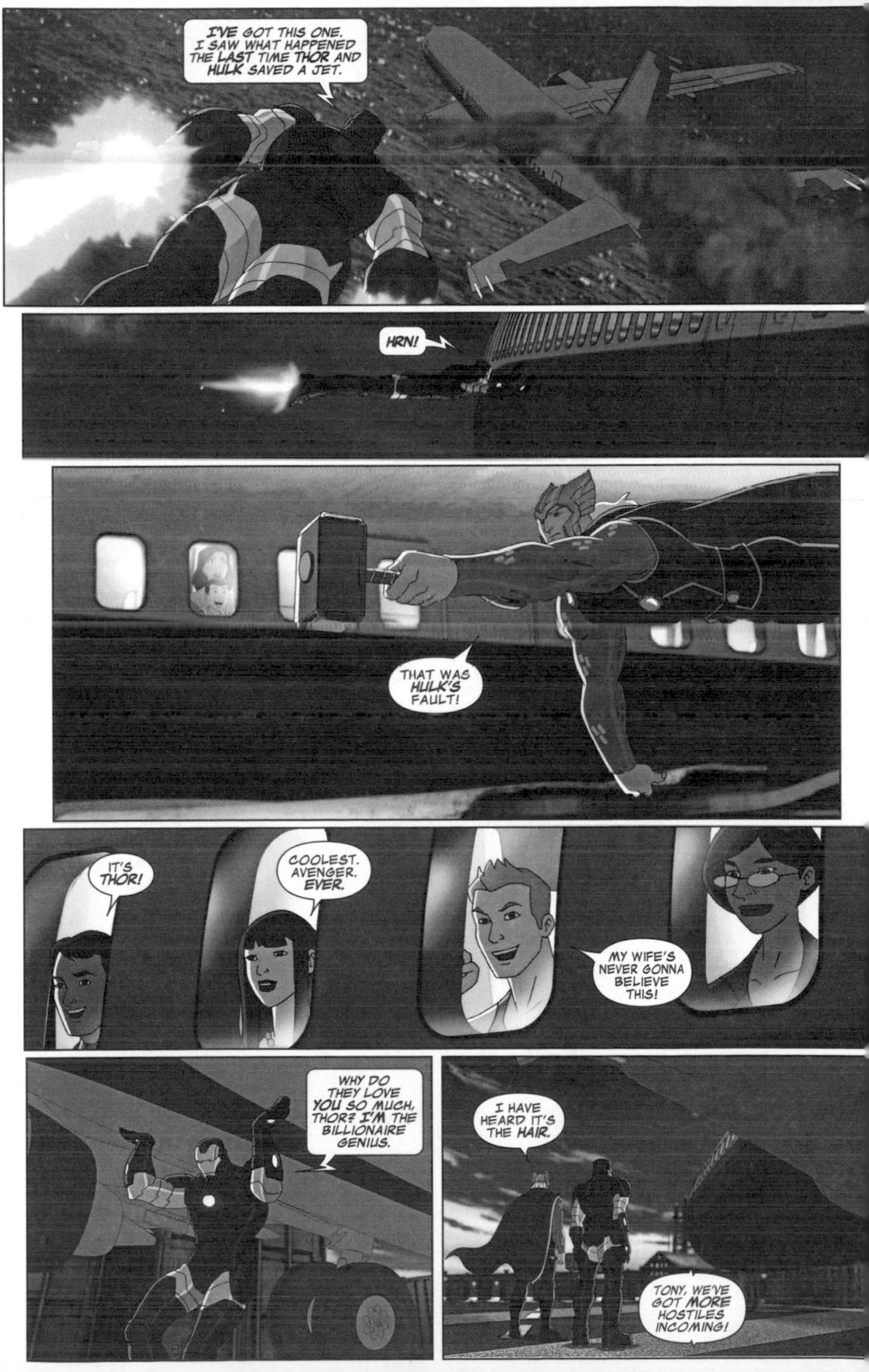
I'VE GOT THIS ONE. I SAW WHAT HAPPENED THE LAST TIME THOR AND HULK SAVED A JET.
HRN!
THAT WAS HULK'S FAULT!
IT'S THOR!
COOLEST. AVENGER. EVER.
MY WIFE'S NEVER GONNA BELIEVE THIS!
WHY DO THEY LOVE YOU SO MUCH, THOR? I'M THE BILLIONAIRE GENIUS.
I HAVE HEARD IT'S THE HAIR.
TONY, WE'VE GOT MORE HOSTILES INCOMING!

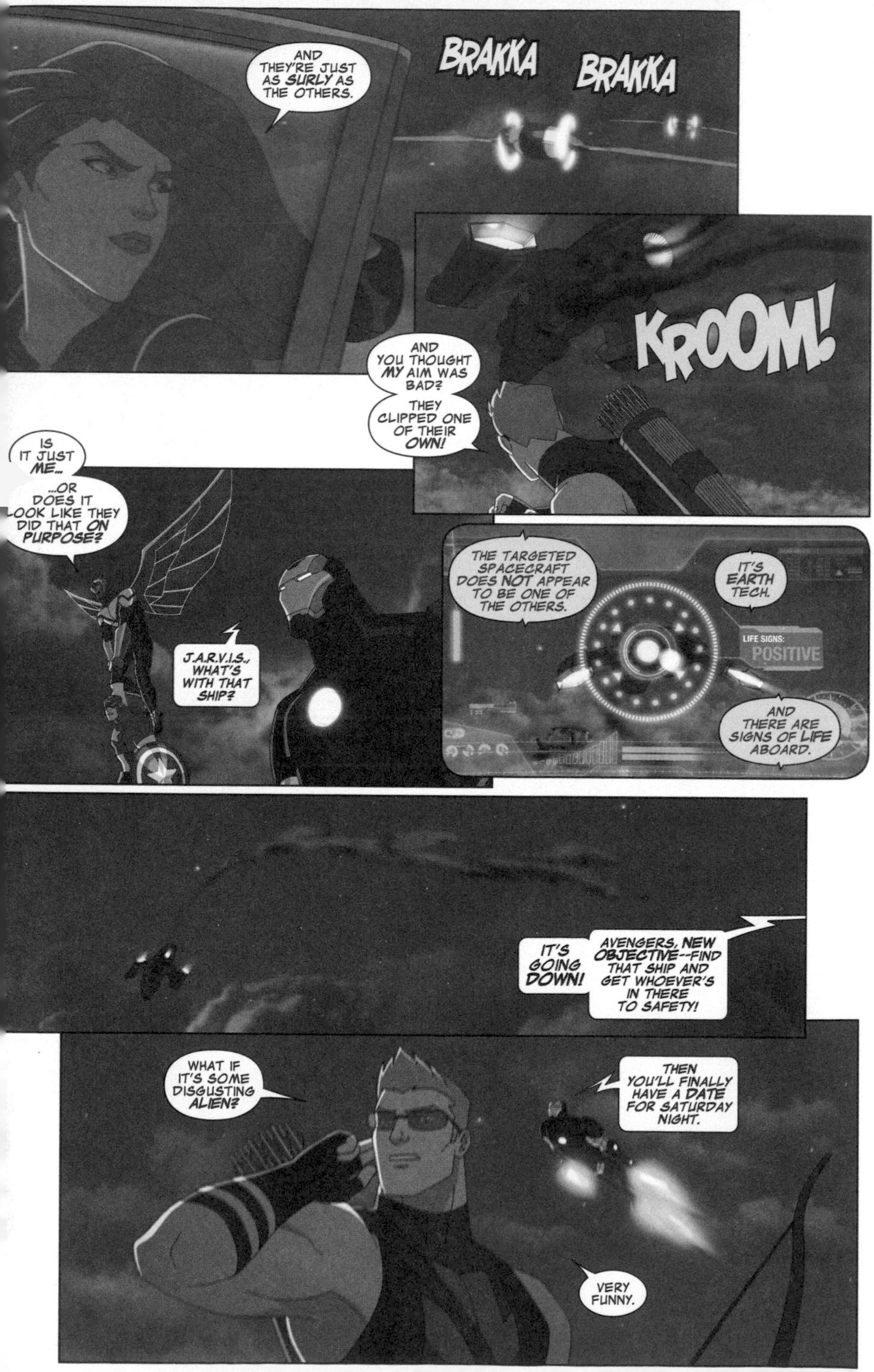
AND THEY'RE JUST AS SURLY AS THE OTHERS.
BRAKKA BRAKKA
KROOM!
AND YOU THOUGHT MY AIM WAS BAD?
THEY CLIPPED ONE OF THEIR OWN!
IS IT JUST ME...
...OR DOES IT LOOK LIKE THEY DID THAT ON PURPOSE?
J.A.R.V.I.S., WHAT'S WITH THAT SHIP?
THE TARGETED SPACECRAFT DOES NOT APPEAR TO BE ONE OF THE OTHERS.
IT'S EARTH TECH.
LIFE SIGNS: POSITIVE
AND THERE ARE SIGNS OF LIFE ABOARD.
IT'S GOING DOWN!
AVENGERS, NEW OBJECTIVE--FIND THAT SHIP AND GET WHOEVER'S IN THERE TO SAFETY!
WHAT IF IT'S SOME DISGUSTING ALIEN?
THEN YOU'LL FINALLY HAVE A DATE FOR SATURDAY NIGHT.
VERY FUNNY.

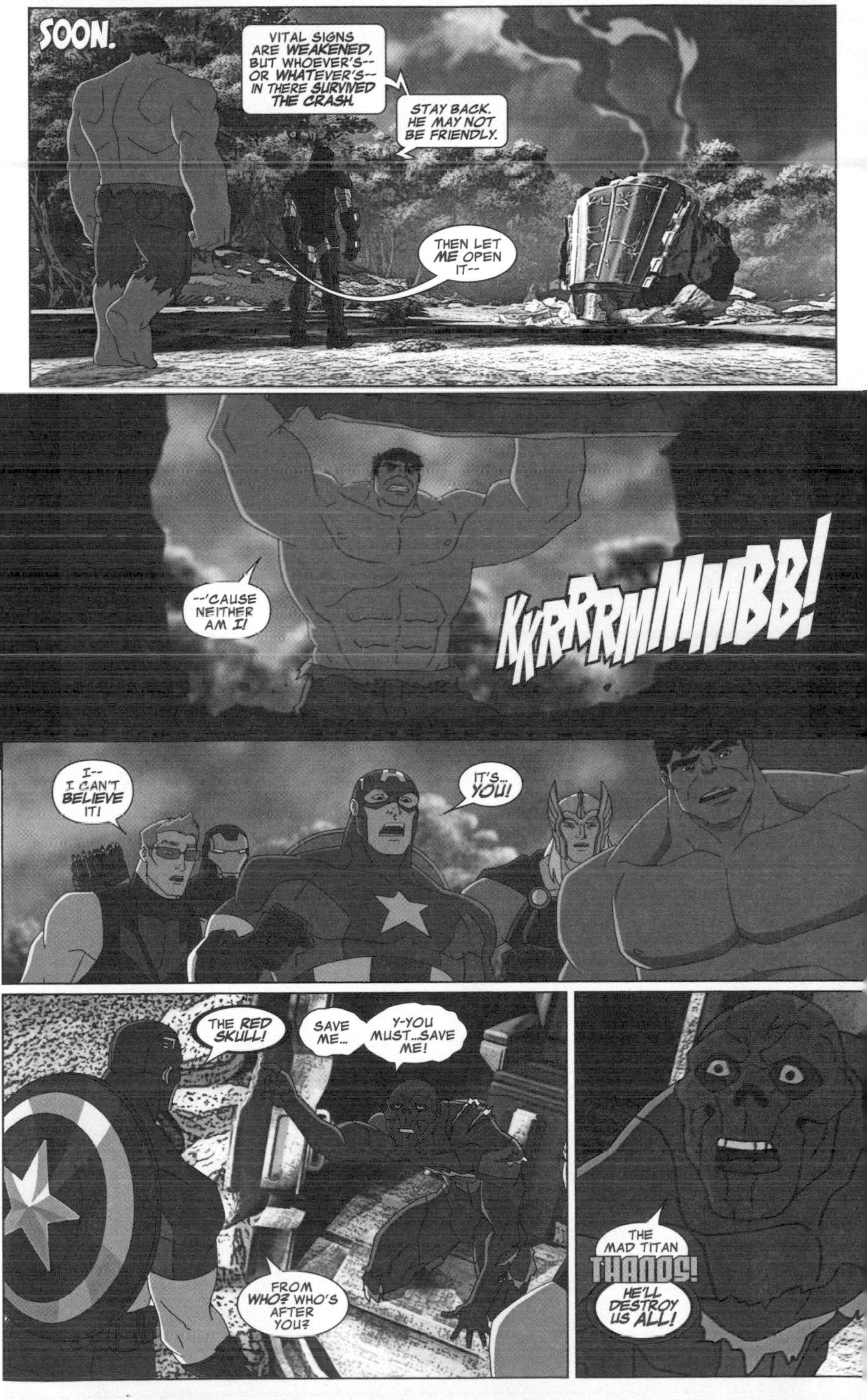
SOON.
VITAL SIGNS ARE WEAKENED, BUT WHOEVER'S-- OR WHATEVER'S-- IN THERE SURVIVED THE CRASH.
STAY BACK. HE MAY NOT BE FRIENDLY.
THEN LET ME OPEN IT--
--'CAUSE NEITHER AM I!
KKRRRMMMBB!
I-- I CAN'T BELIEVE IT!
IT'S... YOU!
THE RED SKULL!
SAVE ME...
Y-YOU MUST...SAVE ME!
FROM WHO? WHO'S AFTER YOU?
THE MAD TITAN THANOS! HE'LL DESTROY US ALL!

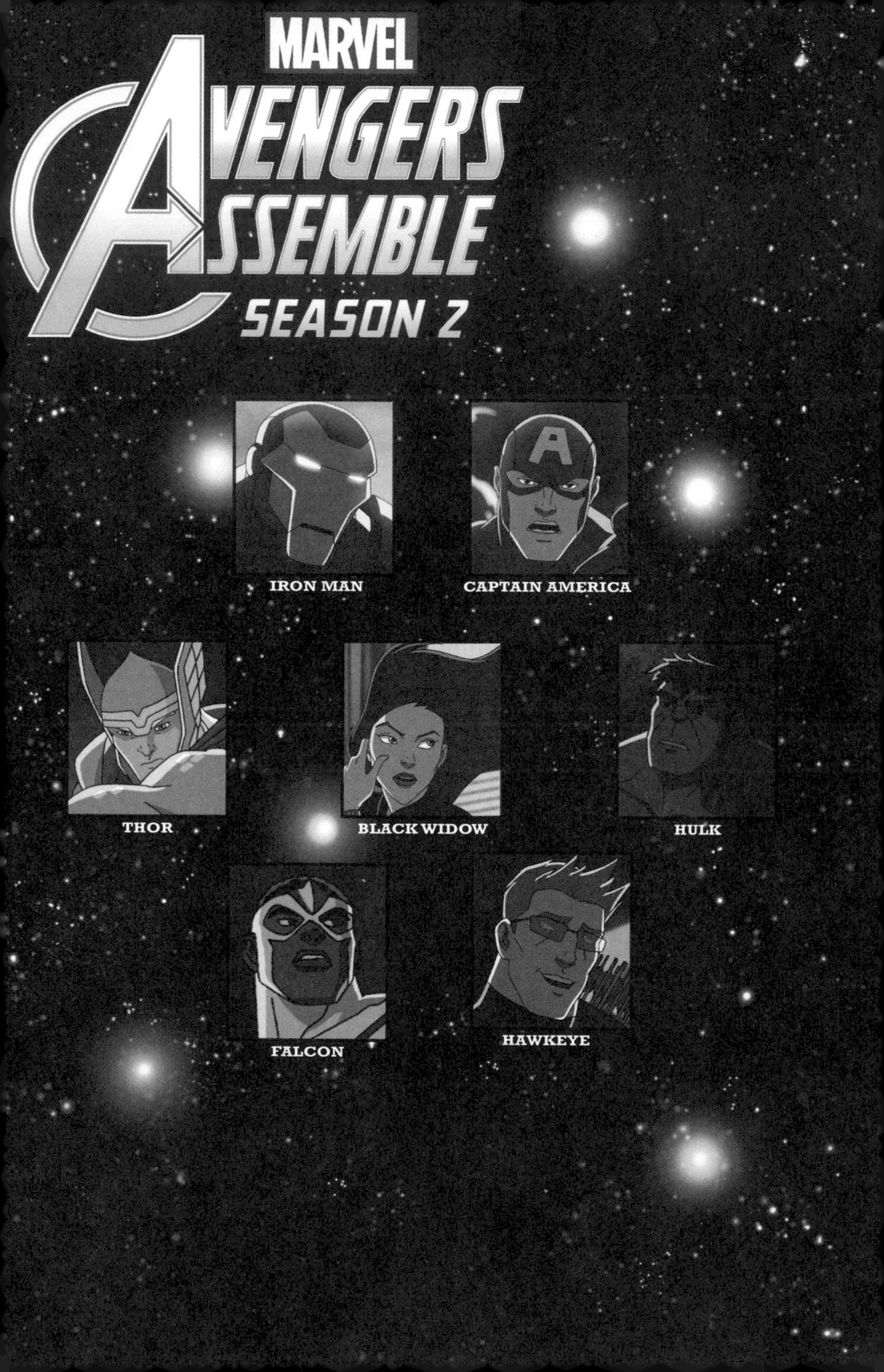
MARVEL
AVENGERS ASSEMBLE
SEASON 2
IRON MAN
CAPTAIN AMERICA
THOR
BLACK WIDOW
HULK
FALCON
HAWKEYE

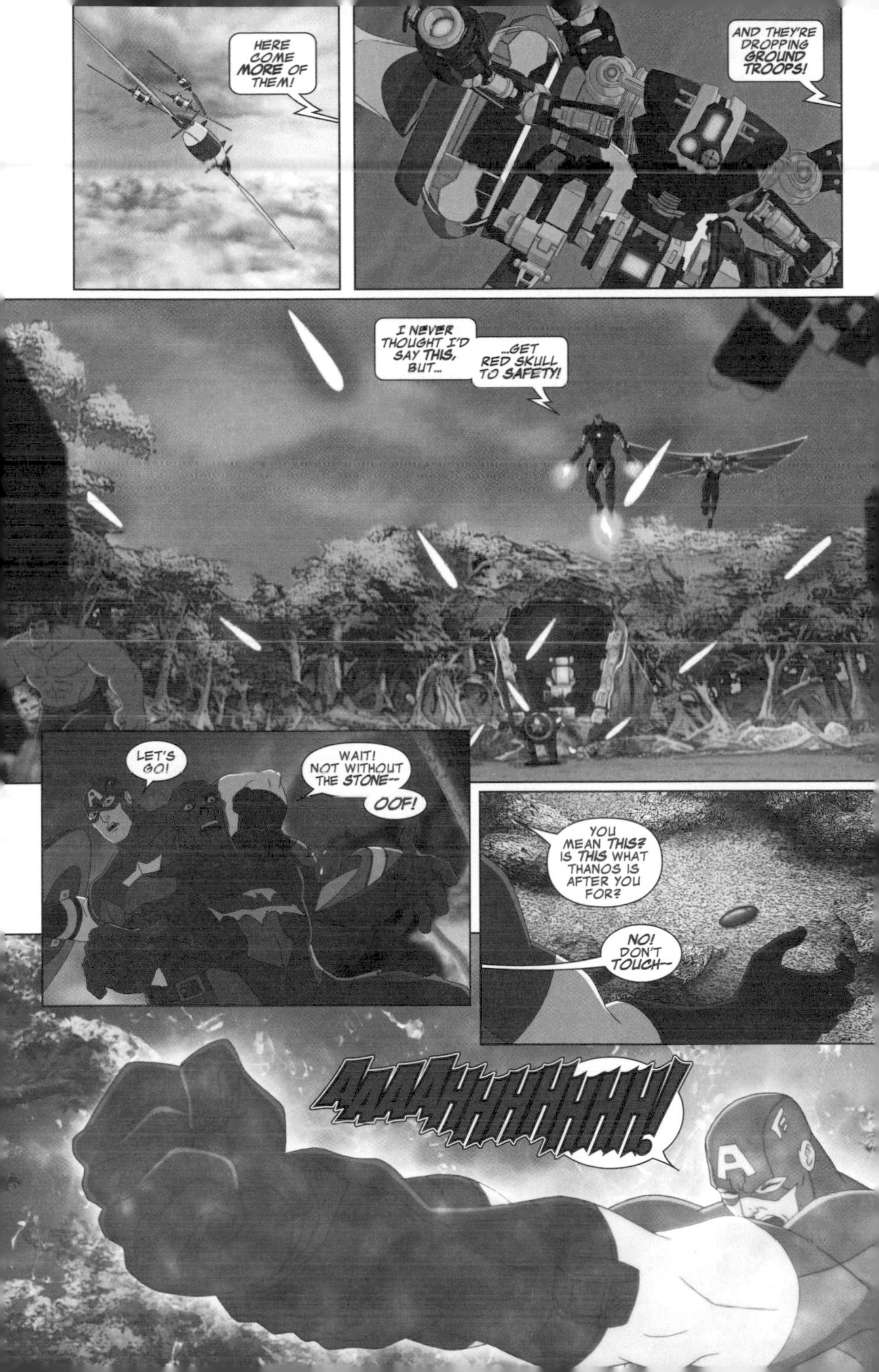
HERE COME MORE OF THEM!
AND THEY'RE DROPPING GROUND TROOPS!
I NEVER THOUGHT I'D SAY THIS, BUT...
...GET RED SKULL TO SAFETY!
LET'S GO!
WAIT! NOT WITHOUT THE STONE--
OOF!
YOU MEAN THIS? IS THIS WHAT THANOS IS AFTER YOU FOR?
NO! DON'T TOUCH--
AAAAHHHHHHHH!

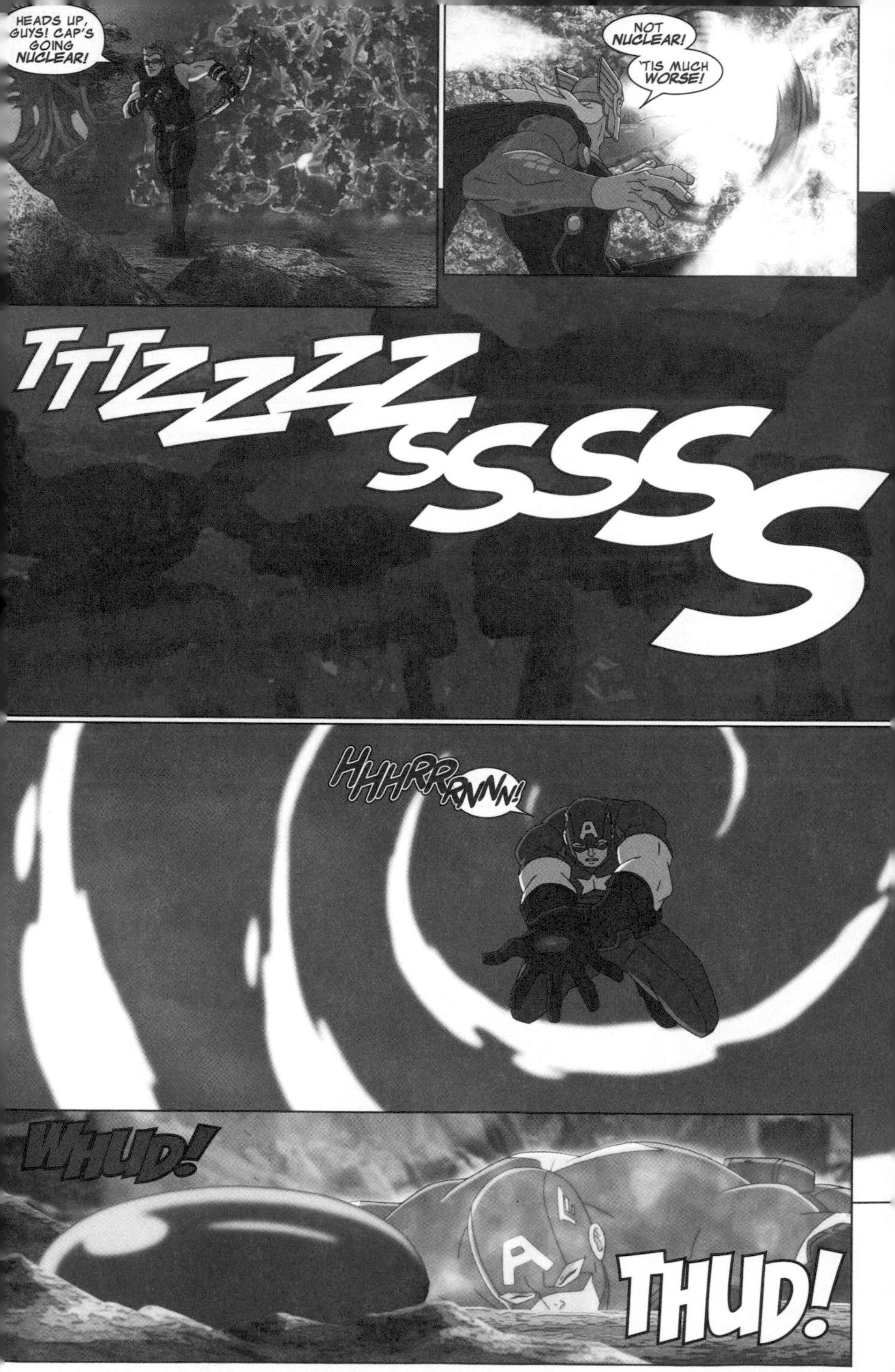
HEADS UP, GUYS! CAP'S GOING NUCLEAR!
NOT NUCLEAR!
'TIS MUCH WORSE!
TTTZZZZSSSSS
HHHRRRNNN!
WHUD!
THUD!

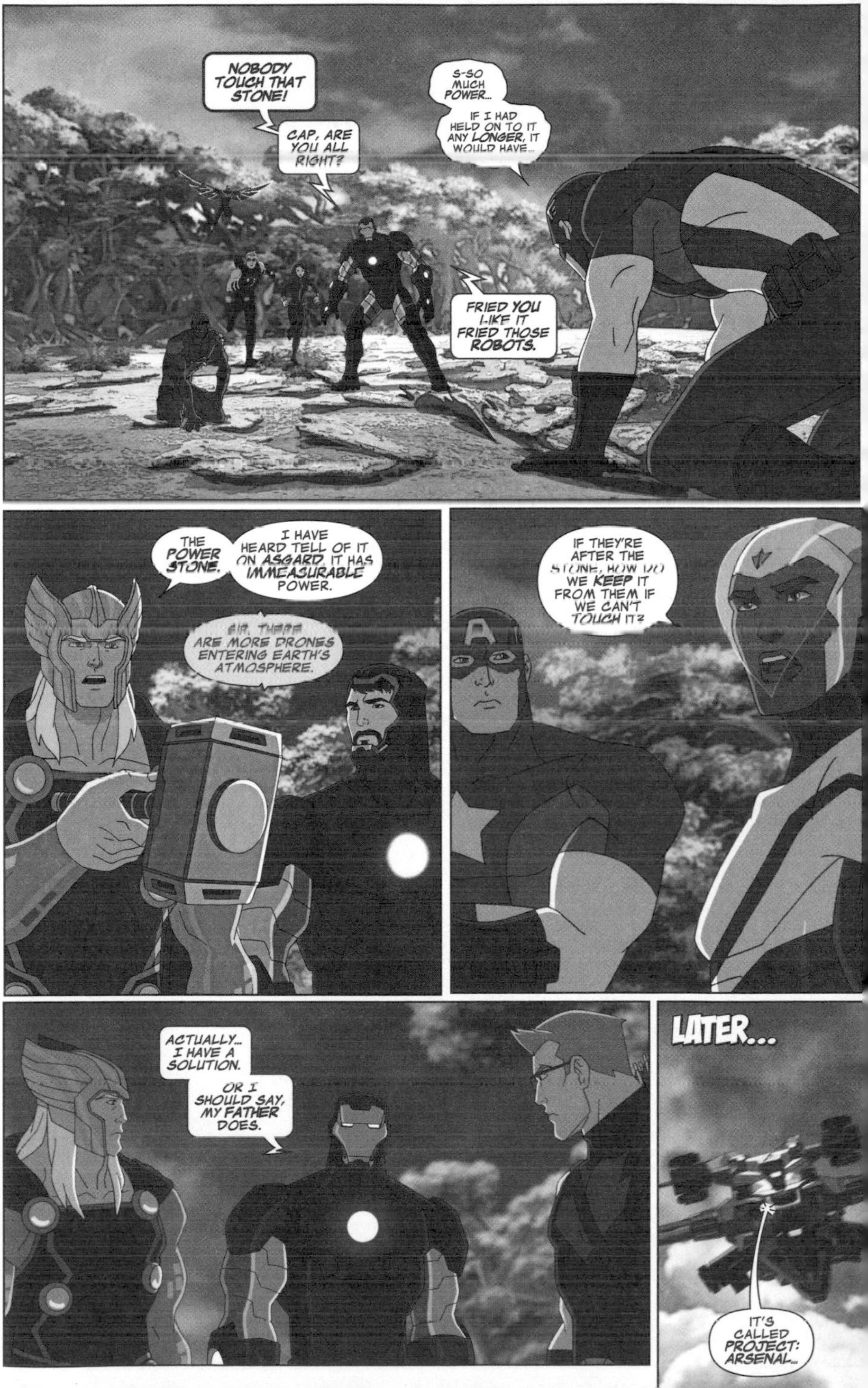
NOBODY TOUCH THAT STONE!
CAP, ARE YOU ALL RIGHT?
S-SO MUCH POWER...
IF I HAD HELD ON TO IT ANY LONGER, IT WOULD HAVE...
FRIED YOU LIKE IT FRIED THOSE ROBOTS.
THE POWER STONE.
I HAVE HEARD TELL OF IT ON ASGARD. IT HAS IMMEASURABLE POWER.
SIR, THERE ARE MORE DRONES ENTERING EARTH'S ATMOSPHERE.
IF THEY'RE AFTER THE STONE, HOW DO WE KEEP IT FROM THEM IF WE CAN'T TOUCH IT?
ACTUALLY... I HAVE A SOLUTION.
OR I SHOULD SAY, MY FATHER DOES.
LATER...
IT'S CALLED PROJECT: ARSENAL...

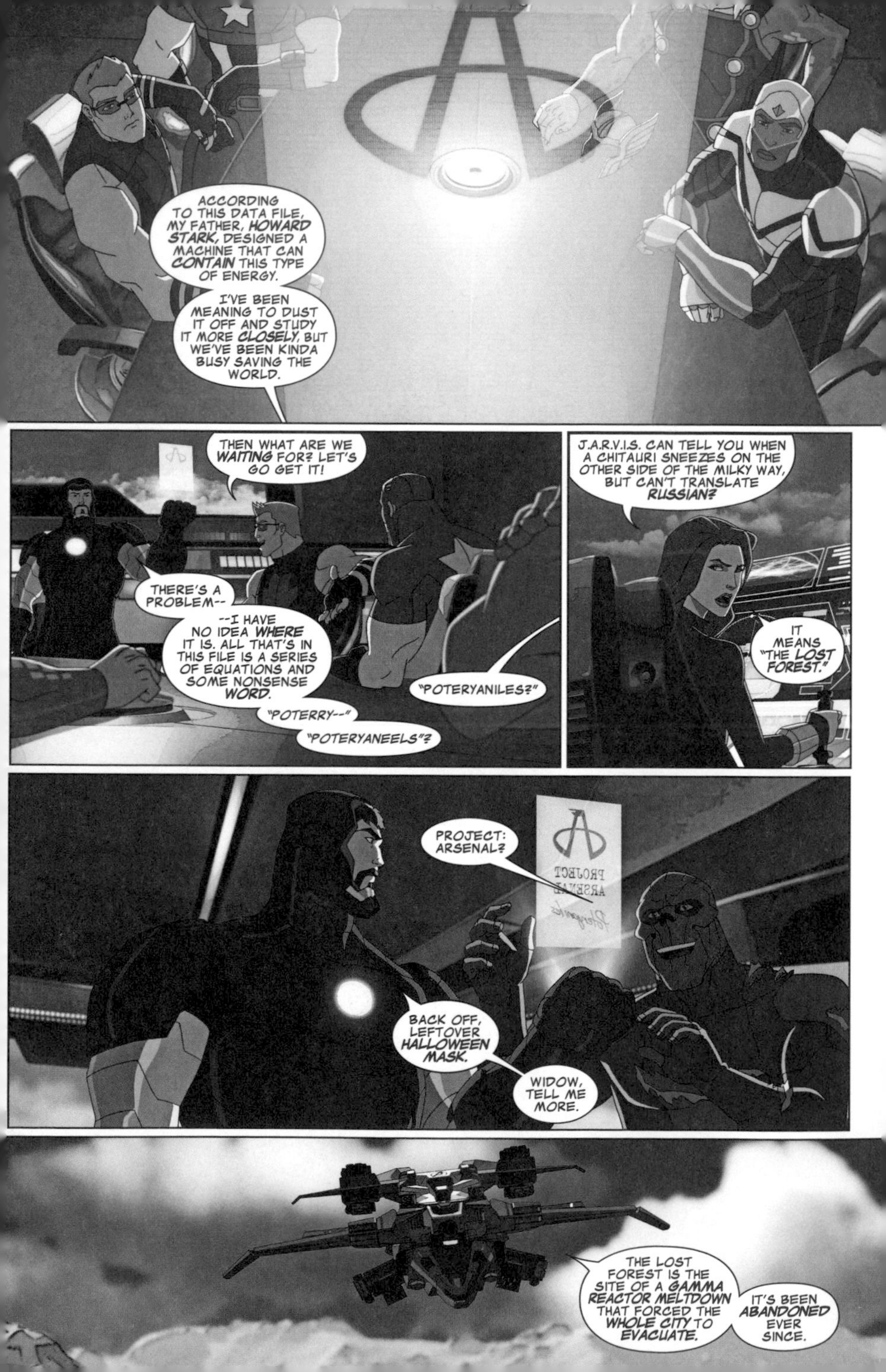
ACCORDING TO THIS DATA FILE, MY FATHER, HOWARD STARK, DESIGNED A MACHINE THAT CAN CONTAIN THIS TYPE OF ENERGY.
I'VE BEEN MEANING TO DUST IT OFF AND STUDY IT MORE CLOSELY, BUT WE'VE BEEN KINDA BUSY SAVING THE WORLD.
THEN WHAT ARE WE WAITING FOR? LET'S GO GET IT!
THERE'S A PROBLEM--
--I HAVE NO IDEA WHERE IT IS. ALL THAT'S IN THIS FILE IS A SERIES OF EQUATIONS AND SOME NONSENSE WORD.
"POTERRY--"
"POTERYANEELS"?
"POTERYANILES?"
J.A.R.V.I.S. CAN TELL YOU WHEN A CHITAURI SNEEZES ON THE OTHER SIDE OF THE MILKY WAY, BUT CAN'T TRANSLATE RUSSIAN?
IT MEANS "THE LOST FOREST."
PROJECT: ARSENAL?
BACK OFF, LEFTOVER HALLOWEEN MASK.
WIDOW, TELL ME MORE.
THE LOST FOREST IS THE SITE OF A GAMMA REACTOR MELTDOWN THAT FORCED THE WHOLE CITY TO EVACUATE.
IT'S BEEN ABANDONED EVER SINCE.

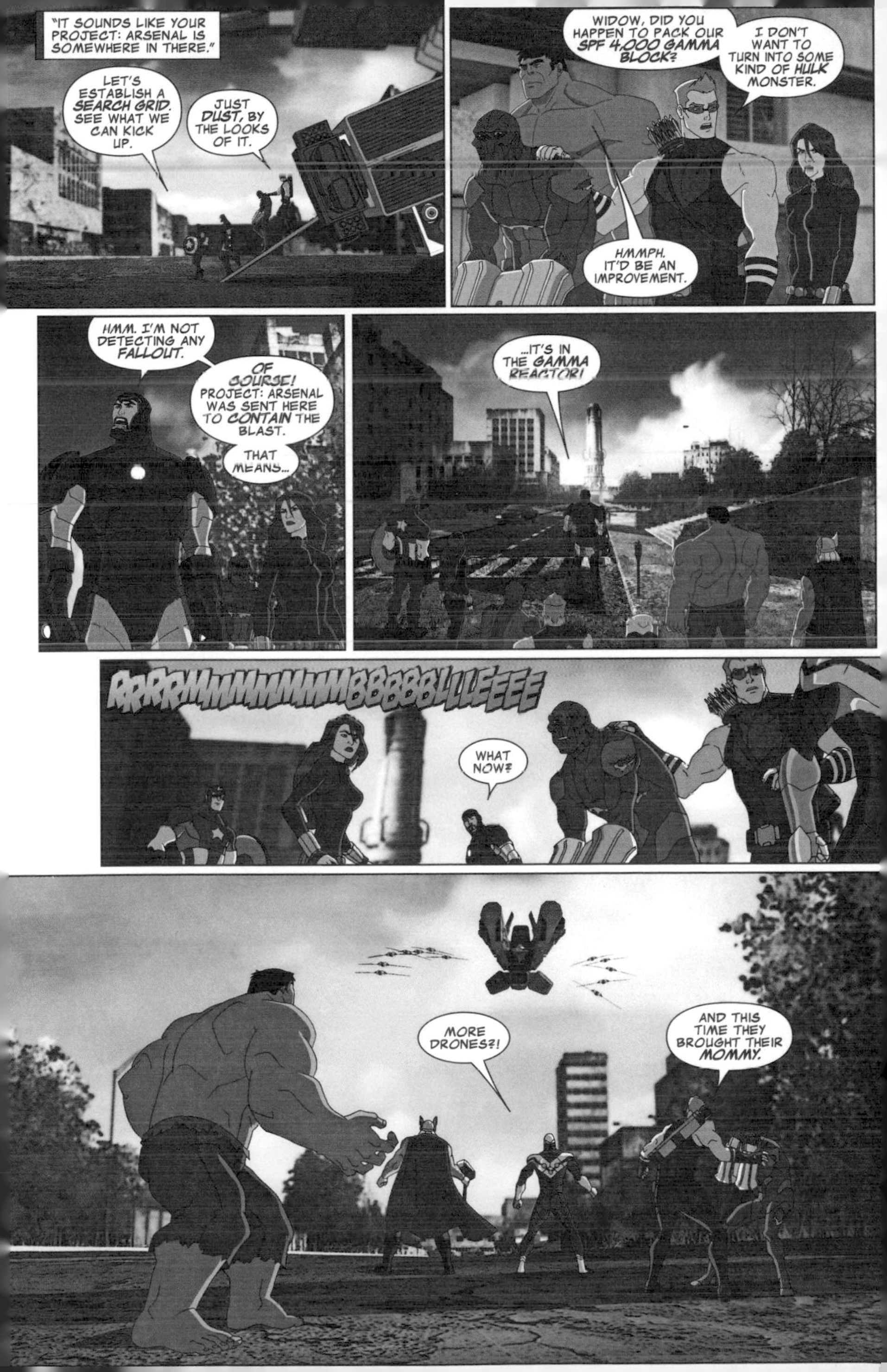
"IT SOUNDS LIKE YOUR PROJECT: ARSENAL IS SOMEWHERE IN THERE."
LET'S ESTABLISH A SEARCH GRID. SEE WHAT WE CAN KICK UP.
JUST DUST, BY THE LOOKS OF IT.
WIDOW, DID YOU HAPPEN TO PACK OUR SPF 4,000 GAMMA BLOCK?
I DON'T WANT TO TURN INTO SOME KIND OF HULK MONSTER.
HMMPH. IT'D BE AN IMPROVEMENT.
HMM. I'M NOT DETECTING ANY FALLOUT.
OF COURSE! PROJECT: ARSENAL WAS SENT HERE TO CONTAIN THE BLAST.
THAT MEANS...
...IT'S IN THE GAMMA REACTOR!
RRRRMMMMMMMMBBBBBLLLEEEE
WHAT NOW?
MORE DRONES?!
AND THIS TIME THEY BROUGHT THEIR MOMMY.

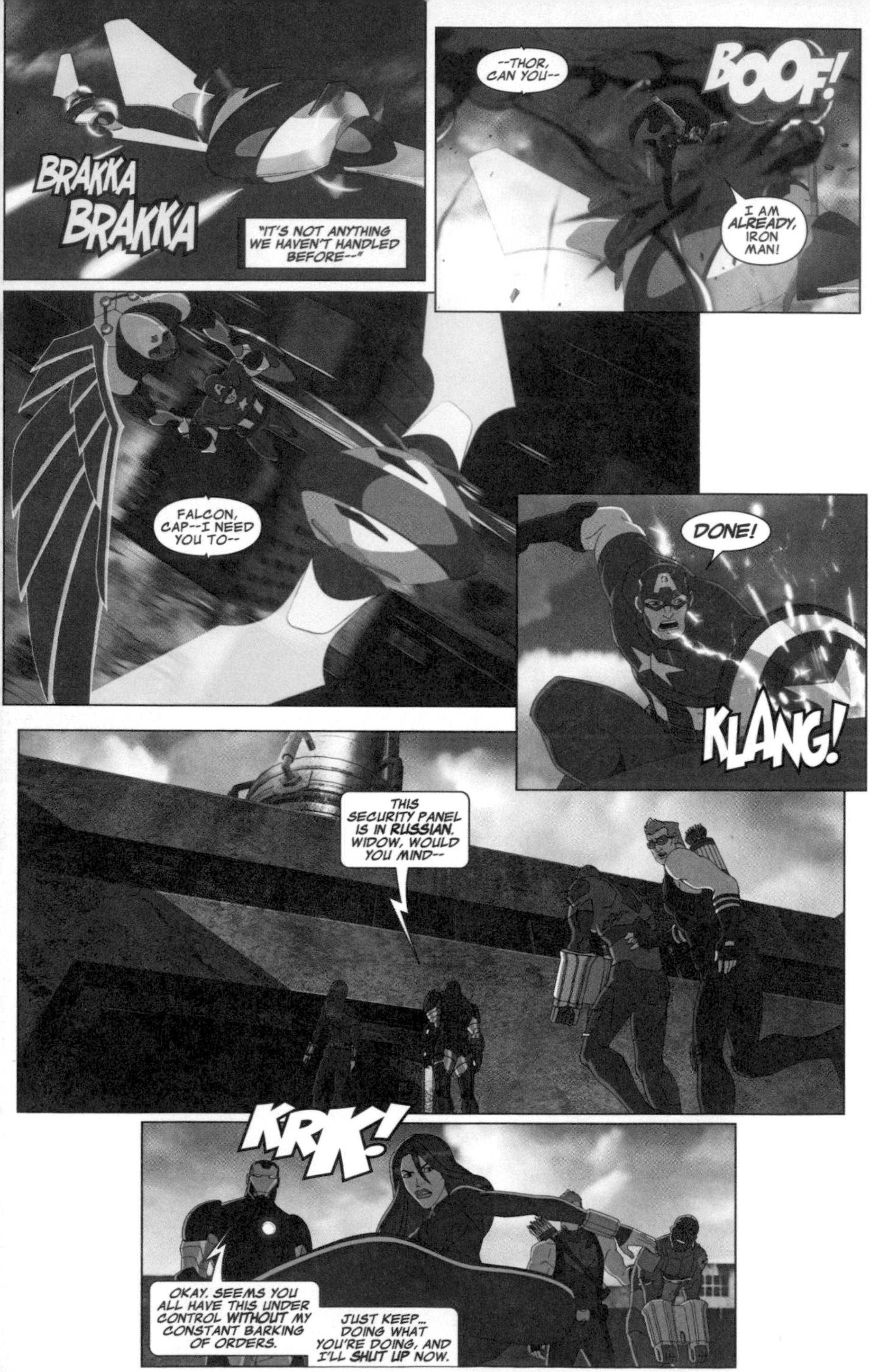
BRAKKA
BRAKKA
"IT'S NOT ANYTHING WE HAVEN'T HANDLED BEFORE--"
--THOR, CAN YOU--
BOOF!
I AM ALREADY, IRON MAN!
FALCON, CAP--I NEED YOU TO--
DONE!
KLANG!
THIS SECURITY PANEL IS IN RUSSIAN. WIDOW, WOULD YOU MIND--
KRK!
OKAY. SEEMS YOU ALL HAVE THIS UNDER CONTROL WITHOUT MY CONSTANT BARKING OF ORDERS.
JUST KEEP... DOING WHAT YOU'RE DOING, AND I'LL SHUT UP NOW.

LOOKS LIKE SOMEONE'S BEEN SAVING ON THEIR CLEANING BILLS.
THERE IT IS!
THE GAMMA REACTOR!
BOOM!
KROOM!
BY THE SOUNDS OF IT OUTSIDE, WE'D BETTER HURRY.
AND BE CAREFUL. IT WON'T TAKE MUCH TO SET IT OFF.
BBRRRMMMM!
REACTOR CORE OVERLOAD IN SIXTY SECONDS.
YOU MEAN LIKE THAT?
EXACTLY.

LOOK AROUND. THERE'S GOT TO BE A FAIL-SAFE SOMEWHERE.
HEY...
...DOES ANYONE ELSE SEE THAT?
THERE'S SOMETHING IN THERE!
IT'S ARSENAL! HAS TO BE!
THAT'S WHAT'S BEEN KEEPING THE GAMMA RADIATION IN CHECK!
THIRTY SECONDS.
QUICK! THE STONE!
SKULL, I THINK YOU'RE ONTO SOMETHING.
THINK YOU CAN HANDLE SOME GAMMA RAYS, HULK?
PUNY GAMMA RAYS!
TAKE THE STONE TO ARSENAL. YOU'RE STRONG ENOUGH TO HANDLE IT FOR A WHILE, BUT MAKE IT QUICK!
HRFF!
STAND BACK!
THUD!
THUD!
THUD!
FIFTEEN SECONDS.

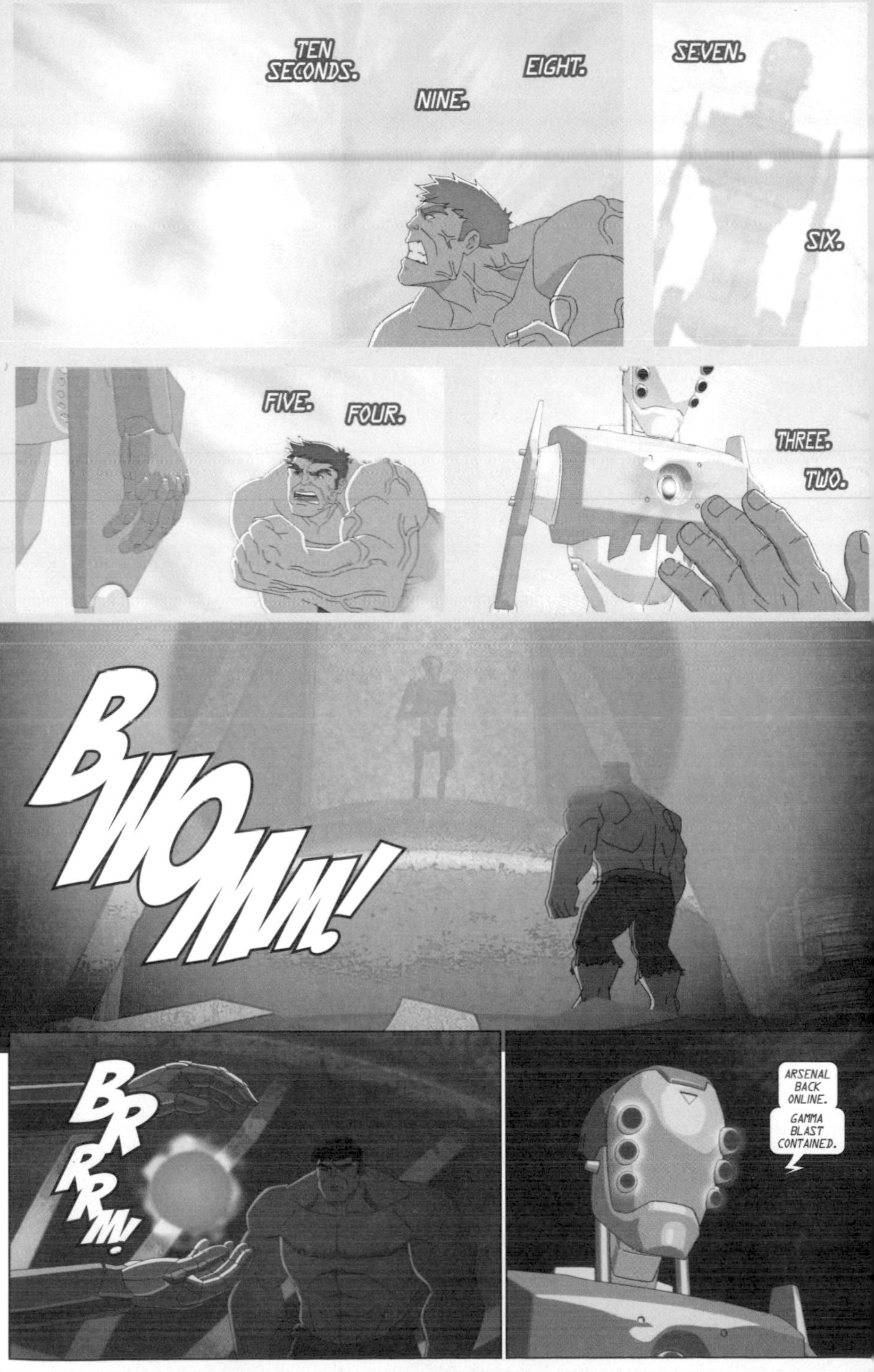
TEN SECONDS.
NINE.
EIGHT.
SEVEN.
SIX.
FIVE.
FOUR.
THREE.
TWO.
BWOMM!
BRRRM!
ARSENAL BACK ONLINE.
GAMMA BLAST CONTAINED.

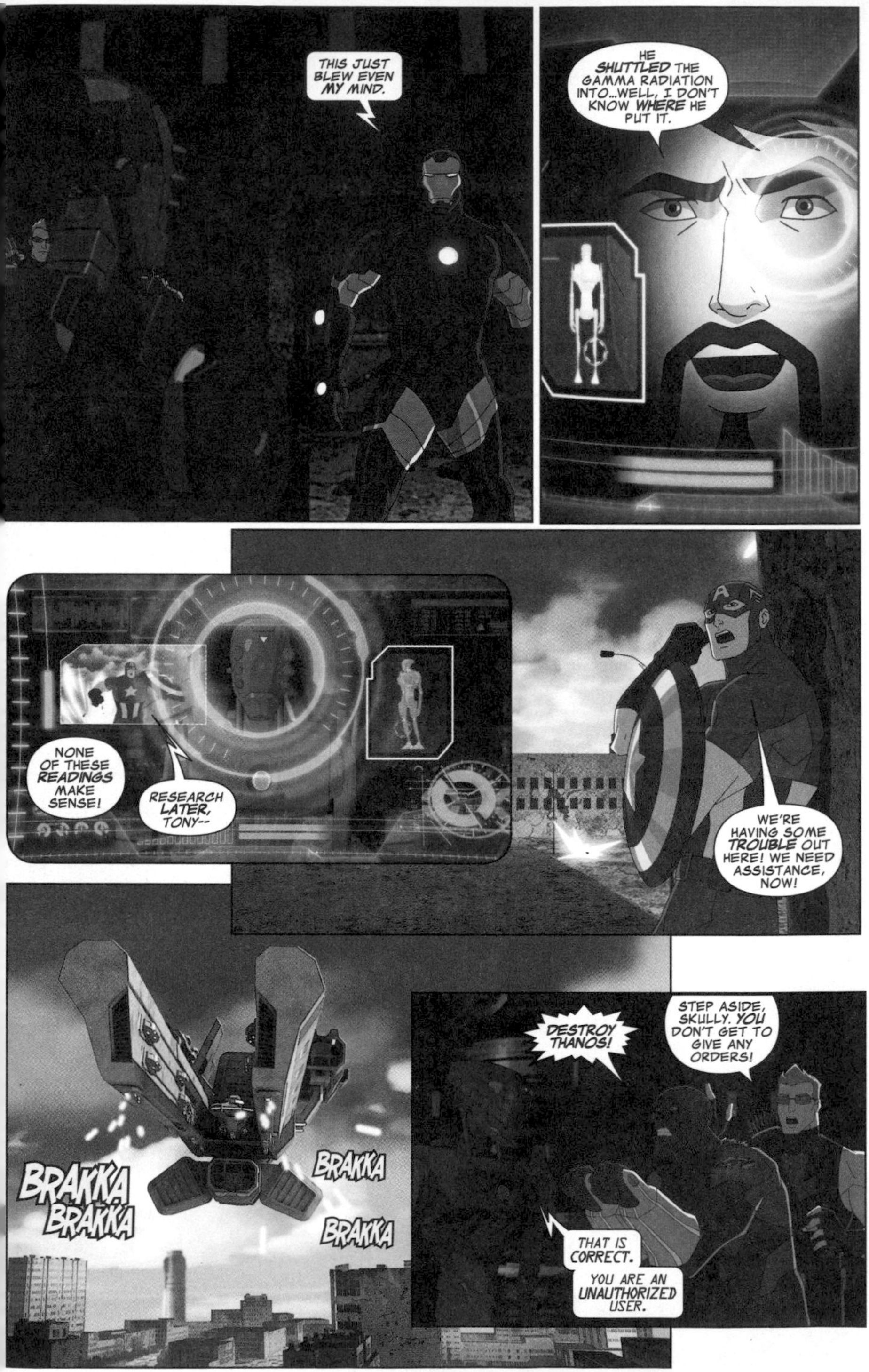
THIS JUST BLEW EVEN MY MIND.
HE SHUTTLED THE GAMMA RADIATION INTO...WELL, I DON'T KNOW WHERE HE PUT IT.
NONE OF THESE READINGS MAKE SENSE!
RESEARCH LATER, TONY--
WE'RE HAVING SOME TROUBLE OUT HERE! WE NEED ASSISTANCE, NOW!
BRAKKA
BRAKKA BRAKKA
BRAKKA
DESTROY THANOS!
STEP ASIDE, SKULLY. YOU DON'T GET TO GIVE ANY ORDERS!
THAT IS CORRECT.
YOU ARE AN UNAUTHORIZED USER.

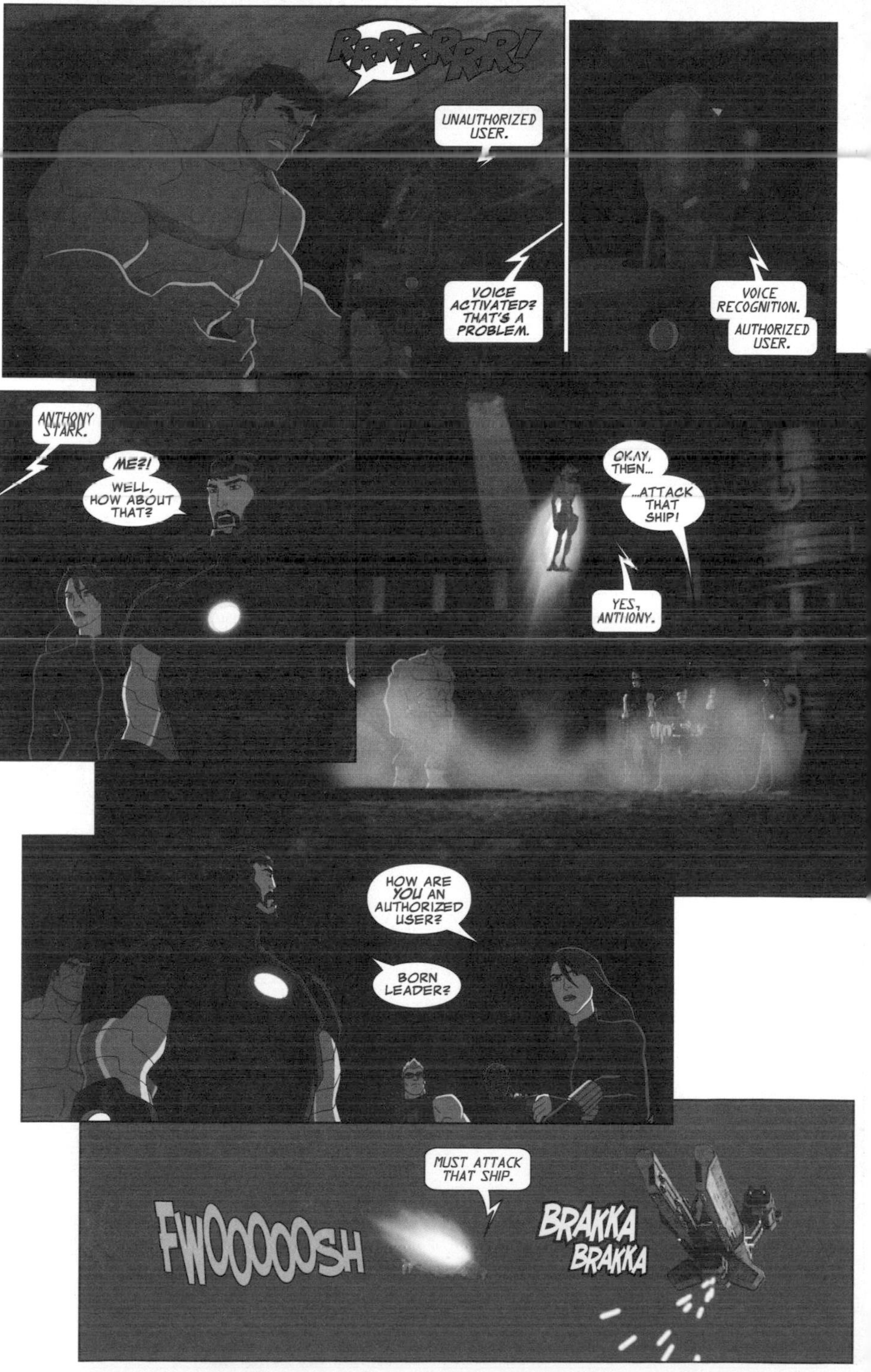
RRRRRRRR!
UNAUTHORIZED USER.
VOICE ACTIVATED? THAT'S A PROBLEM.
VOICE RECOGNITION.
AUTHORIZED USER.
ANTHONY STARK.
ME?! WELL, HOW ABOUT THAT?
OKAY, THEN...
...ATTACK THAT SHIP!
YES, ANTHONY.
HOW ARE YOU AN AUTHORIZED USER?
BORN LEADER?
MUST ATTACK THAT SHIP.
FWOOOOOSH
BRAKKA BRAKKA

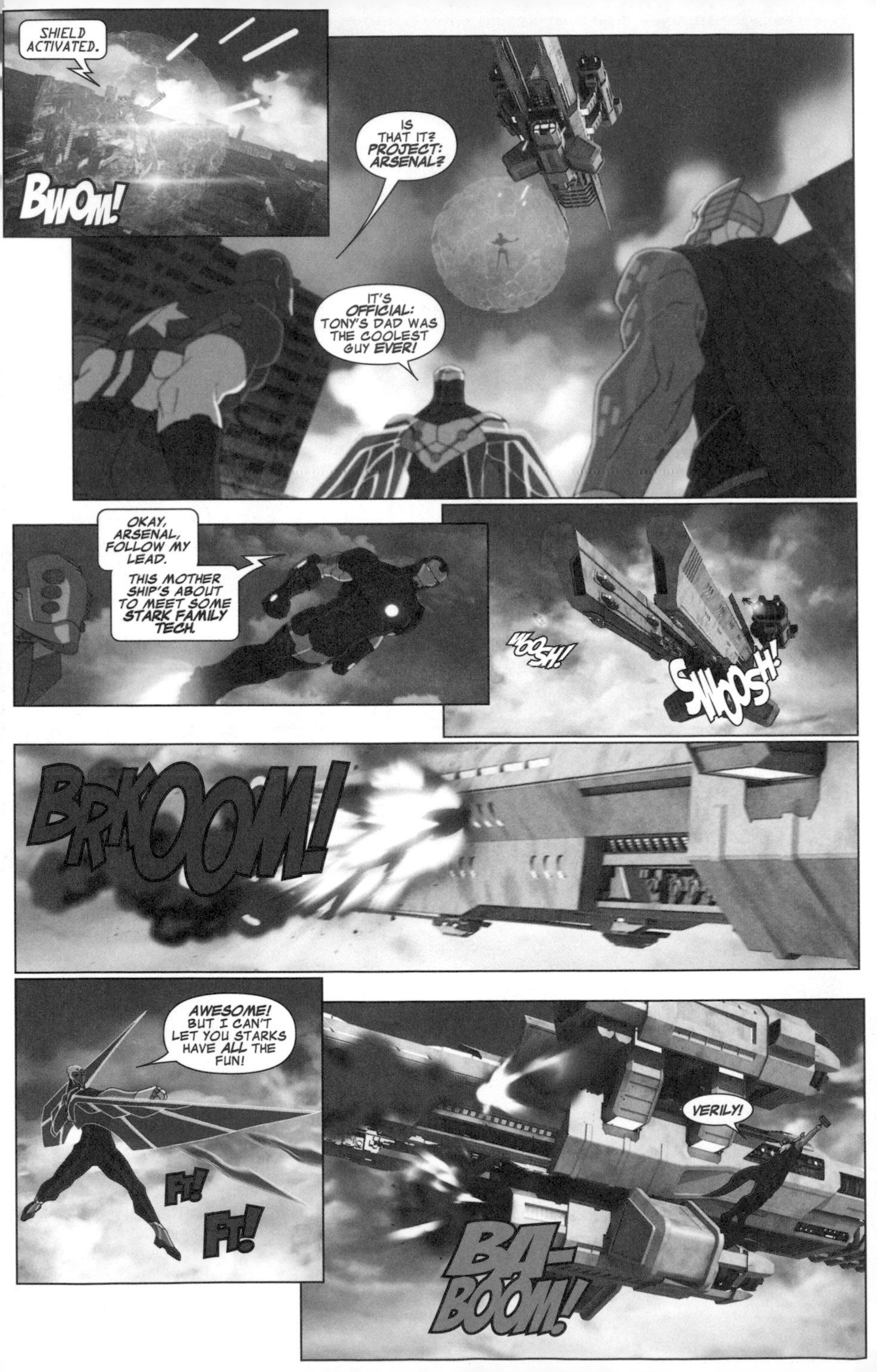
SHIELD ACTIVATED.
BWOM!
IS THAT IT? PROJECT: ARSENAL?
IT'S OFFICIAL: TONY'S DAD WAS THE COOLEST GUY EVER!
OKAY, ARSENAL, FOLLOW MY LEAD.
THIS MOTHER SHIP'S ABOUT TO MEET SOME STARK FAMILY TECH.
WOOSH!
SHOOSH!
BRKOOM!
AWESOME! BUT I CAN'T LET YOU STARKS HAVE ALL THE FUN!
FT!
FT!
VERILY!
BA-BOOM!

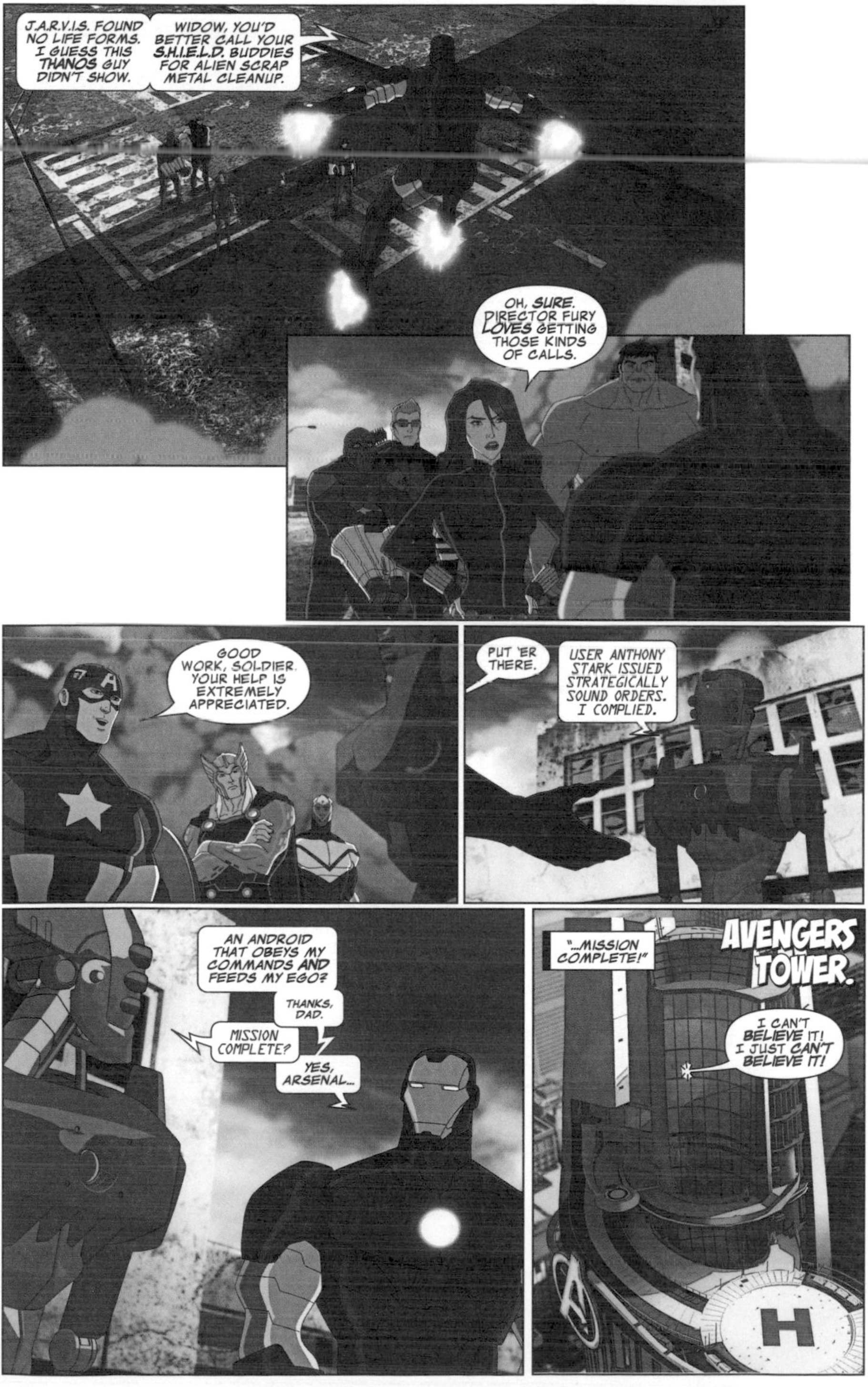
J.A.R.V.I.S. FOUND NO LIFE FORMS. I GUESS THIS THANOS GUY DIDN'T SHOW.
WIDOW, YOU'D BETTER CALL YOUR S.H.I.E.L.D. BUDDIES FOR ALIEN SCRAP METAL CLEANUP.
OH, SURE. DIRECTOR FURY LOVES GETTING THOSE KINDS OF CALLS.
GOOD WORK, SOLDIER. YOUR HELP IS EXTREMELY APPRECIATED.
PUT 'ER THERE.
USER ANTHONY STARK ISSUED STRATEGICALLY SOUND ORDERS. I COMPLIED.
AN ANDROID THAT OBEYS MY COMMANDS AND FEEDS MY EGO?
THANKS, DAD.
MISSION COMPLETE?
YES, ARSENAL...
"...MISSION COMPLETE!"
AVENGERS TOWER.
I CAN'T BELIEVE IT! I JUST CAN'T BELIEVE IT!

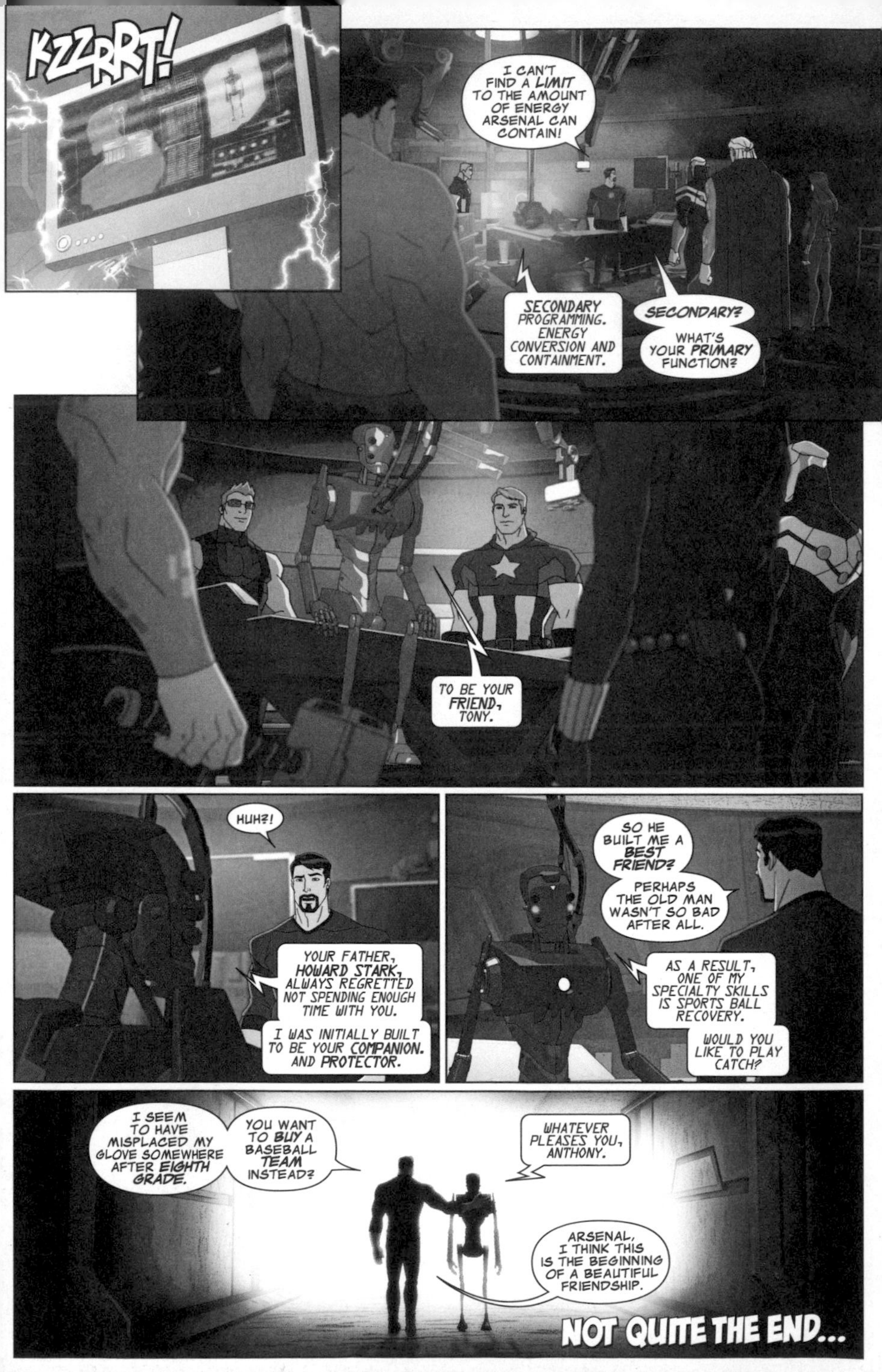
KZZRRT!
I CAN'T FIND A LIMIT TO THE AMOUNT OF ENERGY ARSENAL CAN CONTAIN!
SECONDARY PROGRAMMING. ENERGY CONVERSION AND CONTAINMENT.
SECONDARY?
WHAT'S YOUR PRIMARY FUNCTION?
TO BE YOUR FRIEND, TONY.
HUH?!
YOUR FATHER, HOWARD STARK, ALWAYS REGRETTED NOT SPENDING ENOUGH TIME WITH YOU.
I WAS INITIALLY BUILT TO BE YOUR COMPANION. AND PROTECTOR.
SO HE BUILT ME A BEST FRIEND?
PERHAPS THE OLD MAN WASN'T SO BAD AFTER ALL.
AS A RESULT, ONE OF MY SPECIALTY SKILLS IS SPORTS BALL RECOVERY.
WOULD YOU LIKE TO PLAY CATCH?
I SEEM TO HAVE MISPLACED MY GLOVE SOMEWHERE AFTER EIGHTH GRADE.
YOU WANT TO BUY A BASEBALL TEAM INSTEAD?
WHATEVER PLEASES YOU, ANTHONY.
ARSENAL, I THINK THIS IS THE BEGINNING OF A BEAUTIFUL FRIENDSHIP.
NOT QUITE THE END...

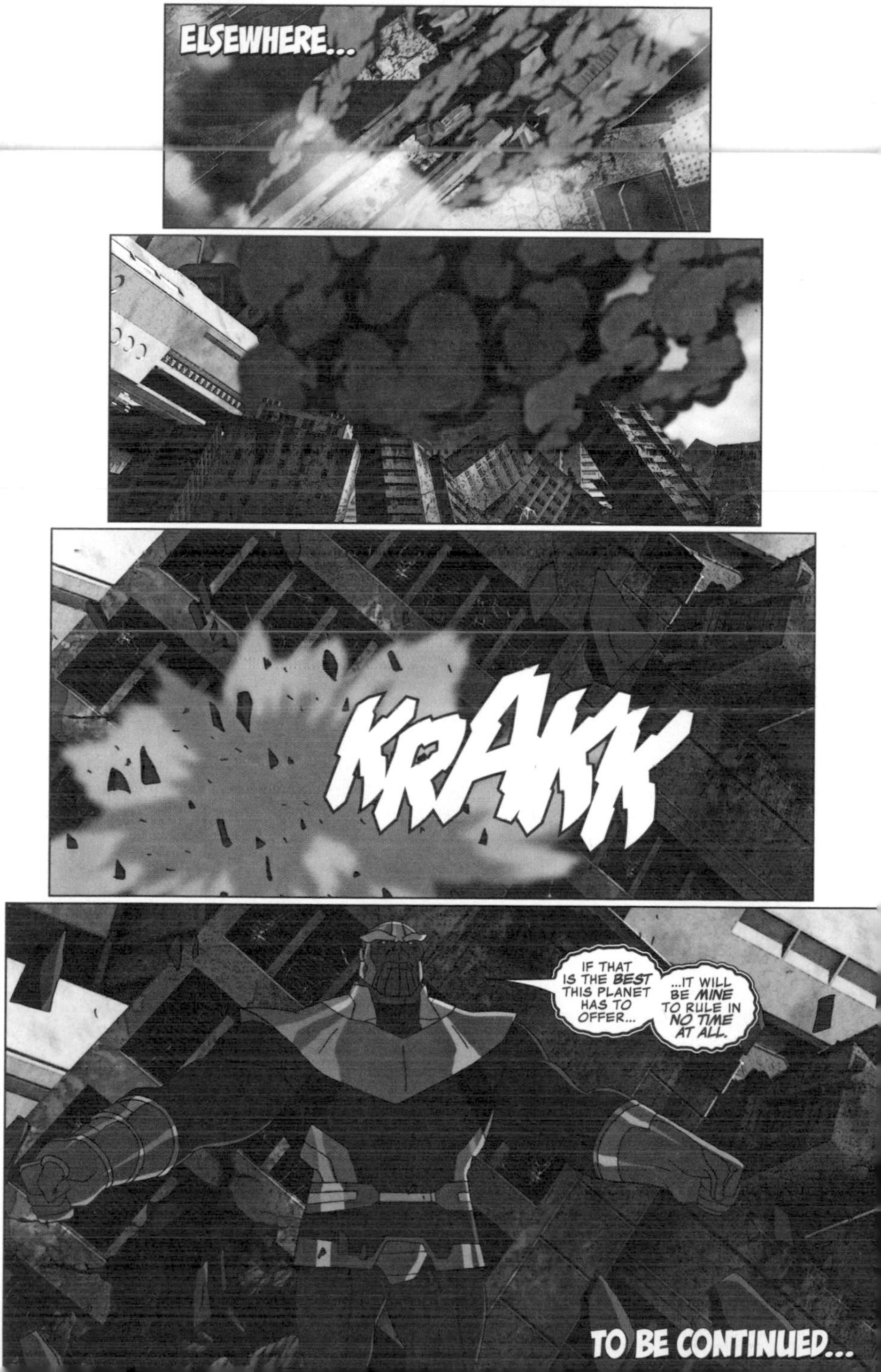
ELSEWHERE...
KRAKK
IF THAT IS THE BEST THIS PLANET HAS TO OFFER...
...IT WILL BE MINE TO RULE IN NO TIME AT ALL.
TO BE CONTINUED...

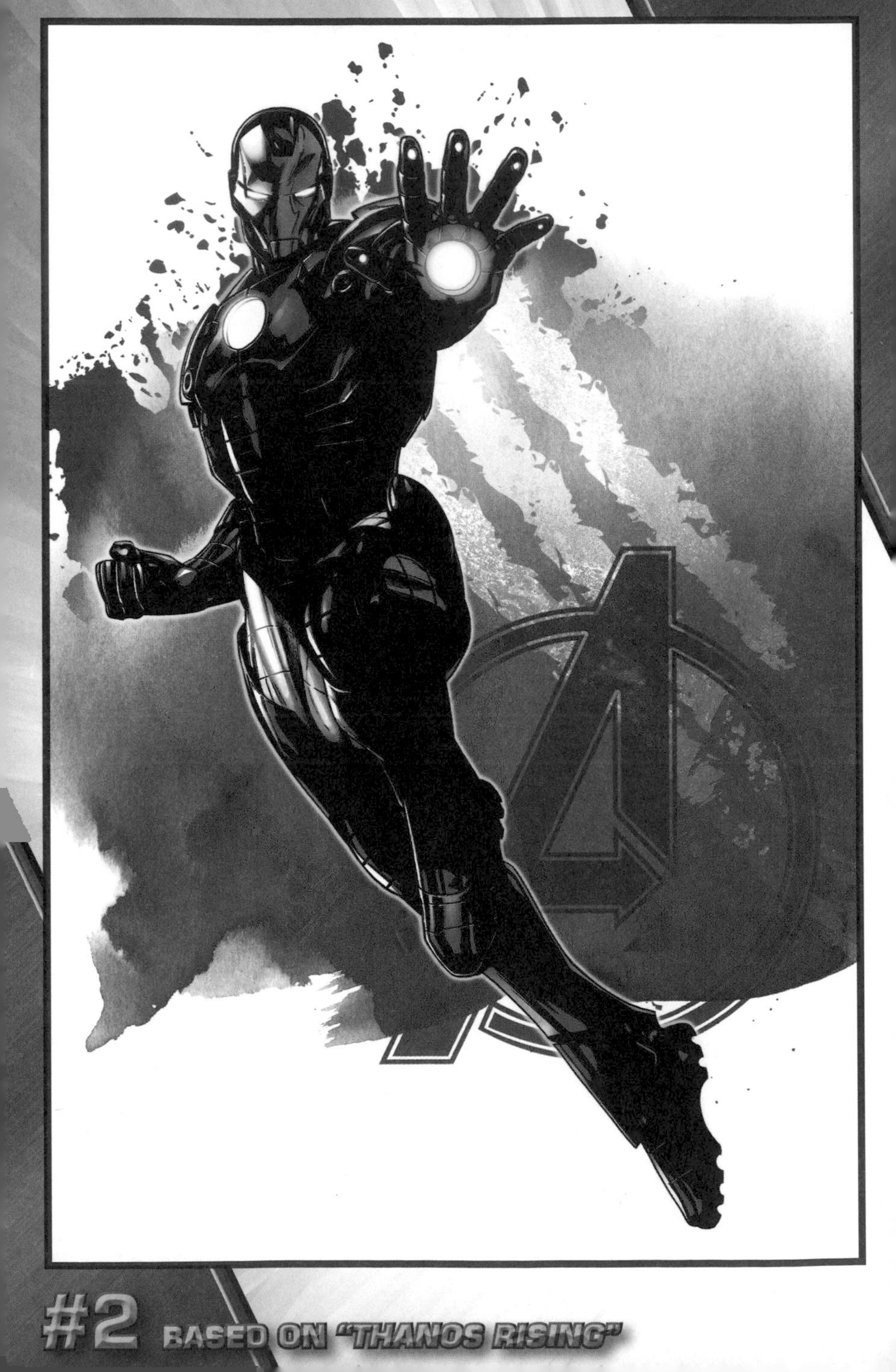

#2 BASED ON "THANOS RISING"

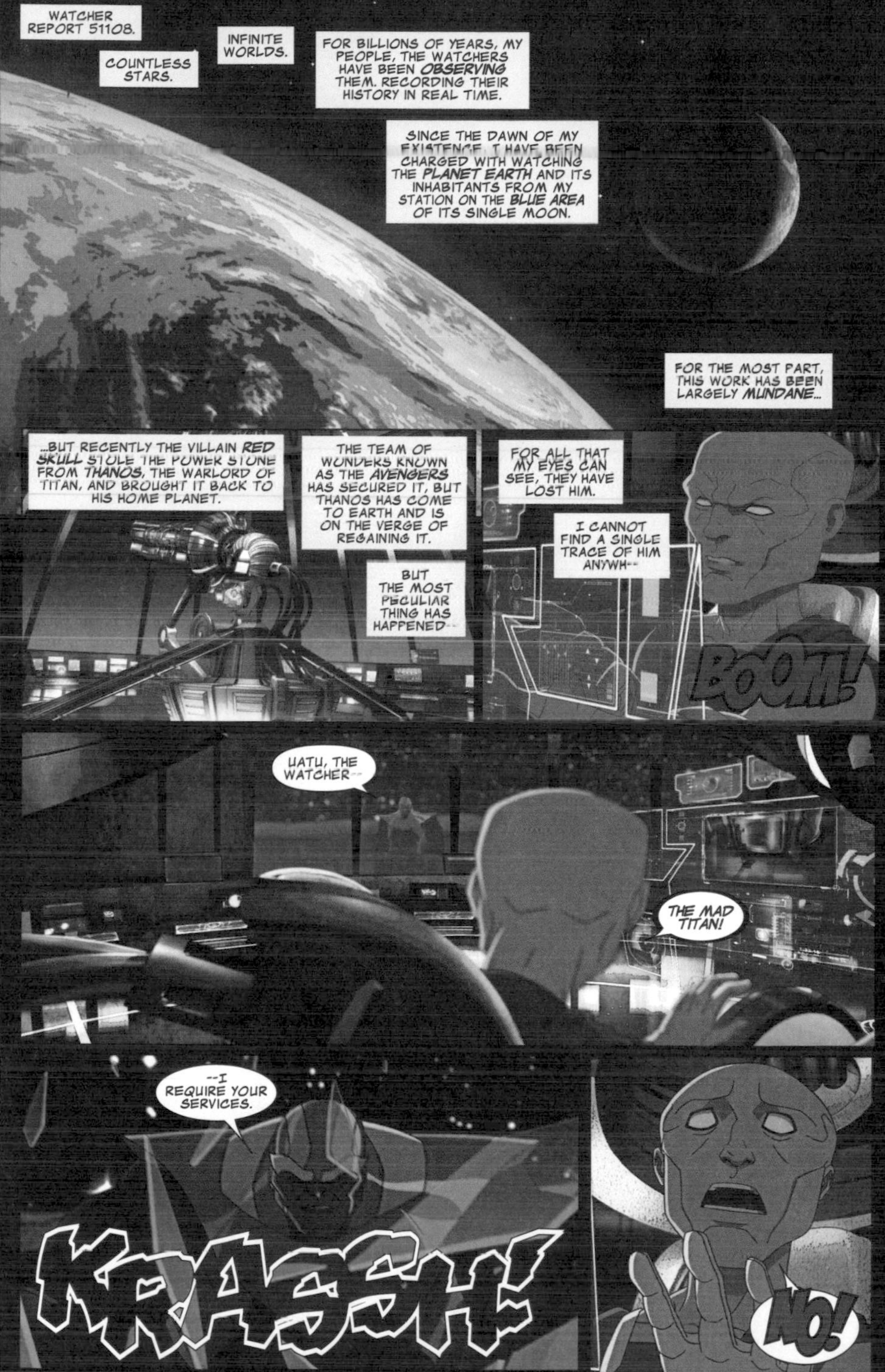
WATCHER REPORT 51108.
COUNTLESS STARS.
INFINITE WORLDS.
FOR BILLIONS OF YEARS, MY PEOPLE, THE WATCHERS HAVE BEEN *OBSERVING* THEM. RECORDING THEIR HISTORY IN REAL TIME.
SINCE THE DAWN OF MY EXISTENCE, I HAVE BEEN CHARGED WITH WATCHING THE *PLANET EARTH* AND ITS INHABITANTS FROM MY STATION ON THE *BLUE AREA* OF ITS SINGLE MOON.
FOR THE MOST PART, THIS WORK HAS BEEN LARGELY *MUNDANE*...
...BUT RECENTLY THE VILLAIN *RED SKULL* STOLE THE POWER STONE FROM *THANOS*, THE WARLORD OF TITAN, AND BROUGHT IT BACK TO HIS HOME PLANET.
THE TEAM OF WONDERS KNOWN AS THE *AVENGERS* HAS SECURED IT, BUT THANOS HAS COME TO EARTH AND IS ON THE VERGE OF REGAINING IT.
BUT THE MOST PECULIAR THING HAS HAPPENED--
FOR ALL THAT MY EYES CAN SEE, THEY HAVE LOST HIM.
I CANNOT FIND A SINGLE TRACE OF HIM ANYWH--
BOOM!
UATU, THE WATCHER--
THE MAD TITAN!
--I REQUIRE YOUR SERVICES.
KRASSH!
NO!

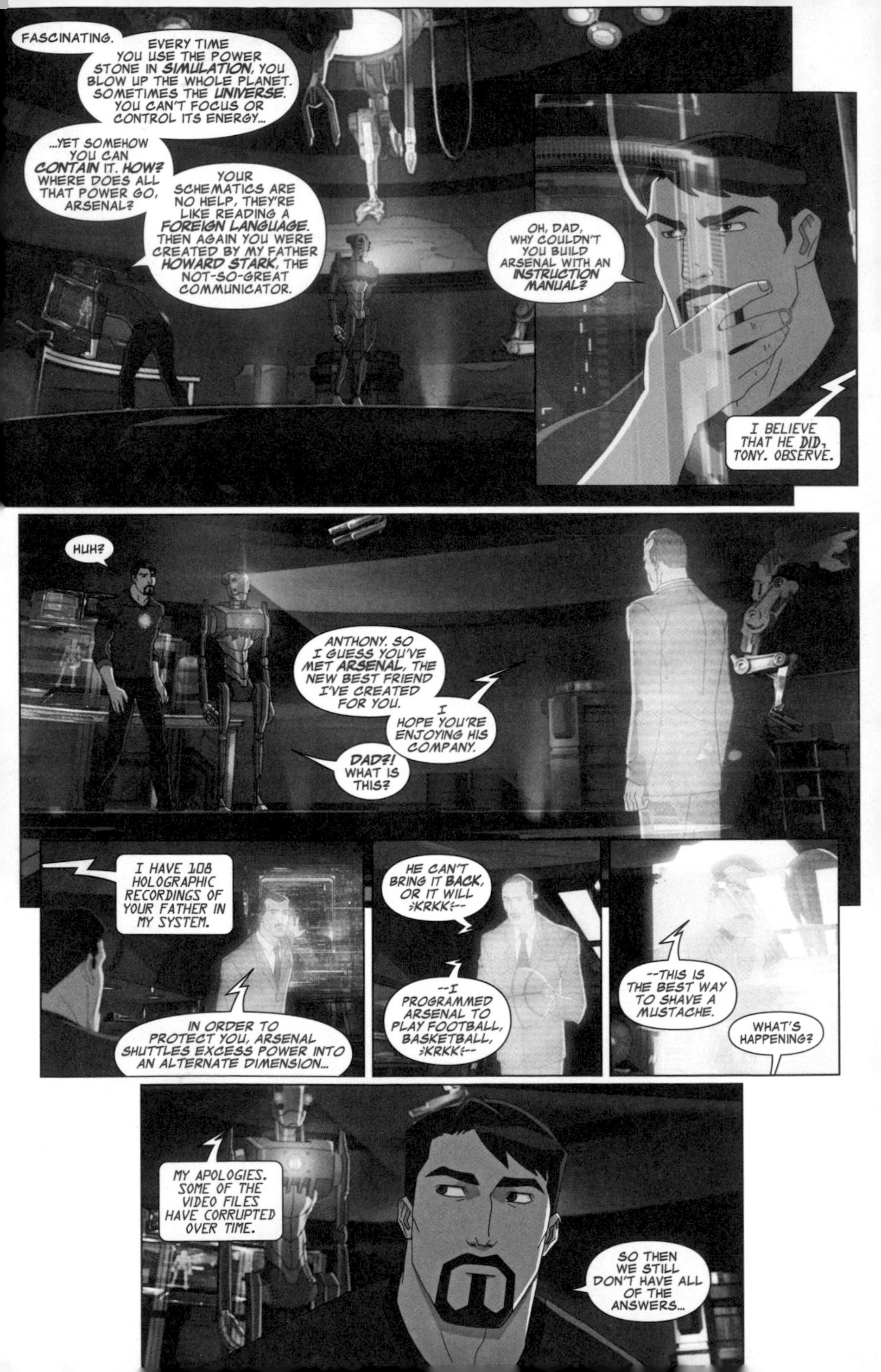
FASCINATING.
EVERY TIME YOU USE THE POWER STONE IN SIMULATION, YOU BLOW UP THE WHOLE PLANET. SOMETIMES THE UNIVERSE. YOU CAN'T FOCUS OR CONTROL ITS ENERGY...
...YET SOMEHOW YOU CAN CONTAIN IT. HOW? WHERE DOES ALL THAT POWER GO, ARSENAL?
YOUR SCHEMATICS ARE NO HELP, THEY'RE LIKE READING A FOREIGN LANGUAGE. THEN AGAIN YOU WERE CREATED BY MY FATHER HOWARD STARK, THE NOT-SO-GREAT COMMUNICATOR.
OH, DAD, WHY COULDN'T YOU BUILD ARSENAL WITH AN INSTRUCTION MANUAL?
I BELIEVE THAT HE DID, TONY. OBSERVE.
HUH?
ANTHONY. SO I GUESS YOU'VE MET ARSENAL, THE NEW BEST FRIEND I'VE CREATED FOR YOU.
I HOPE YOU'RE ENJOYING HIS COMPANY.
DAD?! WHAT IS THIS?
I HAVE 108 HOLOGRAPHIC RECORDINGS OF YOUR FATHER IN MY SYSTEM.
IN ORDER TO PROTECT YOU, ARSENAL SHUTTLES EXCESS POWER INTO AN ALTERNATE DIMENSION...
HE CAN'T BRING IT BACK, OR IT WILL ›KRKK‹--
--I PROGRAMMED ARSENAL TO PLAY FOOTBALL, BASKETBALL, ›KRKK‹--
--THIS IS THE BEST WAY TO SHAVE A MUSTACHE.
WHAT'S HAPPENING?
MY APOLOGIES. SOME OF THE VIDEO FILES HAVE CORRUPTED OVER TIME.
SO THEN WE STILL DON'T HAVE ALL OF THE ANSWERS...

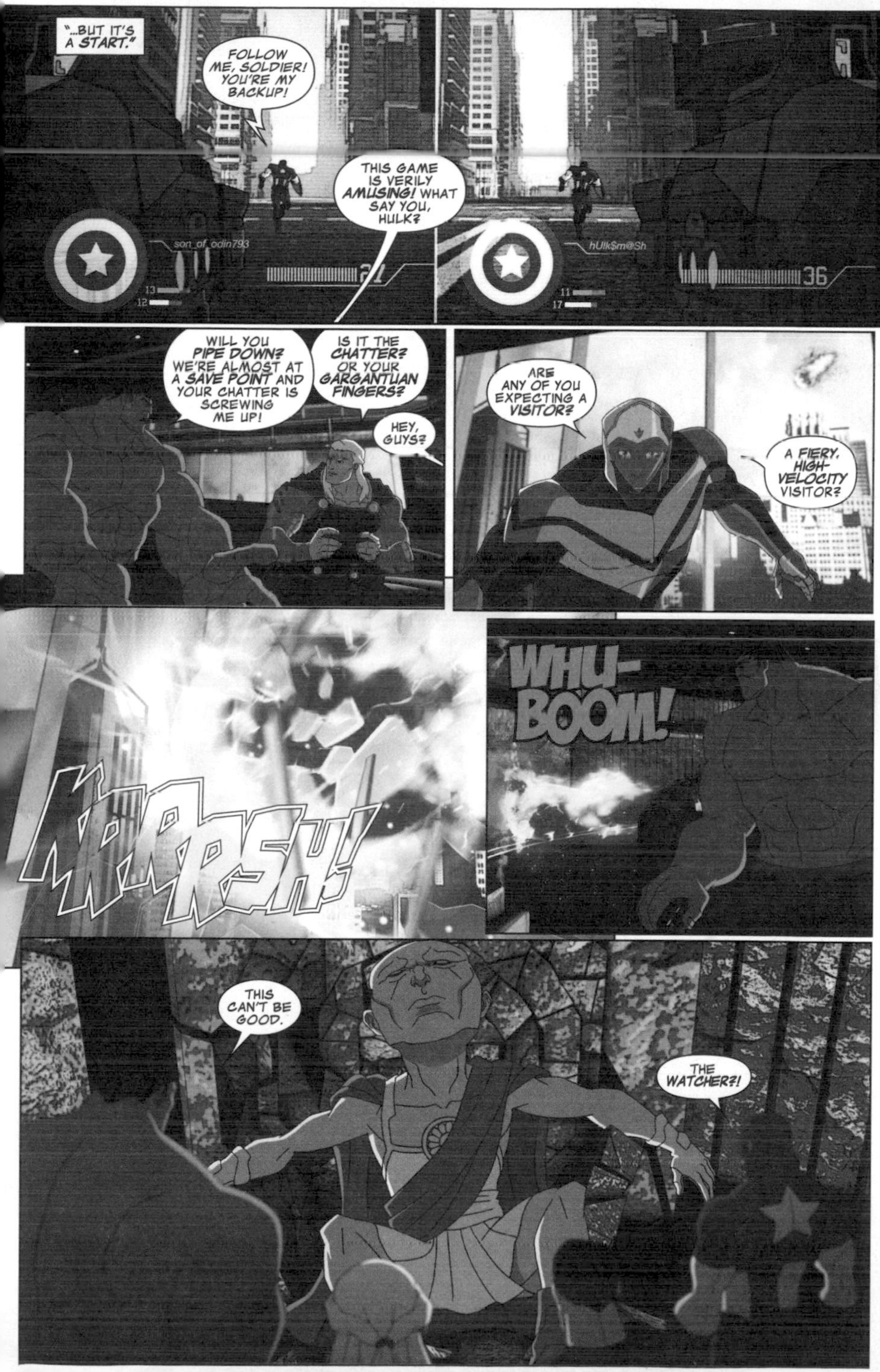
"...BUT IT'S A START."
FOLLOW ME, SOLDIER! YOU'RE MY BACKUP!
THIS GAME IS VERILY AMUSING! WHAT SAY YOU, HULK?
son_of_odin793
21
hUlk$m@Sh
36
WILL YOU PIPE DOWN? WE'RE ALMOST AT A SAVE POINT AND YOUR CHATTER IS SCREWING ME UP!
IS IT THE CHATTER? OR YOUR GARGANTUAN FINGERS?
HEY, GUYS?
ARE ANY OF YOU EXPECTING A VISITOR?
A FIERY, HIGH-VELOCITY VISITOR?
KRASH!
WHU-BOOM!
THIS CAN'T BE GOOD.
THE WATCHER?!

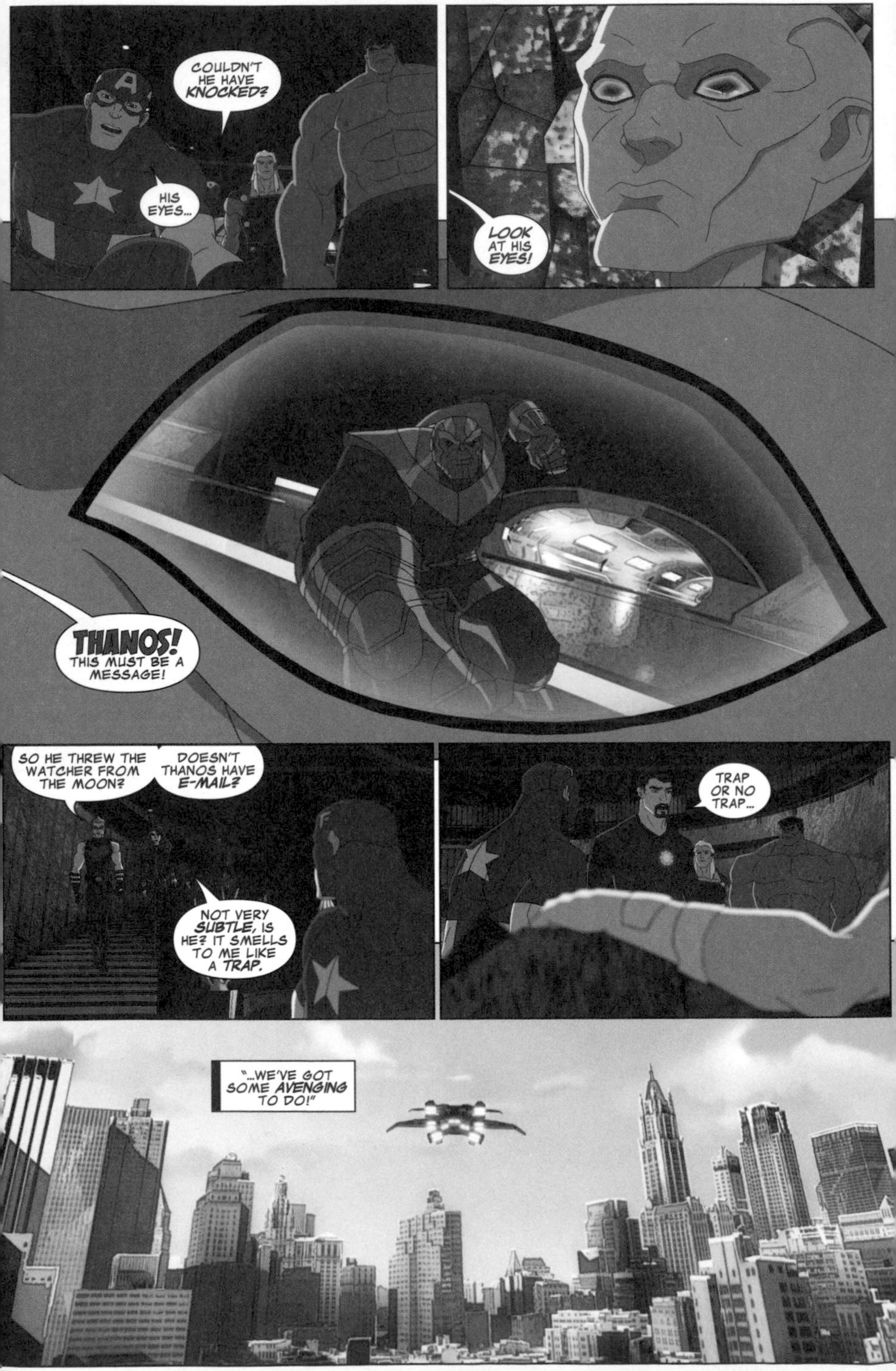
COULDN'T HE HAVE KNOCKED?
HIS EYES...
LOOK AT HIS EYES!
THANOS! THIS MUST BE A MESSAGE!
SO HE THREW THE WATCHER FROM THE MOON?
DOESN'T THANOS HAVE E-MAIL?
NOT VERY SUBTLE, IS HE? IT SMELLS TO ME LIKE A TRAP.
TRAP OR NO TRAP...
"...WE'VE GOT SOME AVENGING TO DO!"

IF THE POWER STONE IS WHAT THANOS WANTS...
...WHY ARE WE BRINGING THE ROBOT THAT'S CARRYING IT AROUND IN ITS CHEST?
IT'S A CALCULATED RISK. IF ALL ELSE FAILS, THE POWER STONE IS THE ONLY THING THAT CAN STOP HIM.
AND HOW ARE WE SUPPOSED TO FIGHT HIM ON THE MOON WITHOUT SPACESUITS OR ANYTHING?
THE BLUE AREA OF THE MOON HAS AN EARTH-LIKE ENVIRONMENT. WE'LL BE FINE.
YOU HAVE ALL THE ANSWERS, DON'T YOU?
WARNING! WARNING! INCOMING OBJECT!
NOT ALL OF THEM.
COLLISION IMMINENT!
KRAK!
CRASH!
SO...
...YOU HAVE RECEIVED MY INVITATION.

RUNCCH!
AND YOU BROUGHT THE STONE.
I HAD EXPECTED SUCH FOOLISHNESS.
EH?
IT'S A TRICK!
BWOM!
SSSHHHHHMMMMM
A SECOND SHIP?

NICE JOB ON THAT TRAP, WIDOW.
A DECOY SHIP? A BOOBY-TRAPPED TREASURE?
IT'S SPYCRAFT 101.
THANOS, I PRESUME? I'D SAY IT'S NICE TO FINALLY MEET YOU... BUT I'D BE LYING.
DO YOU REALLY BELIEVE THIS JAIL CAN HOLD THE LIKES OF THANOS OF TITAN?
I DO, YEAH. IT IS STARKTECH AFTER ALL.
I WILL MAKE YOU ONE OFFER--
HAND OVER THE POWER STONE THAT IS RIGHTFULLY MINE AND I WILL SPARE YOUR PLANET.
SORRY, BUT YOU'RE NOT IN A POSITION TO MAKE ANY DEALS.
ON THE CONTRARY...
NYAAAAA!
...I BELIEVE I AM!
BY ODIN'S BEARD! HE'S GOT US!
KRZZKKK!
HNNN...
SEE? HUMAN TECHNOLOGY IS MERE CHILD'S PLAY.
BWOM!

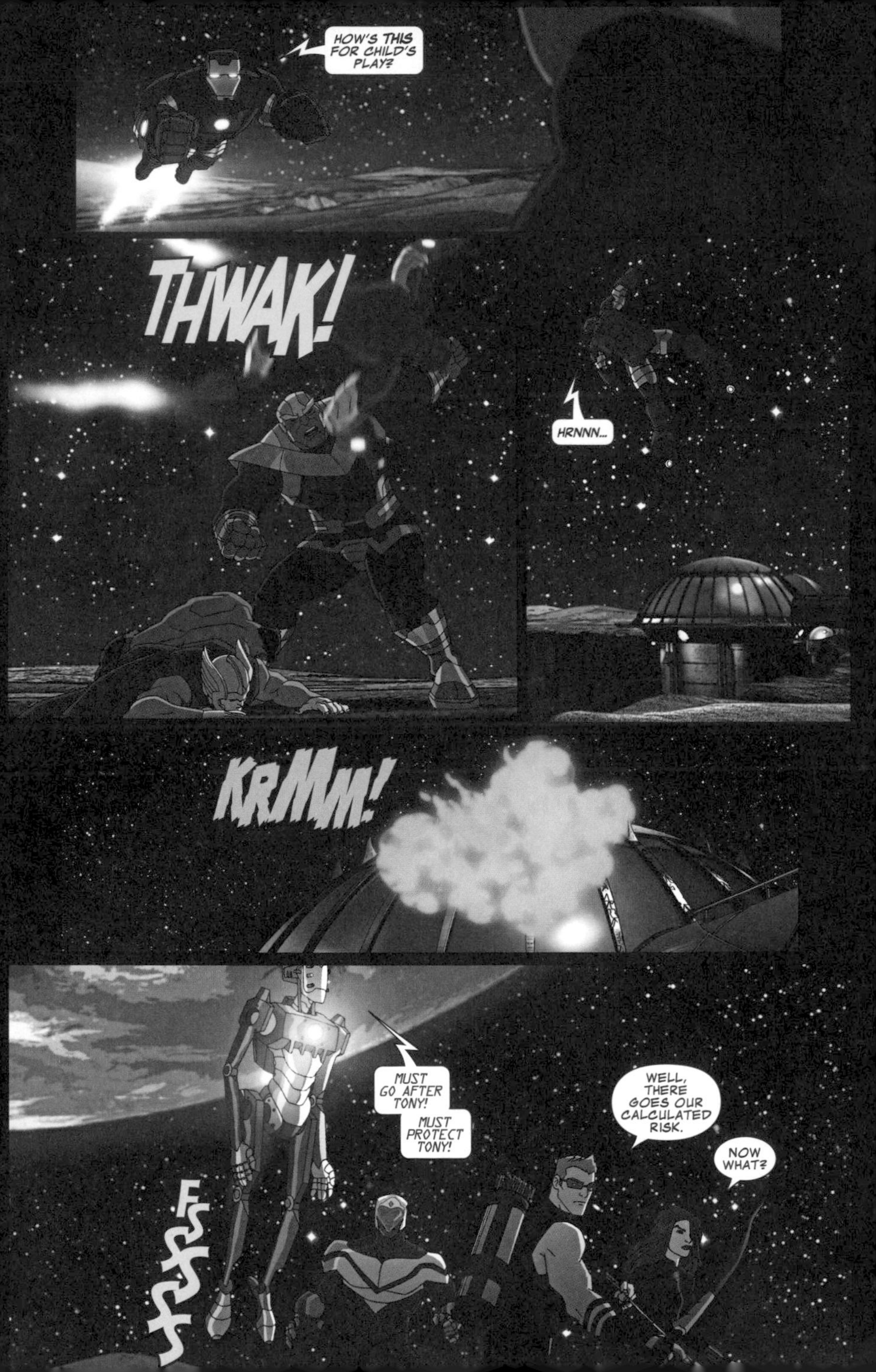
HOW'S THIS FOR CHILD'S PLAY?
THWAK!
HRNNN...
KRMM!
MUST GO AFTER TONY!
MUST PROTECT TONY!
WELL, THERE GOES OUR CALCULATED RISK.
NOW WHAT?
FSSS

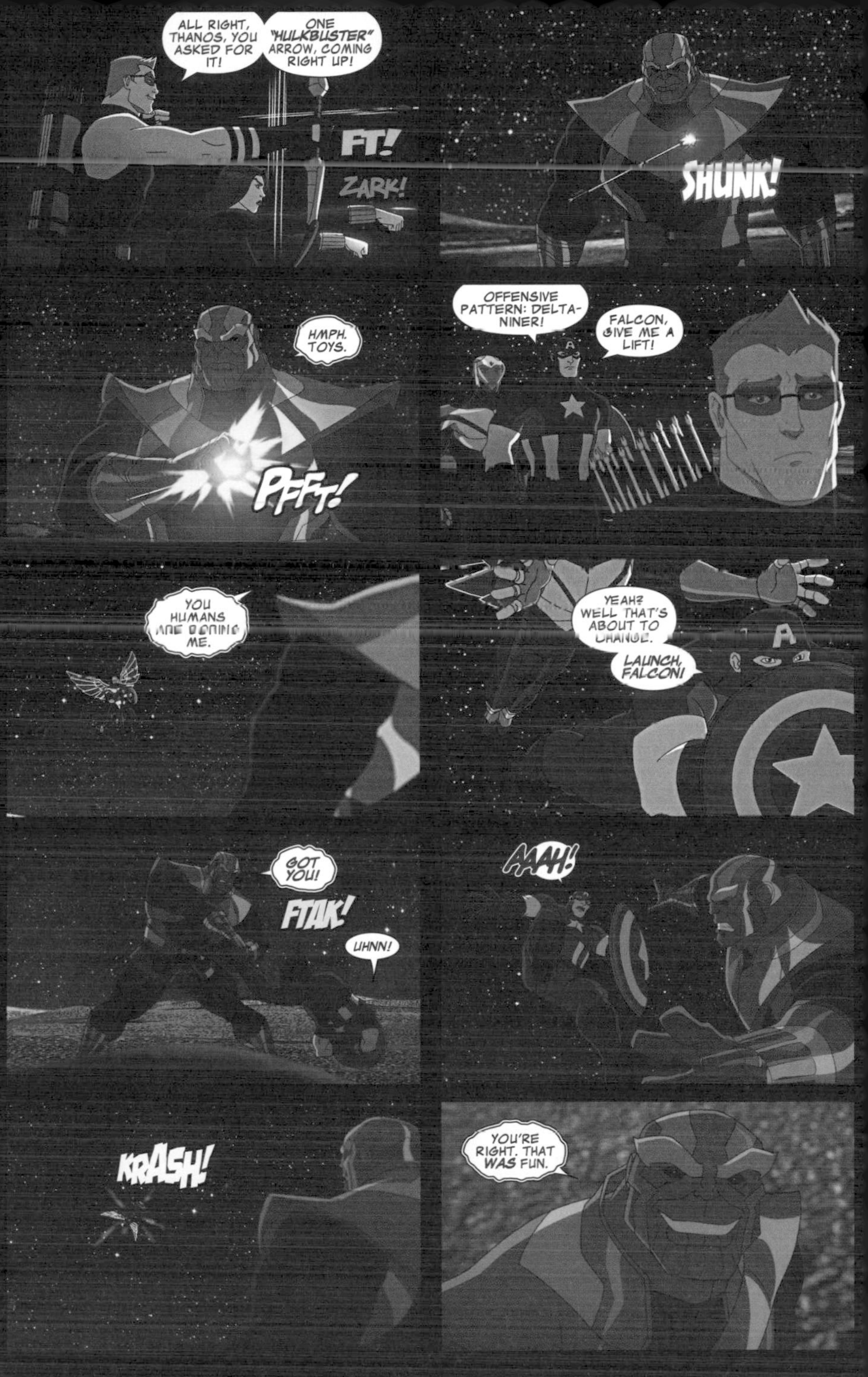

ALL RIGHT, THANOS, YOU ASKED FOR IT!
ONE "HULKBUSTER" ARROW, COMING RIGHT UP!
FT!
ZARK!
SHUNK!
HMPH. TOYS.
PFFT!
OFFENSIVE PATTERN: DELTA-NINER!
FALCON, GIVE ME A LIFT!
YOU HUMANS ARE BORING ME.
YEAH? WELL THAT'S ABOUT TO CHANGE.
LAUNCH, FALCON!
GOT YOU!
FTAK!
UHNN!
AAAH!
KRASH!
YOU'RE RIGHT. THAT WAS FUN.

TONY, ARE YOU ALL RIGHT?
I THINK SO. LUCKILY THE WATCHER'S CITADEL BROKE MY FALL.
OUCH.
IS IT TIME FOR ME TO EMPLOY THE POWER STONE?
AND BLOW UP THE MOON? I DON'T THINK SO.
NOT WITHOUT A WAY TO FOCUS ITS ENERGY.
PERHAPS THE WATCHER'S EQUIPMENT WILL PROVIDE A SOLUTION.
THE WATCHER'S--?
ARSENAL, I DON'T THINK I'VE EVER SAID THIS TO ANYONE BUT MYSELF...
...BUT YOU'RE A GENIUS!
UATU, DO YOU MIND IF I BORROW SOME OF YOUR STUFF?
I CANNOT INTERFERE. I CAN ONLY OBSERVE.

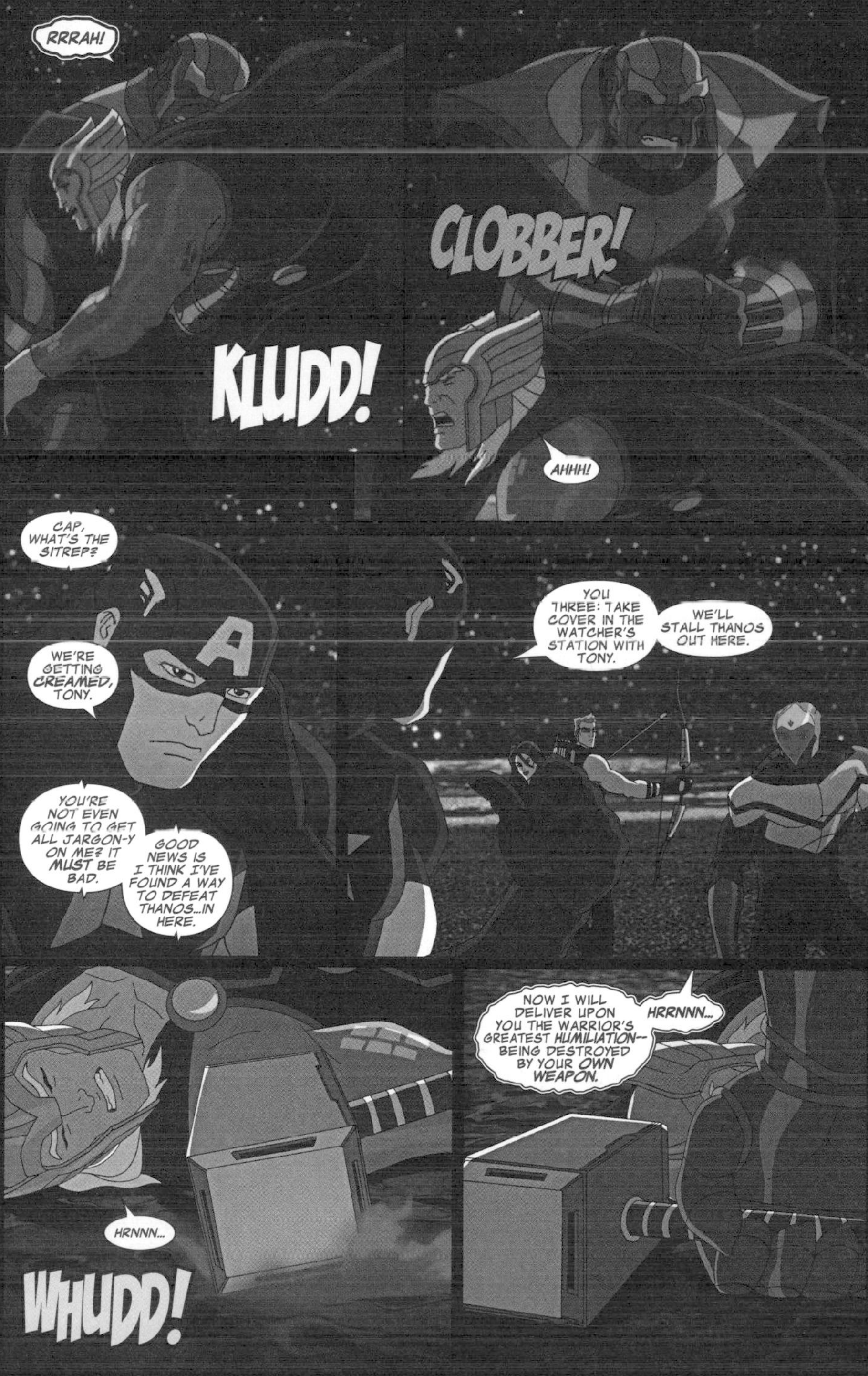
RRRAH!
CLOBBER!
KLUDD!
AHHH!
CAP, WHAT'S THE SITREP?
WE'RE GETTING CREAMED, TONY.
YOU'RE NOT EVEN GOING TO GET ALL JARGON-Y ON ME? IT MUST BE BAD.
GOOD NEWS IS I THINK I'VE FOUND A WAY TO DEFEAT THANOS...IN HERE.
YOU THREE: TAKE COVER IN THE WATCHER'S STATION WITH TONY.
WE'LL STALL THANOS OUT HERE.
HRNNN...
WHUDD!
NOW I WILL DELIVER UPON YOU THE WARRIOR'S GREATEST HUMILIATION--BEING DESTROYED BY YOUR OWN WEAPON.
HRRNNN...

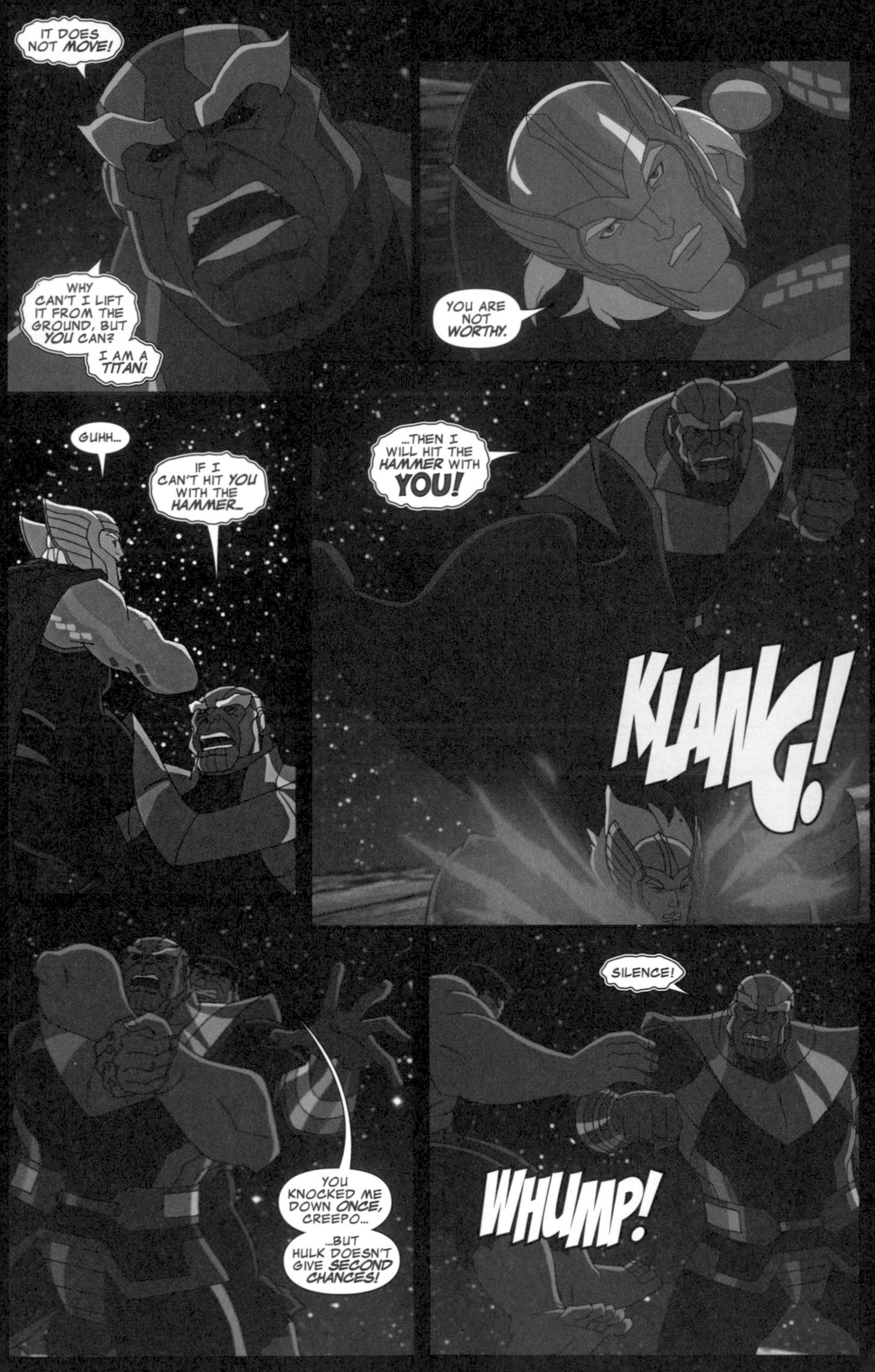
IT DOES NOT MOVE!
WHY CAN'T I LIFT IT FROM THE GROUND, BUT YOU CAN?
I AM A TITAN!
YOU ARE NOT WORTHY.
GUHH...
IF I CAN'T HIT YOU WITH THE HAMMER...
...THEN I WILL HIT THE HAMMER WITH YOU!
KLANG!
YOU KNOCKED ME DOWN ONCE, CREEPO...
...BUT HULK DOESN'T GIVE SECOND CHANCES!
SILENCE!
WHUMP!

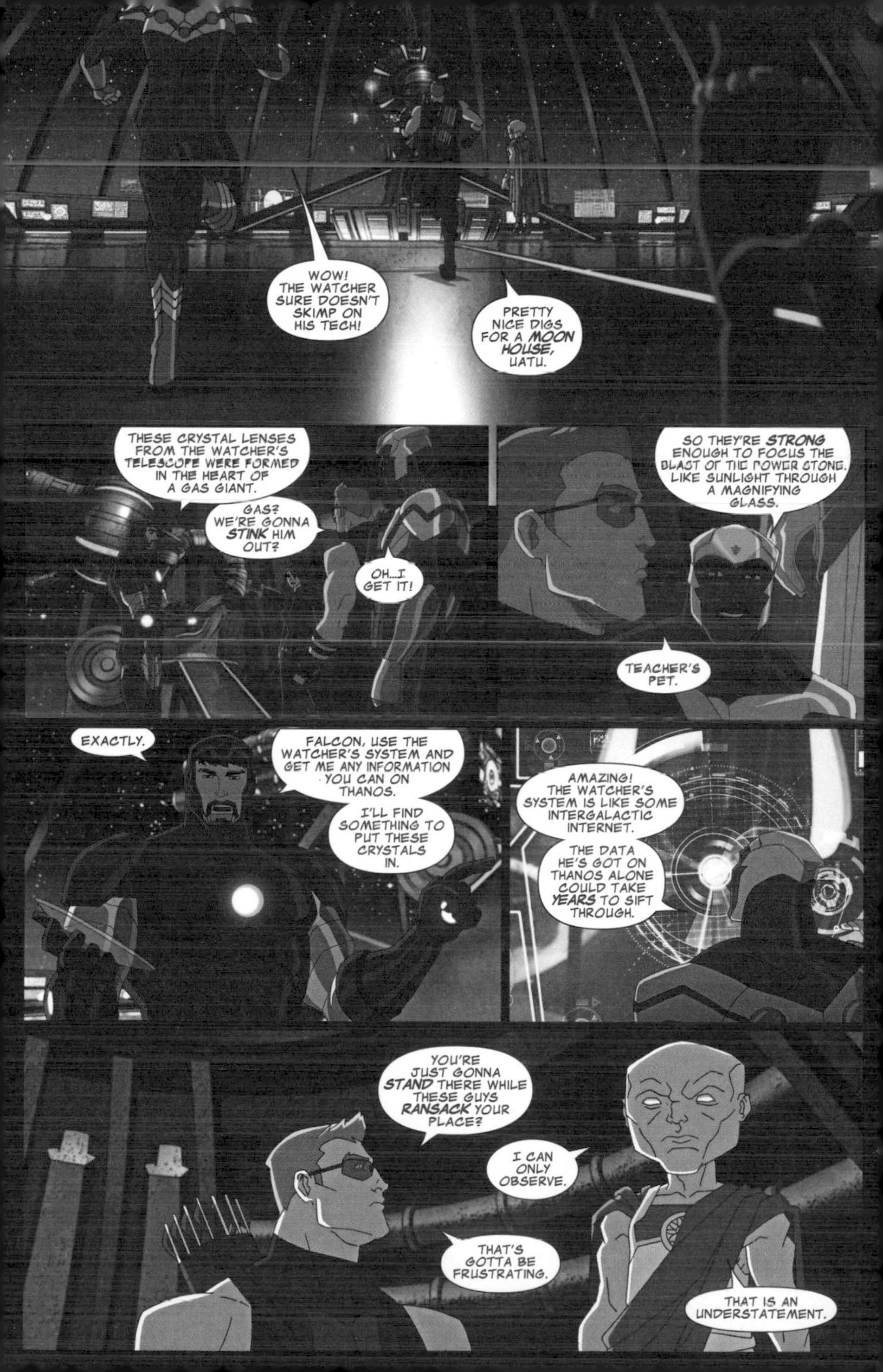
WOW! THE WATCHER SURE DOESN'T SKIMP ON HIS TECH!
PRETTY NICE DIGS FOR A MOON HOUSE, UATU.
THESE CRYSTAL LENSES FROM THE WATCHER'S TELESCOPE WERE FORMED IN THE HEART OF A GAS GIANT.
GAS? WE'RE GONNA STINK HIM OUT?
OH...I GET IT!
SO THEY'RE STRONG ENOUGH TO FOCUS THE BLAST OF THE POWER STONE. LIKE SUNLIGHT THROUGH A MAGNIFYING GLASS.
TEACHER'S PET.
EXACTLY.
FALCON, USE THE WATCHER'S SYSTEM AND GET ME ANY INFORMATION YOU CAN ON THANOS.
I'LL FIND SOMETHING TO PUT THESE CRYSTALS IN.
AMAZING! THE WATCHER'S SYSTEM IS LIKE SOME INTERGALACTIC INTERNET.
THE DATA HE'S GOT ON THANOS ALONE COULD TAKE YEARS TO SIFT THROUGH.
YOU'RE JUST GONNA STAND THERE WHILE THESE GUYS RANSACK YOUR PLACE?
I CAN ONLY OBSERVE.
THAT'S GOTTA BE FRUSTRATING.
THAT IS AN UNDERSTATEMENT.

THROOM!
HULK? BIG GUY, ARE YOU OKAY?
THUD!
IF YOU'RE THE MIGHTIEST THE EARTH HAS TO OFFER, YOUR PLANET IS DOOMED.
NOW GIVE ME THE POWER STONE...
...OR SUFFER THE CONSEQUENCES!
BOOM!
MOONQUAKE! MOONQUAKE!
NO! I ONLY NEEDED A COUPLE MORE MINUTES!
RUMBLE RUMBLE RUMBLE

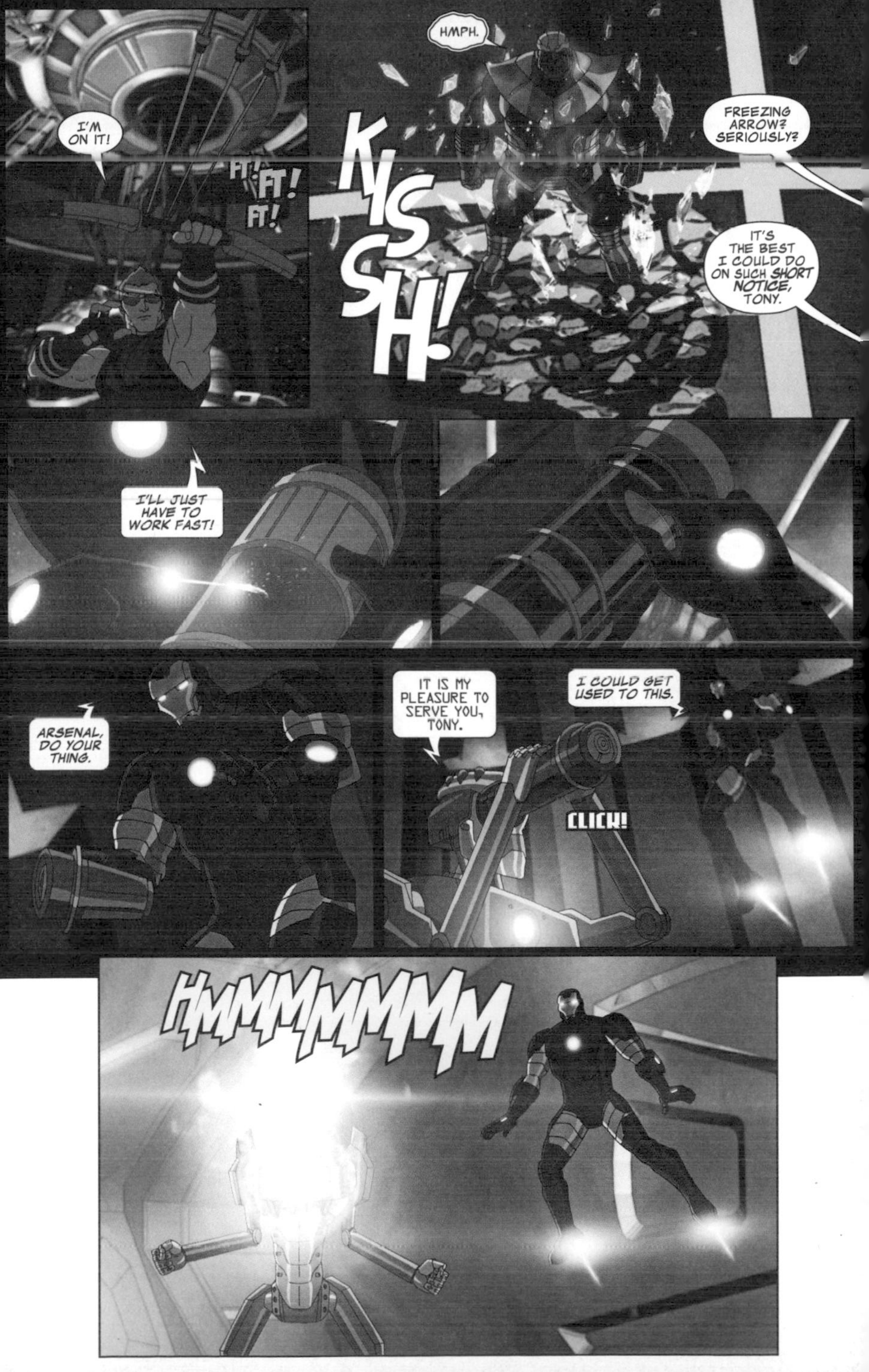
I'M ON IT!
FT! FT! FT!
HMPH.
KRSSH!
FREEZING ARROW? SERIOUSLY?
IT'S THE BEST I COULD DO ON SUCH SHORT NOTICE, TONY.
I'LL JUST HAVE TO WORK FAST!
ARSENAL, DO YOUR THING.
IT IS MY PLEASURE TO SERVE YOU, TONY.
I COULD GET USED TO THIS.
CLICK!
HMMMMMMMM

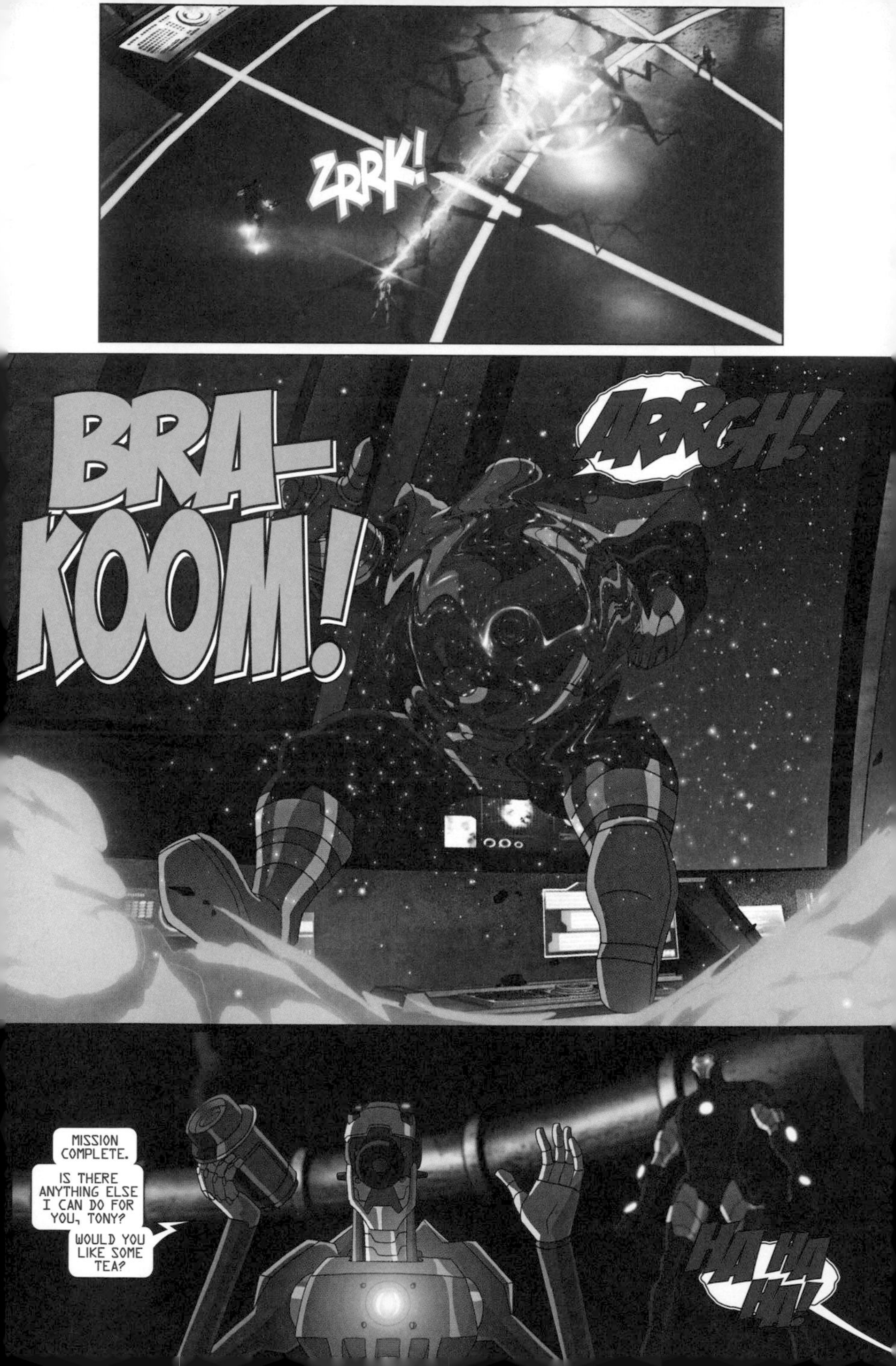
ZRRK!
BRA-KOOM!
ARRGH!
MISSION COMPLETE.
IS THERE ANYTHING ELSE I CAN DO FOR YOU, TONY?
WOULD YOU LIKE SOME TEA?
HA HA HA!

YOU THOUGHT I'D COME FOR THE POWER STONE WITHOUT A WAY TO CONTAIN IT?
BEHOLD...
...THE INFINITY GAUNTLET!
WHAT'S HAPPENING TO TONY'S THREEPIO?
HEY! THAT'S MY BIRTHDAY PRESENT! PUT HIM DOWN, THANOS!
HE HAS THAT WHICH BELONGS TO ME.
THE POWER STONE IS MINE!
VOOOSH!

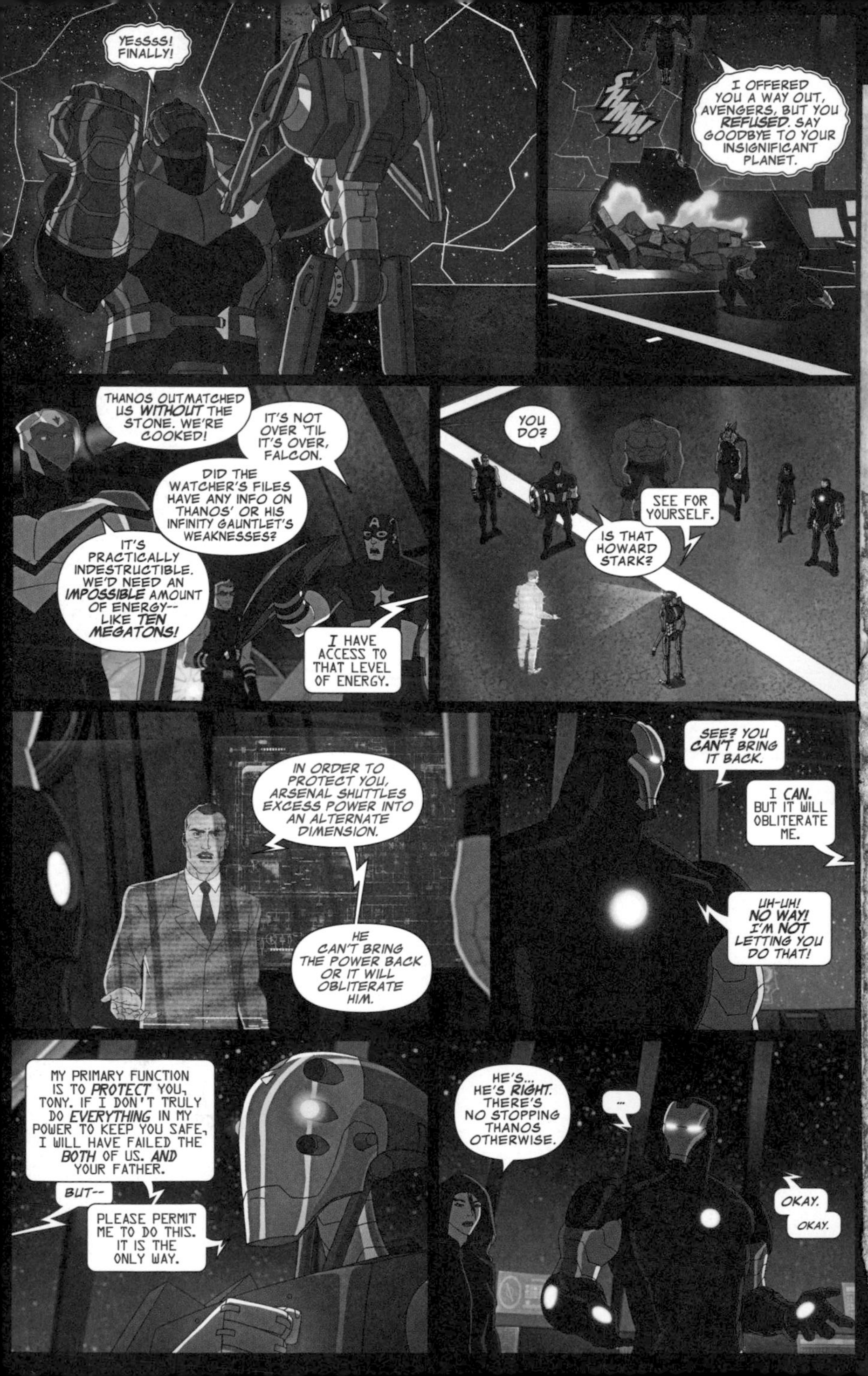
YESSSS! FINALLY!
FWMM!
I OFFERED YOU A WAY OUT, AVENGERS, BUT YOU REFUSED. SAY GOODBYE TO YOUR INSIGNIFICANT PLANET.
THANOS OUTMATCHED US WITHOUT THE STONE. WE'RE COOKED!
IT'S NOT OVER 'TIL IT'S OVER, FALCON.
DID THE WATCHER'S FILES HAVE ANY INFO ON THANOS' OR HIS INFINITY GAUNTLET'S WEAKNESSES?
IT'S PRACTICALLY INDESTRUCTIBLE. WE'D NEED AN IMPOSSIBLE AMOUNT OF ENERGY-- LIKE TEN MEGATONS!
I HAVE ACCESS TO THAT LEVEL OF ENERGY.
YOU DO?
SEE FOR YOURSELF.
IS THAT HOWARD STARK?
IN ORDER TO PROTECT YOU, ARSENAL SHUTTLES EXCESS POWER INTO AN ALTERNATE DIMENSION.
HE CAN'T BRING THE POWER BACK OR IT WILL OBLITERATE HIM.
SEE? YOU CAN'T BRING IT BACK.
I CAN. BUT IT WILL OBLITERATE ME.
UH-UH! NO WAY! I'M NOT LETTING YOU DO THAT!
MY PRIMARY FUNCTION IS TO PROTECT YOU, TONY. IF I DON'T TRULY DO EVERYTHING IN MY POWER TO KEEP YOU SAFE, I WILL HAVE FAILED THE BOTH OF US. AND YOUR FATHER.
BUT--
PLEASE PERMIT ME TO DO THIS. IT IS THE ONLY WAY.
HE'S... HE'S RIGHT. THERE'S NO STOPPING THANOS OTHERWISE.
...
OKAY.
OKAY.

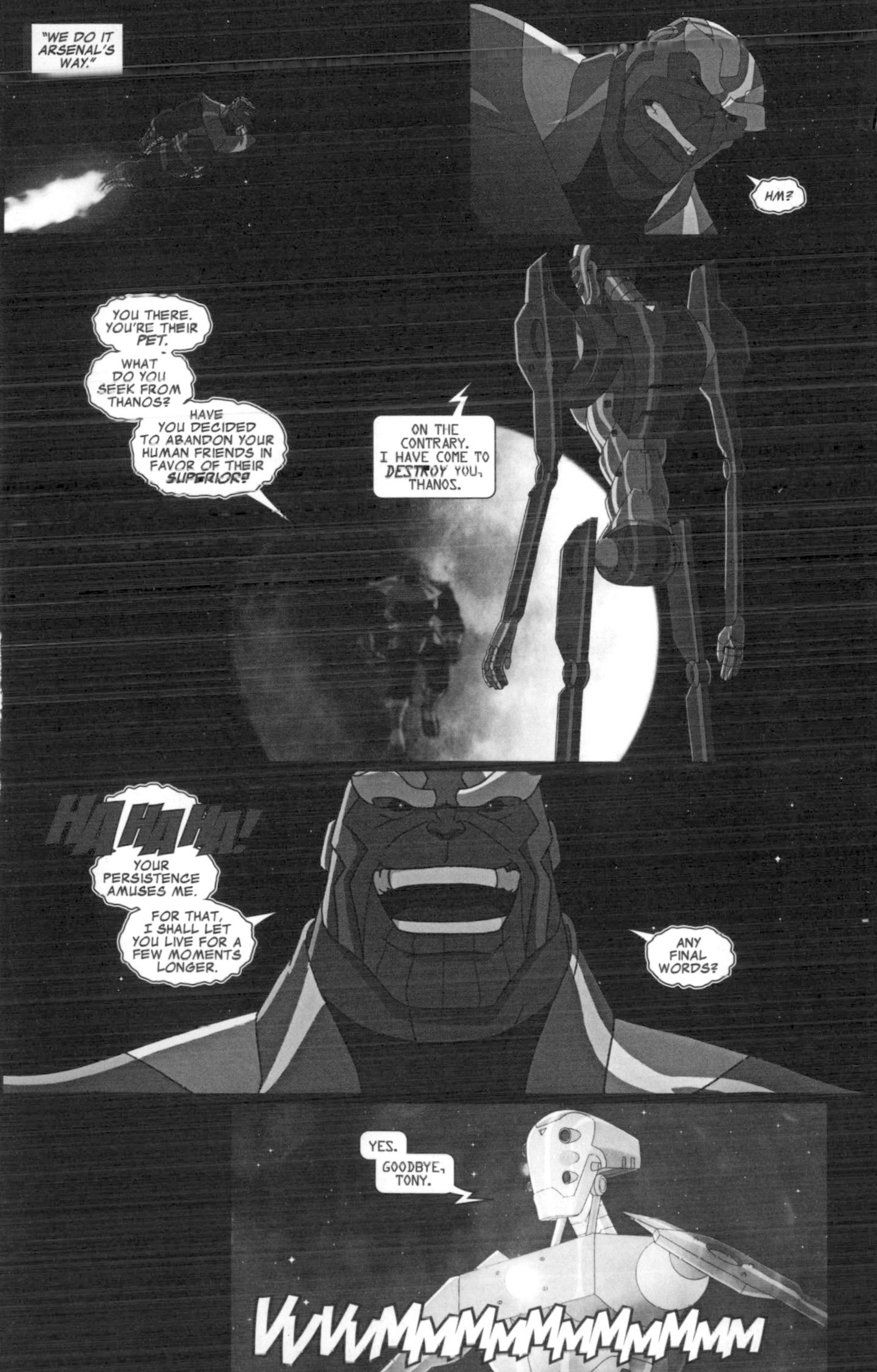
"WE DO IT ARSENAL'S WAY."
HM?
YOU THERE. YOU'RE THEIR PET.
WHAT DO YOU SEEK FROM THANOS?
HAVE YOU DECIDED TO ABANDON YOUR HUMAN FRIENDS IN FAVOR OF THEIR SUPERIOR?
ON THE CONTRARY. I HAVE COME TO DESTROY YOU, THANOS.
HA HA HA!
YOUR PERSISTENCE AMUSES ME.
FOR THAT, I SHALL LET YOU LIVE FOR A FEW MOMENTS LONGER.
ANY FINAL WORDS?
YES. GOODBYE, TONY.
VVVVMMMMMMMMMMMMMM

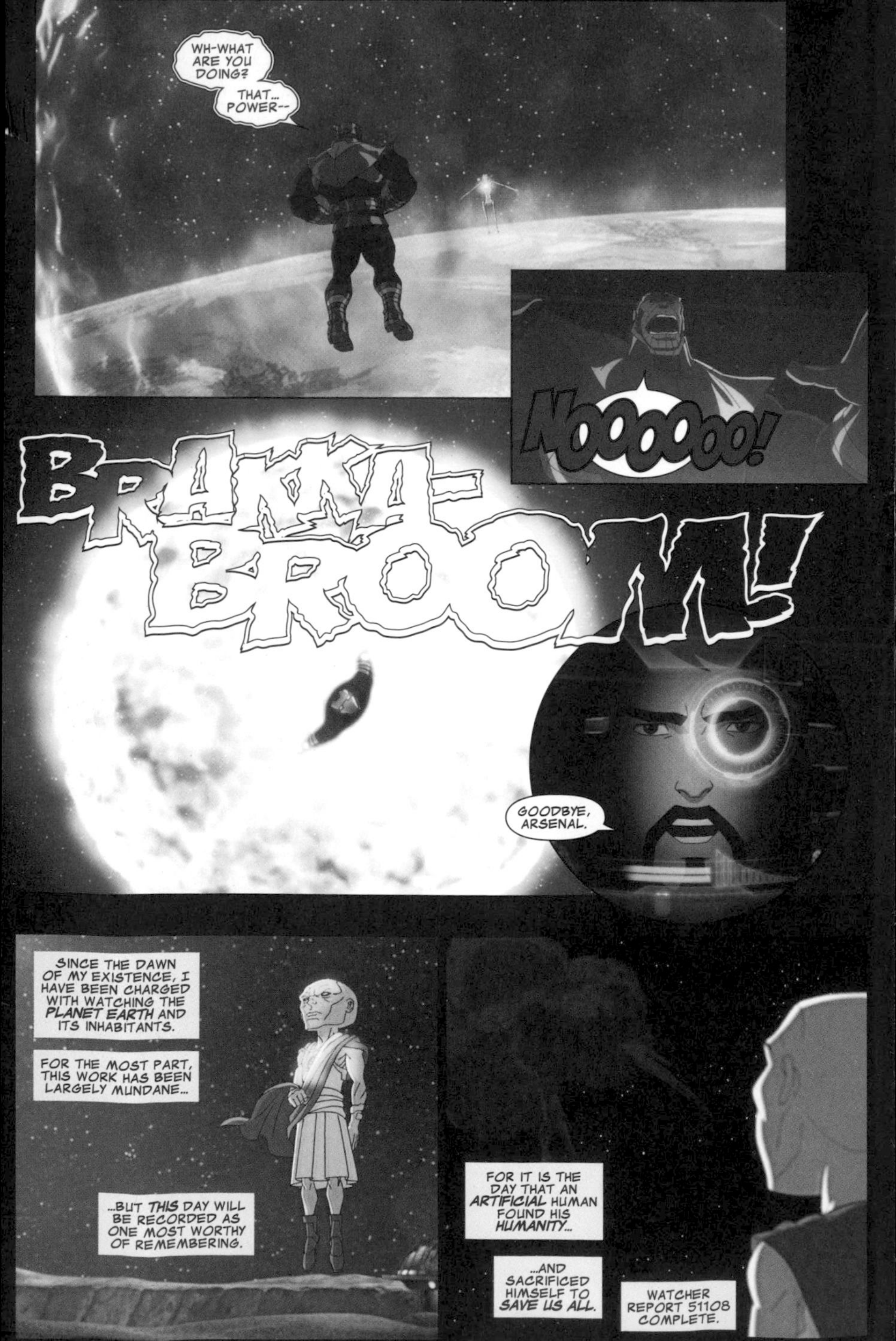
WH-WHAT ARE YOU DOING?
THAT... POWER--
NOOOOOO!
BRAKA-BROOM!
GOODBYE, ARSENAL.
SINCE THE DAWN OF MY EXISTENCE, I HAVE BEEN CHARGED WITH WATCHING THE PLANET EARTH AND ITS INHABITANTS.
FOR THE MOST PART, THIS WORK HAS BEEN LARGELY MUNDANE...
...BUT THIS DAY WILL BE RECORDED AS ONE MOST WORTHY OF REMEMBERING.
FOR IT IS THE DAY THAT AN ARTIFICIAL HUMAN FOUND HIS HUMANITY...
...AND SACRIFICED HIMSELF TO SAVE US ALL.
WATCHER REPORT 51108 COMPLETE.

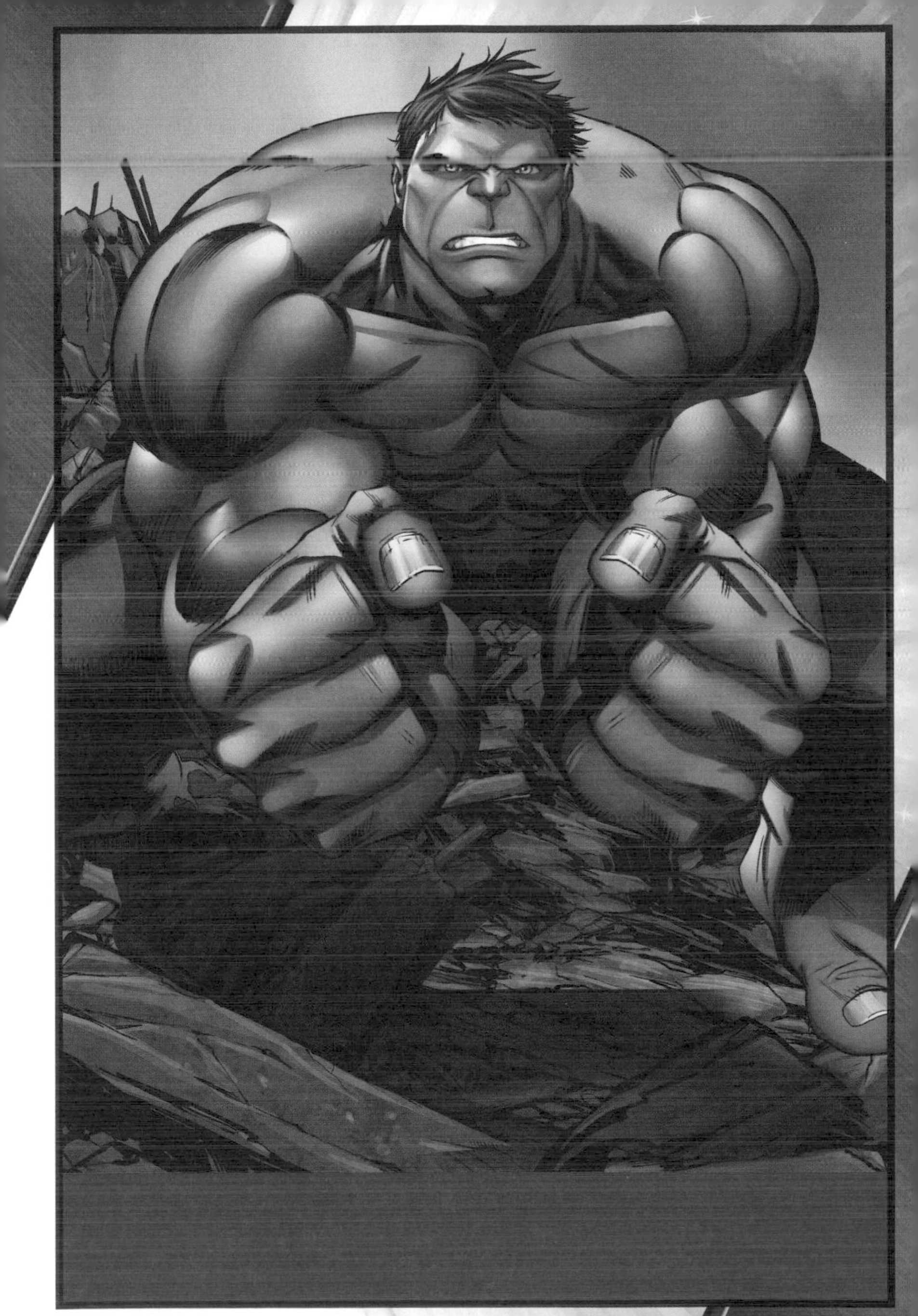

BASED ON "HULK'S DAY OUT" #3

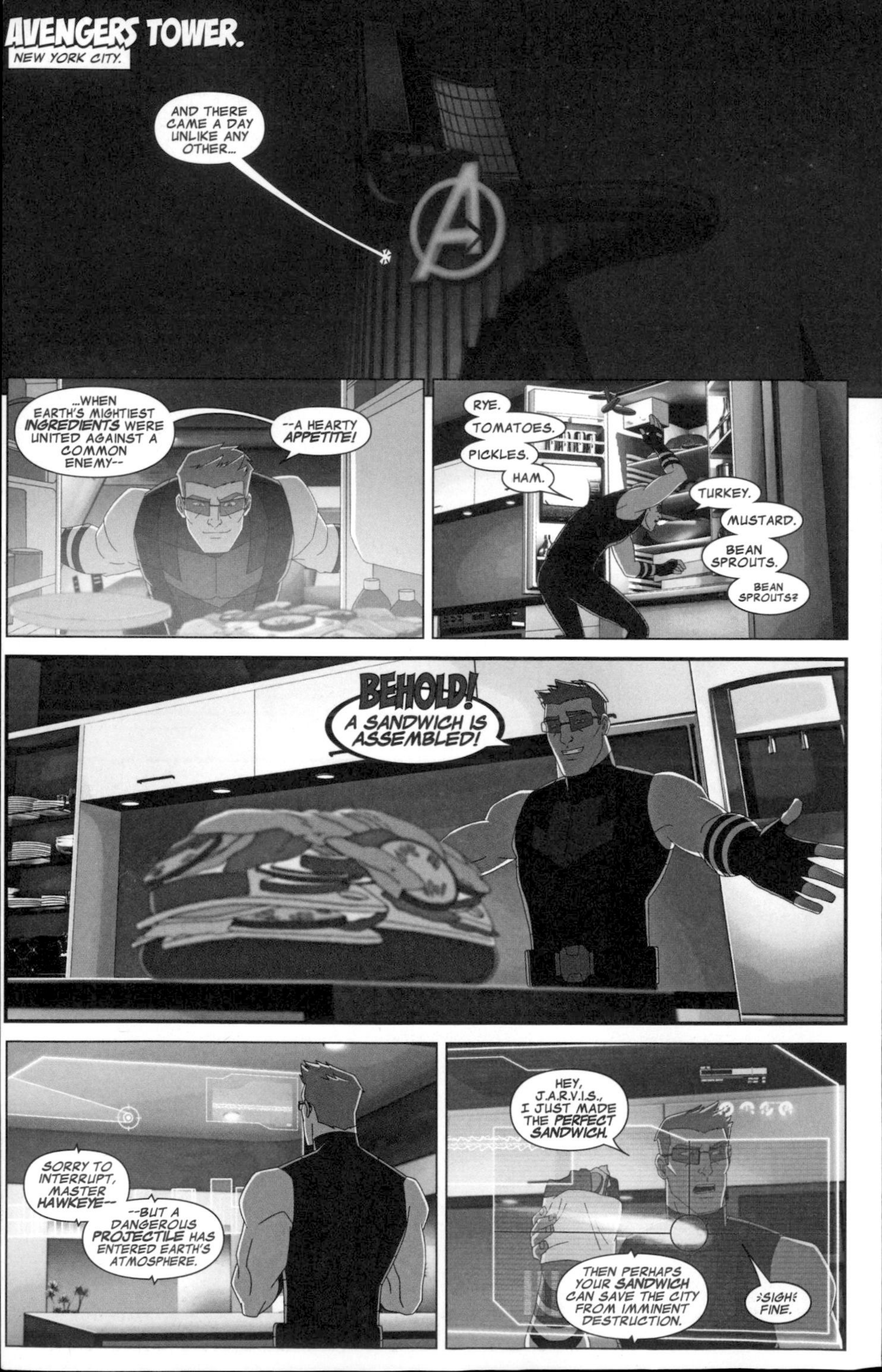

AVENGERS TOWER.
NEW YORK CITY.
AND THERE CAME A DAY UNLIKE ANY OTHER...
...WHEN EARTH'S MIGHTIEST INGREDIENTS WERE UNITED AGAINST A COMMON ENEMY--
--A HEARTY APPETITE!
RYE.
TOMATOES.
PICKLES.
HAM.
TURKEY.
MUSTARD.
BEAN SPROUTS.
BEAN SPROUTS?
BEHOLD! A SANDWICH IS ASSEMBLED!
SORRY TO INTERRUPT, MASTER HAWKEYE--
--BUT A DANGEROUS PROJECTILE HAS ENTERED EARTH'S ATMOSPHERE.
HEY, J.A.R.V.I.S., I JUST MADE THE PERFECT SANDWICH.
THEN PERHAPS YOUR SANDWICH CAN SAVE THE CITY FROM IMMINENT DESTRUCTION.
SIGH FINE.

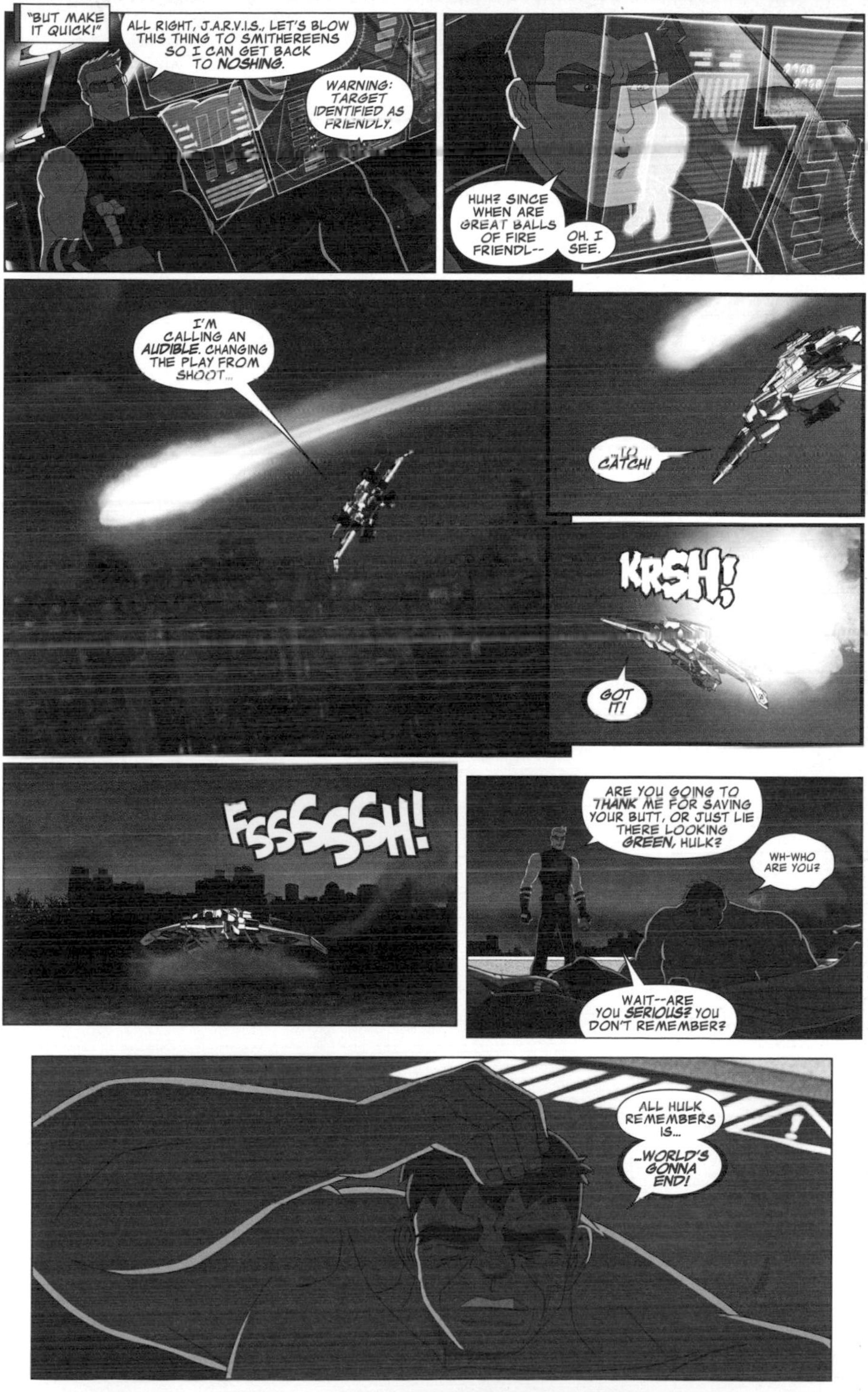
"BUT MAKE IT QUICK!"
ALL RIGHT, J.A.R.V.I.S., LET'S BLOW THIS THING TO SMITHEREENS SO I CAN GET BACK TO NOSHING.
WARNING: TARGET IDENTIFIED AS FRIENDLY.
HUH? SINCE WHEN ARE GREAT BALLS OF FIRE FRIENDL--
OH. I SEE.
I'M CALLING AN AUDIBLE. CHANGING THE PLAY FROM SHOOT...
...TO CATCH!
KRSH!
GOT IT!
FSSSSSH!
ARE YOU GOING TO THANK ME FOR SAVING YOUR BUTT, OR JUST LIE THERE LOOKING GREEN, HULK?
WH-WHO ARE YOU?
WAIT--ARE YOU SERIOUS? YOU DON'T REMEMBER?
ALL HULK REMEMBERS IS...
...WORLD'S GONNA END!

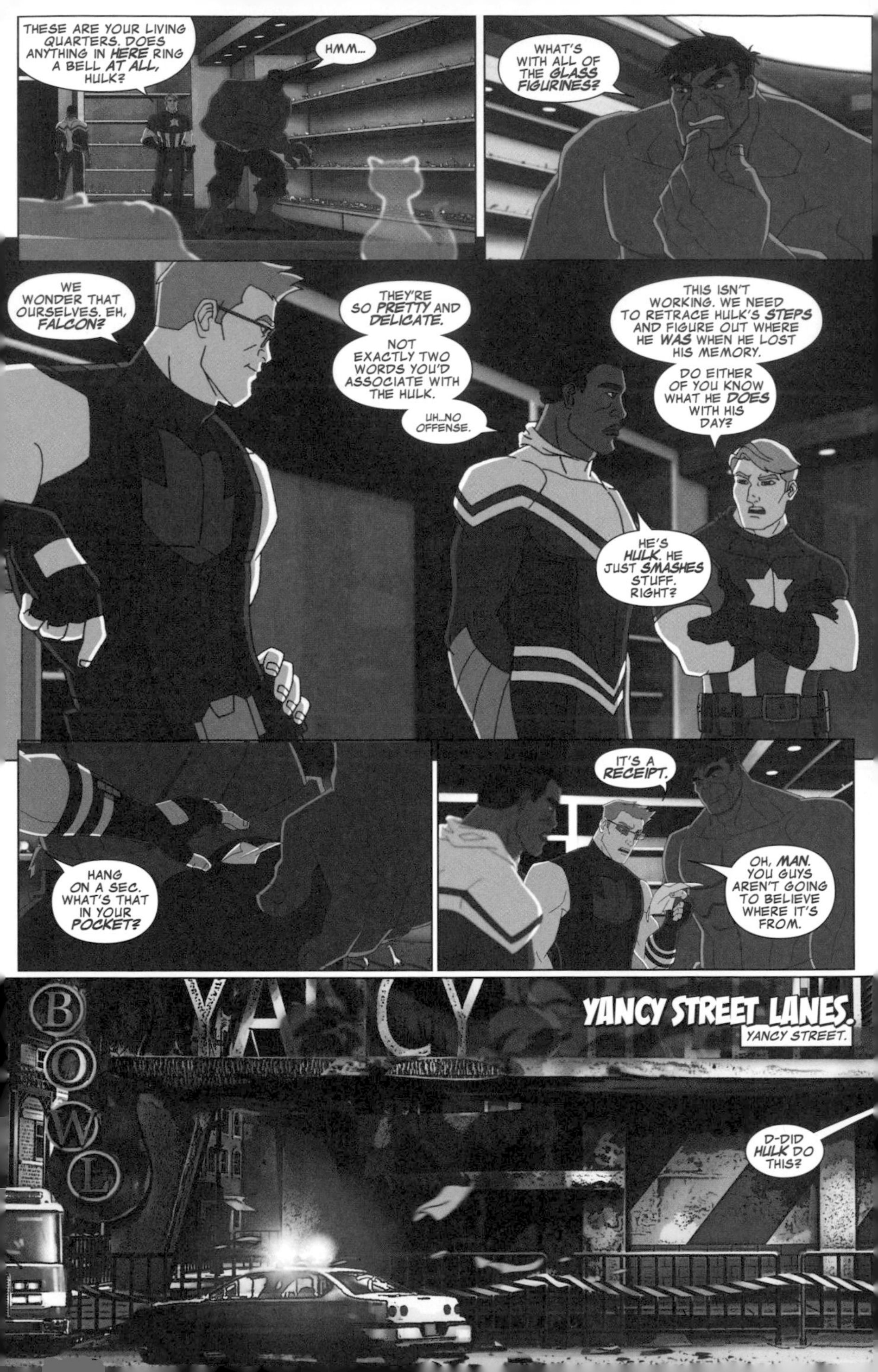
THESE ARE YOUR LIVING QUARTERS. DOES ANYTHING IN HERE RING A BELL AT ALL, HULK?
HMM...
WHAT'S WITH ALL OF THE GLASS FIGURINES?
WE WONDER THAT OURSELVES. EH, FALCON?
THEY'RE SO PRETTY AND DELICATE.
NOT EXACTLY TWO WORDS YOU'D ASSOCIATE WITH THE HULK.
UH...NO OFFENSE.
THIS ISN'T WORKING. WE NEED TO RETRACE HULK'S STEPS AND FIGURE OUT WHERE HE WAS WHEN HE LOST HIS MEMORY.
DO EITHER OF YOU KNOW WHAT HE DOES WITH HIS DAY?
HE'S HULK. HE JUST SMASHES STUFF. RIGHT?
HANG ON A SEC. WHAT'S THAT IN YOUR POCKET?
IT'S A RECEIPT.
OH, MAN. YOU GUYS AREN'T GOING TO BELIEVE WHERE IT'S FROM.
YANCY STREET LANES.
YANCY STREET.
BOWL
YANCY
D-DID HULK DO THIS?

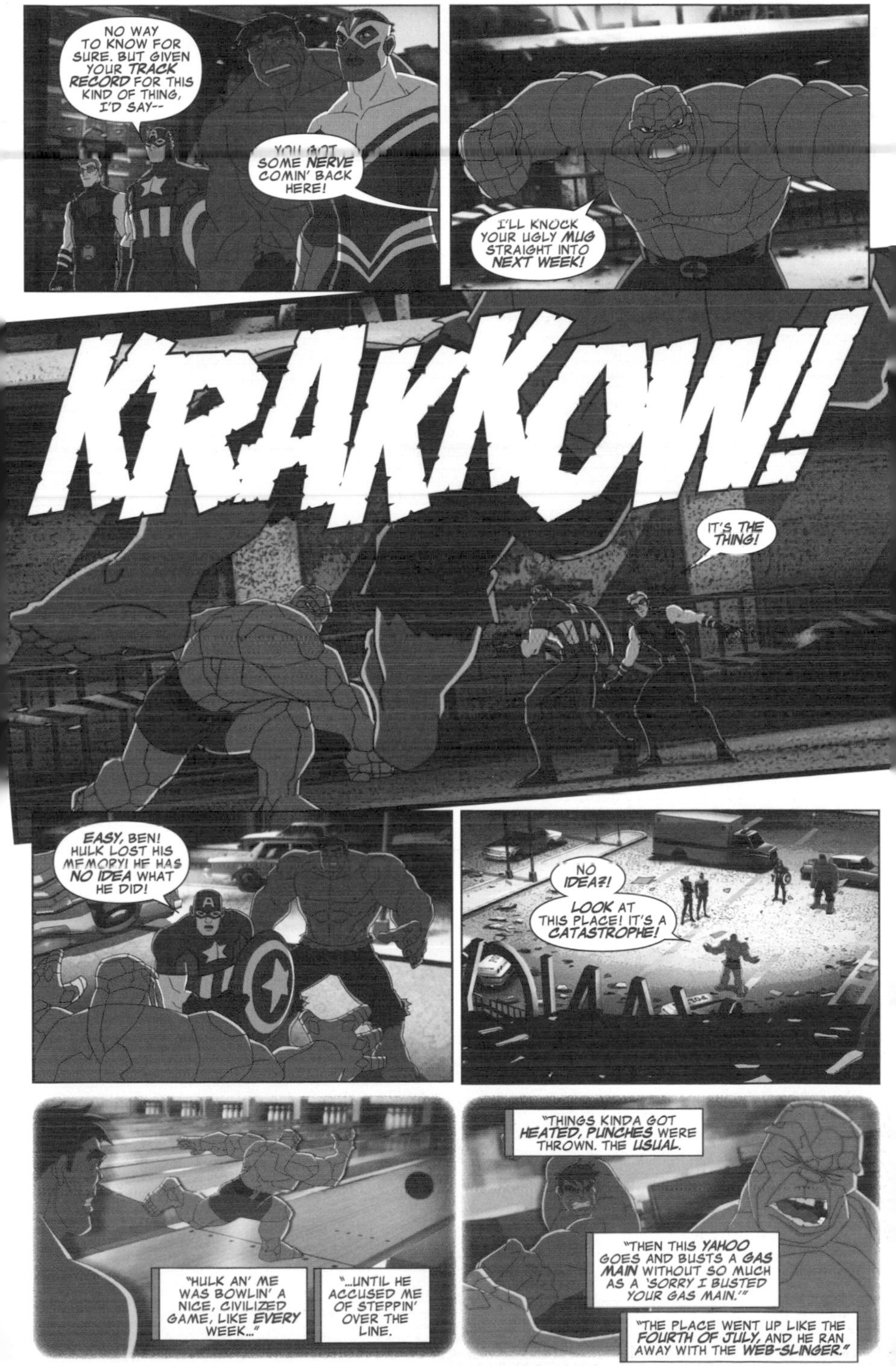
NO WAY TO KNOW FOR SURE. BUT GIVEN YOUR TRACK RECORD FOR THIS KIND OF THING, I'D SAY--
YOU GOT SOME NERVE COMIN' BACK HERE!
I'LL KNOCK YOUR UGLY MUG STRAIGHT INTO NEXT WEEK!
KRAKKOW!
IT'S THE THING!
EASY, BEN! HULK LOST HIS MEMORY! HE HAS NO IDEA WHAT HE DID!
NO IDEA?!
LOOK AT THIS PLACE! IT'S A CATASTROPHE!
"HULK AN' ME WAS BOWLIN' A NICE, CIVILIZED GAME, LIKE EVERY WEEK..."
"...UNTIL HE ACCUSED ME OF STEPPIN' OVER THE LINE.
"THINGS KINDA GOT HEATED, PUNCHES WERE THROWN. THE USUAL.
"THEN THIS YAHOO GOES AND BUSTS A GAS MAIN WITHOUT SO MUCH AS A 'SORRY I BUSTED YOUR GAS MAIN.'"
"THE PLACE WENT UP LIKE THE FOURTH OF JULY, AND HE RAN AWAY WITH THE WEB-SLINGER."

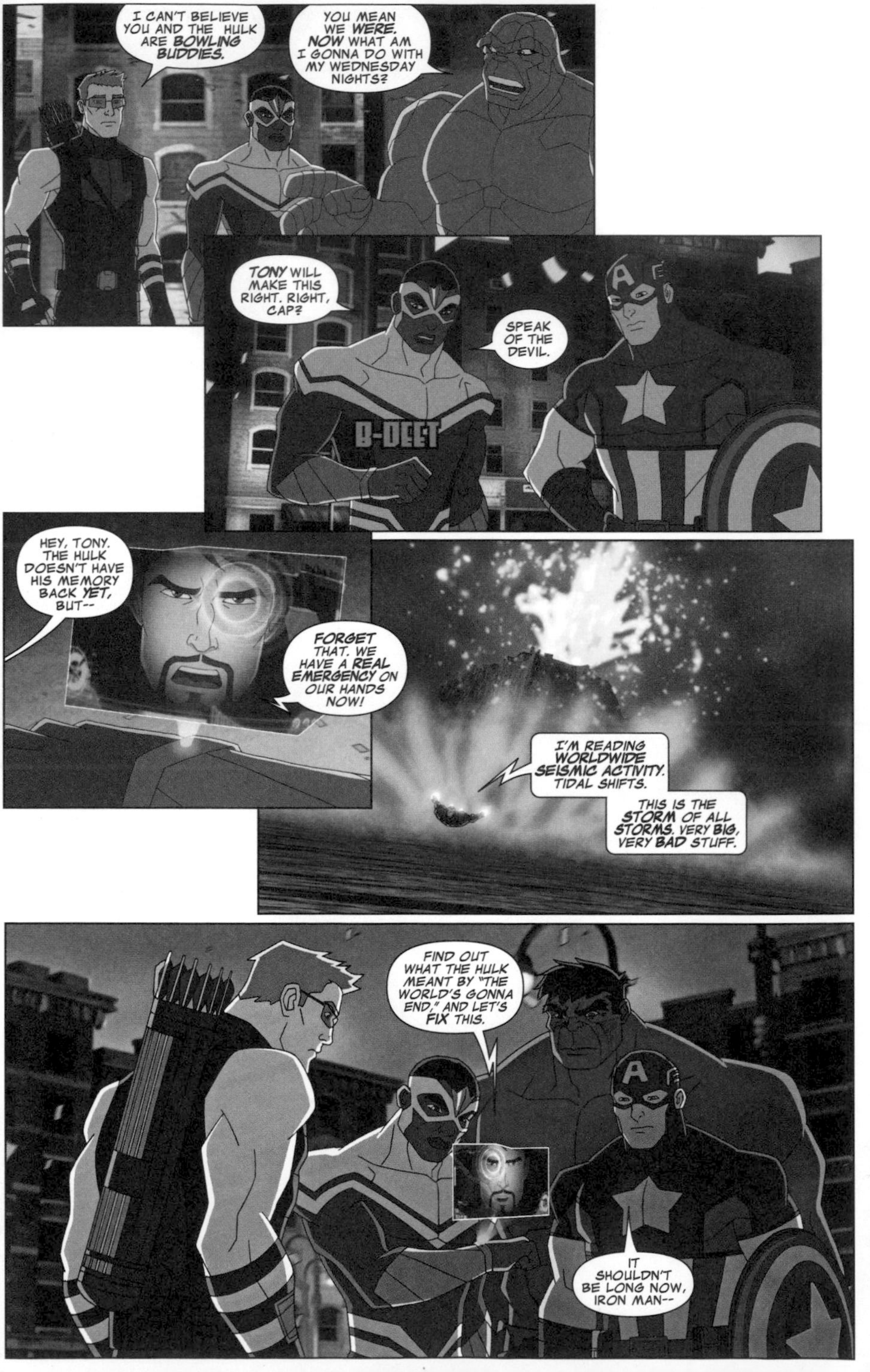
I CAN'T BELIEVE YOU AND THE HULK ARE BOWLING BUDDIES.
YOU MEAN WE WERE. NOW WHAT AM I GONNA DO WITH MY WEDNESDAY NIGHTS?
TONY WILL MAKE THIS RIGHT. RIGHT, CAP?
SPEAK OF THE DEVIL.
B-DEET
HEY, TONY. THE HULK DOESN'T HAVE HIS MEMORY BACK YET, BUT--
FORGET THAT. WE HAVE A REAL EMERGENCY ON OUR HANDS NOW!
I'M READING WORLDWIDE SEISMIC ACTIVITY. TIDAL SHIFTS.
THIS IS THE STORM OF ALL STORMS. VERY BIG, VERY BAD STUFF.
FIND OUT WHAT THE HULK MEANT BY "THE WORLD'S GONNA END," AND LET'S FIX THIS.
IT SHOULDN'T BE LONG NOW, IRON MAN--

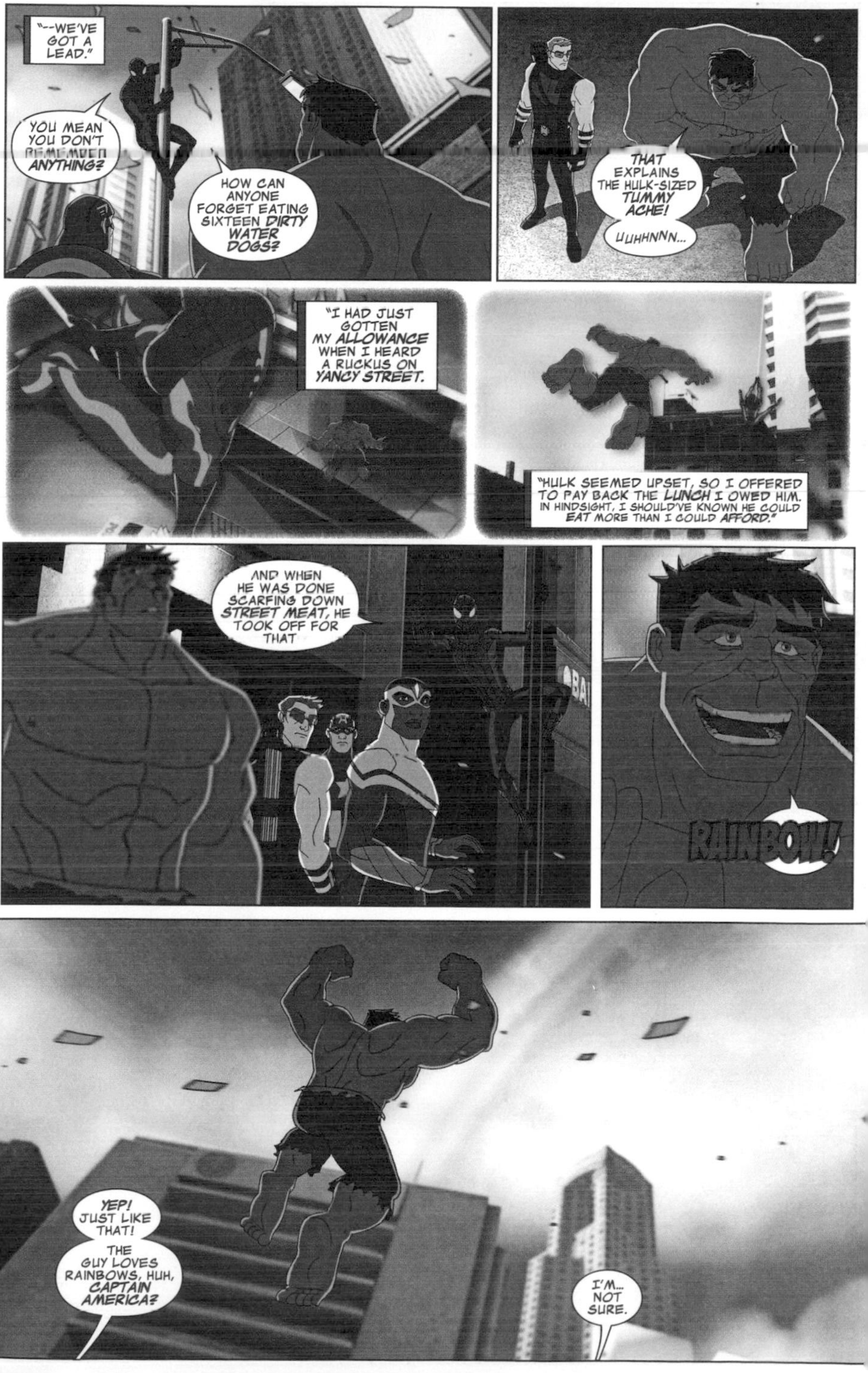
"--WE'VE GOT A LEAD."
YOU MEAN YOU DON'T REMEMBER ANYTHING?
HOW CAN ANYONE FORGET EATING SIXTEEN DIRTY WATER DOGS?
THAT EXPLAINS THE HULK-SIZED TUMMY ACHE!
UUHHNNN...
"I HAD JUST GOTTEN MY ALLOWANCE WHEN I HEARD A RUCKUS ON YANCY STREET.
"HULK SEEMED UPSET, SO I OFFERED TO PAY BACK THE LUNCH I OWED HIM. IN HINDSIGHT, I SHOULD'VE KNOWN HE COULD EAT MORE THAN I COULD AFFORD."
AND WHEN HE WAS DONE SCARFING DOWN STREET MEAT, HE TOOK OFF FOR THAT
RAINBOW!
YEP! JUST LIKE THAT!
THE GUY LOVES RAINBOWS, HUH, CAPTAIN AMERICA?
I'M... NOT SURE.

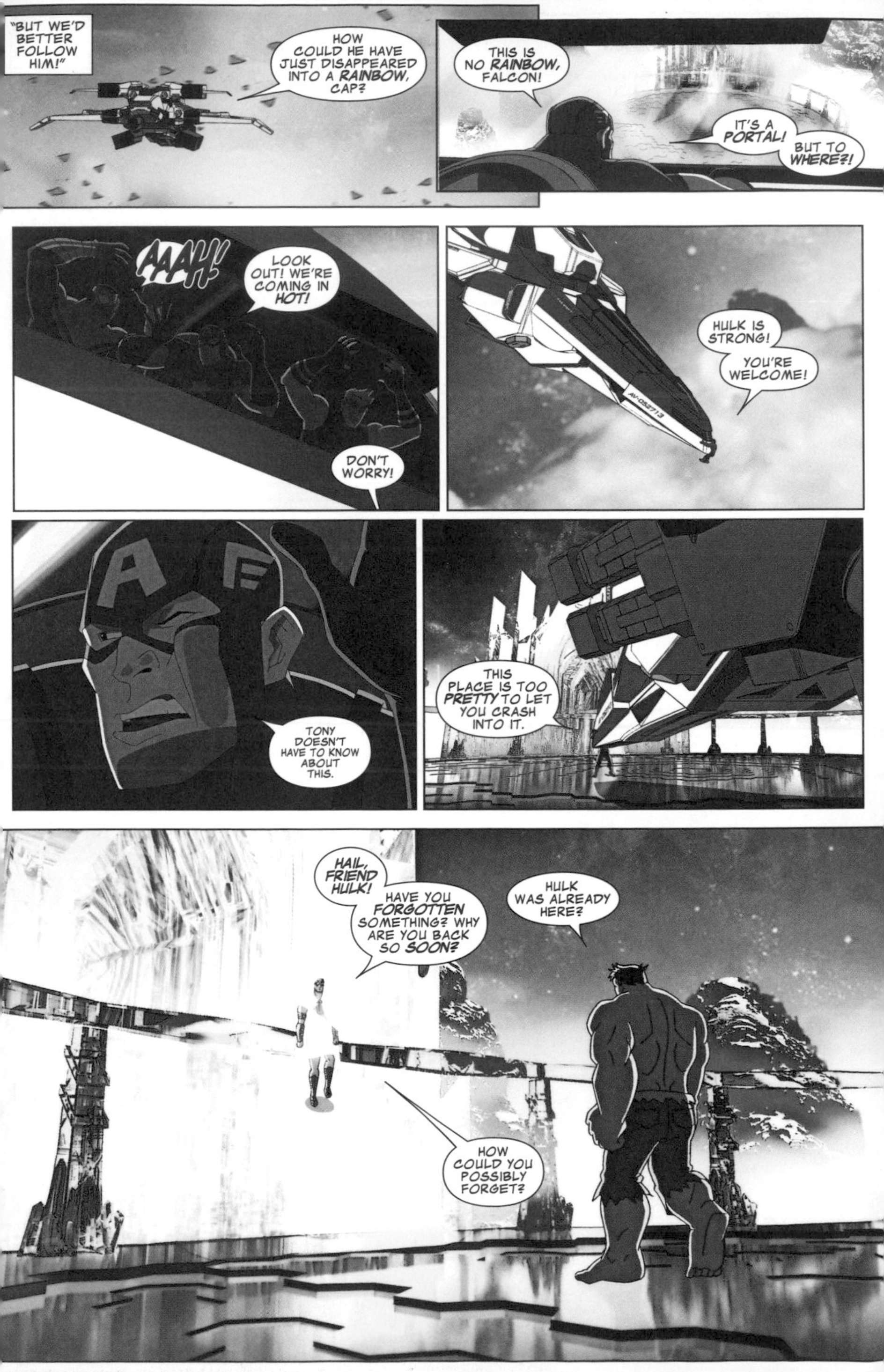
"BUT WE'D BETTER FOLLOW HIM!"
HOW COULD HE HAVE JUST DISAPPEARED INTO A RAINBOW, CAP?
THIS IS NO RAINBOW, FALCON!
IT'S A PORTAL!
BUT TO WHERE?!
AAAH!
LOOK OUT! WE'RE COMING IN HOT!
DON'T WORRY!
HULK IS STRONG!
YOU'RE WELCOME!
TONY DOESN'T HAVE TO KNOW ABOUT THIS.
THIS PLACE IS TOO PRETTY TO LET YOU CRASH INTO IT.
HAIL, FRIEND HULK!
HAVE YOU FORGOTTEN SOMETHING? WHY ARE YOU BACK SO SOON?
HULK WAS ALREADY HERE?
HOW COULD YOU POSSIBLY FORGET?

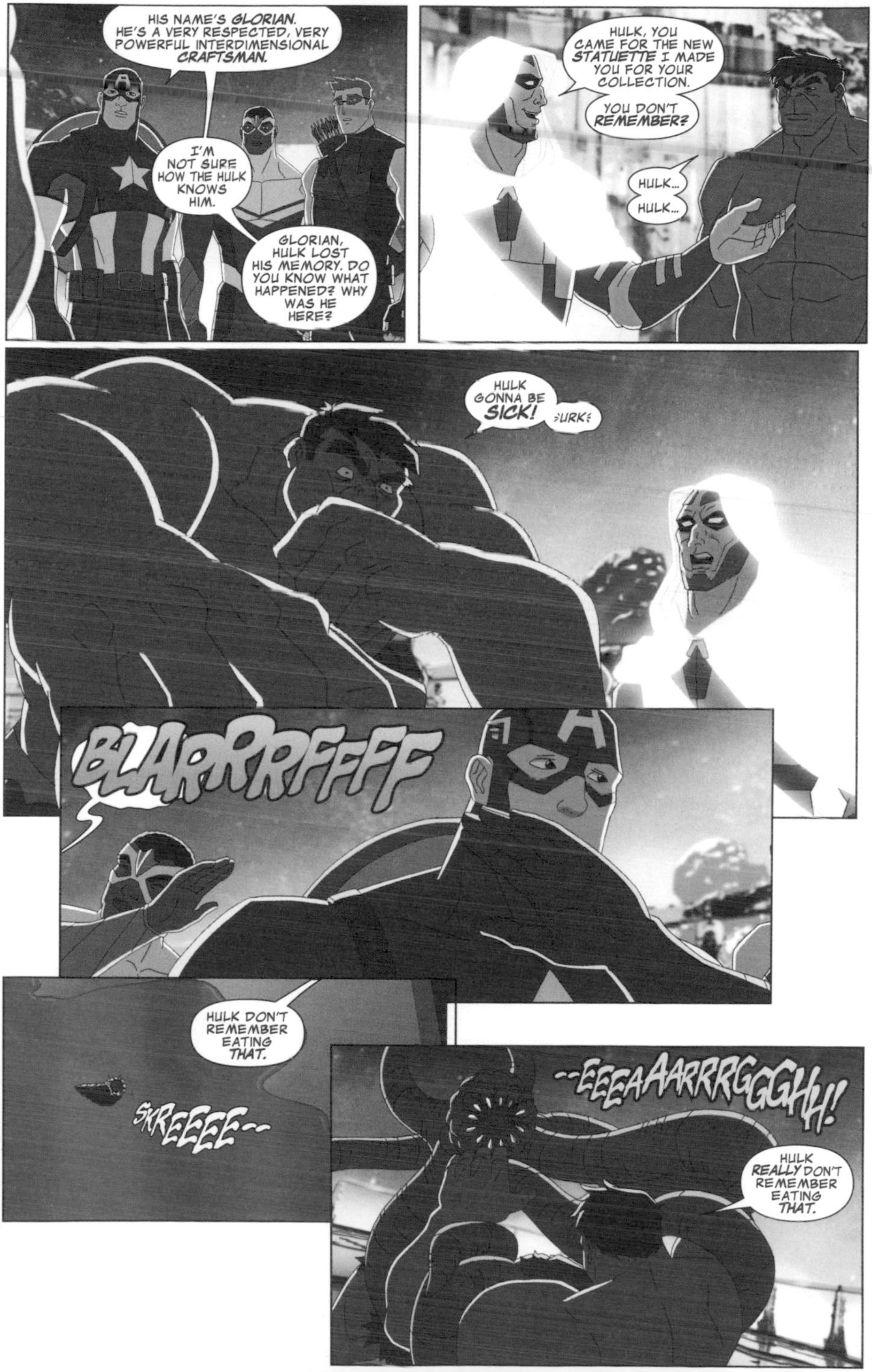
HIS NAME'S GLORIAN. HE'S A VERY RESPECTED, VERY POWERFUL INTERDIMENSIONAL CRAFTSMAN.
I'M NOT SURE HOW THE HULK KNOWS HIM.
GLORIAN, HULK LOST HIS MEMORY. DO YOU KNOW WHAT HAPPENED? WHY WAS HE HERE?
HULK, YOU CAME FOR THE NEW STATUETTE I MADE YOU FOR YOUR COLLECTION.
YOU DON'T REMEMBER?
HULK...
HULK...
HULK GONNA BE SICK!
URK
BLARRRRFFFFF
HULK DON'T REMEMBER EATING THAT.
SKREEEEE--
--EEEAAARRRGGGHH!
HULK REALLY DON'T REMEMBER EATING THAT.

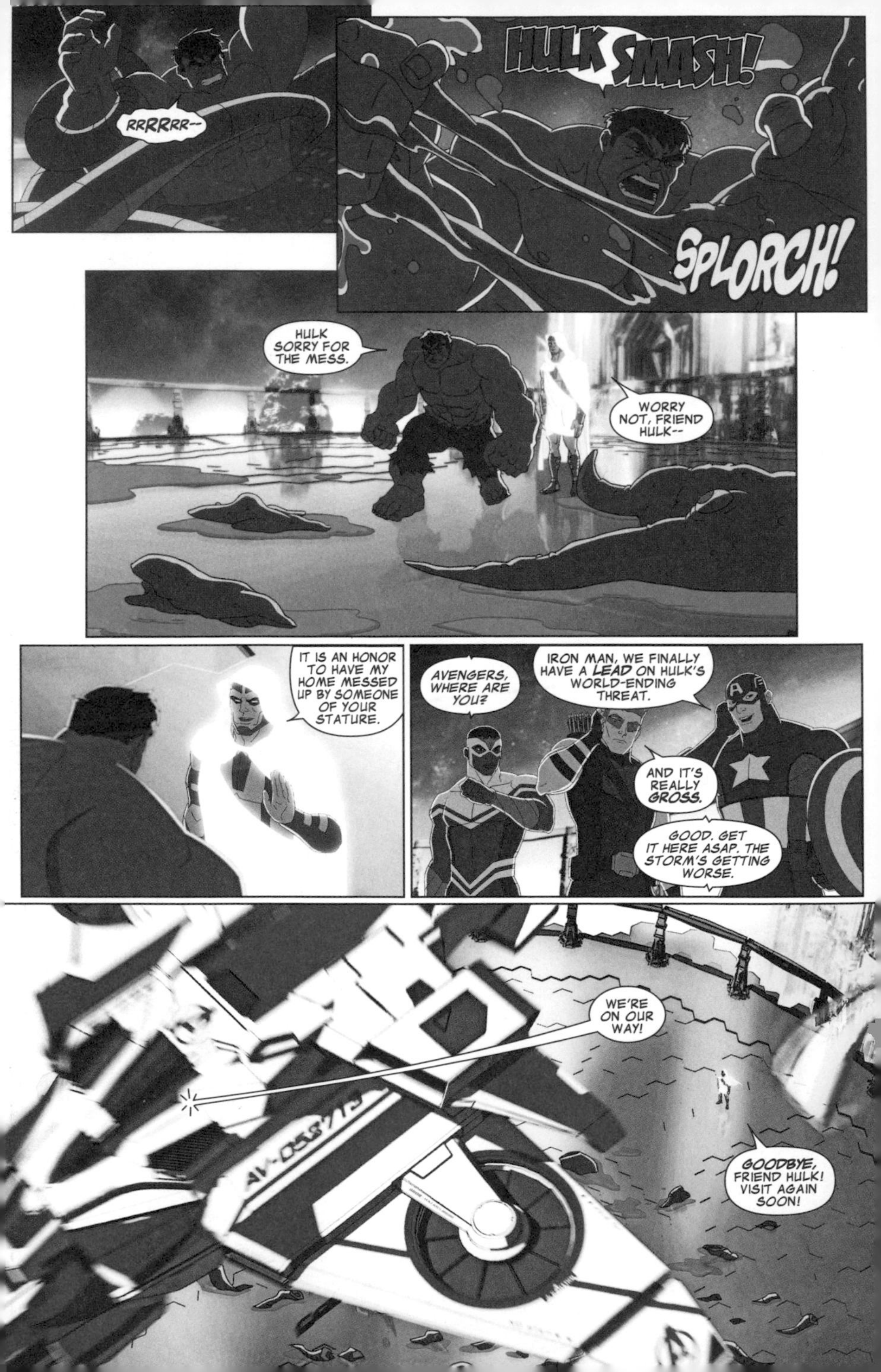
RRRRRR--
HULK SMASH!
SPLORCH!
HULK SORRY FOR THE MESS.
WORRY NOT, FRIEND HULK--
IT IS AN HONOR TO HAVE MY HOME MESSED UP BY SOMEONE OF YOUR STATURE.
AVENGERS, WHERE ARE YOU?
IRON MAN, WE FINALLY HAVE A LEAD ON HULK'S WORLD-ENDING THREAT.
AND IT'S REALLY GROSS.
GOOD. GET IT HERE ASAP. THE STORM'S GETTING WORSE.
WE'RE ON OUR WAY!
GOODBYE, FRIEND HULK! VISIT AGAIN SOON!

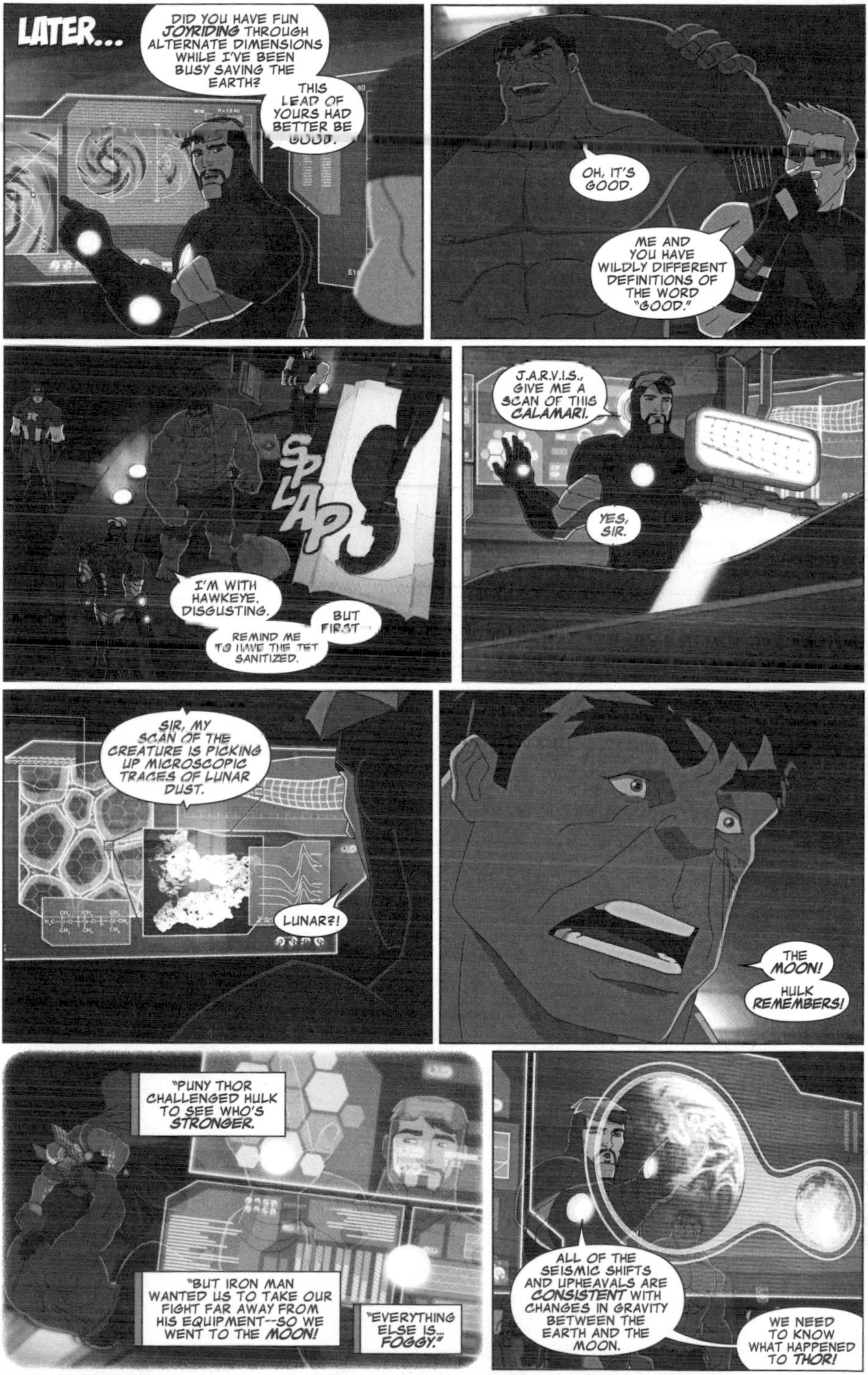
LATER...
DID YOU HAVE FUN JOYRIDING THROUGH ALTERNATE DIMENSIONS WHILE I'VE BEEN BUSY SAVING THE EARTH?
THIS LEAD OF YOURS HAD BETTER BE GOOD.
OH, IT'S GOOD.
ME AND YOU HAVE WILDLY DIFFERENT DEFINITIONS OF THE WORD "GOOD."
SPLAP
I'M WITH HAWKEYE. DISGUSTING.
BUT FIRST...
REMIND ME TO HAVE THE JET SANITIZED.
J.A.R.V.I.S., GIVE ME A SCAN OF THIS CALAMARI.
YES, SIR.
SIR, MY SCAN OF THE CREATURE IS PICKING UP MICROSCOPIC TRACES OF LUNAR DUST.
LUNAR?!
THE MOON!
HULK REMEMBERS!
"PUNY THOR CHALLENGED HULK TO SEE WHO'S STRONGER.
"BUT IRON MAN WANTED US TO TAKE OUR FIGHT FAR AWAY FROM HIS EQUIPMENT--SO WE WENT TO THE MOON!
"EVERYTHING ELSE IS... FOGGY."
ALL OF THE SEISMIC SHIFTS AND UPHEAVALS ARE CONSISTENT WITH CHANGES IN GRAVITY BETWEEN THE EARTH AND THE MOON.
WE NEED TO KNOW WHAT HAPPENED TO THOR!

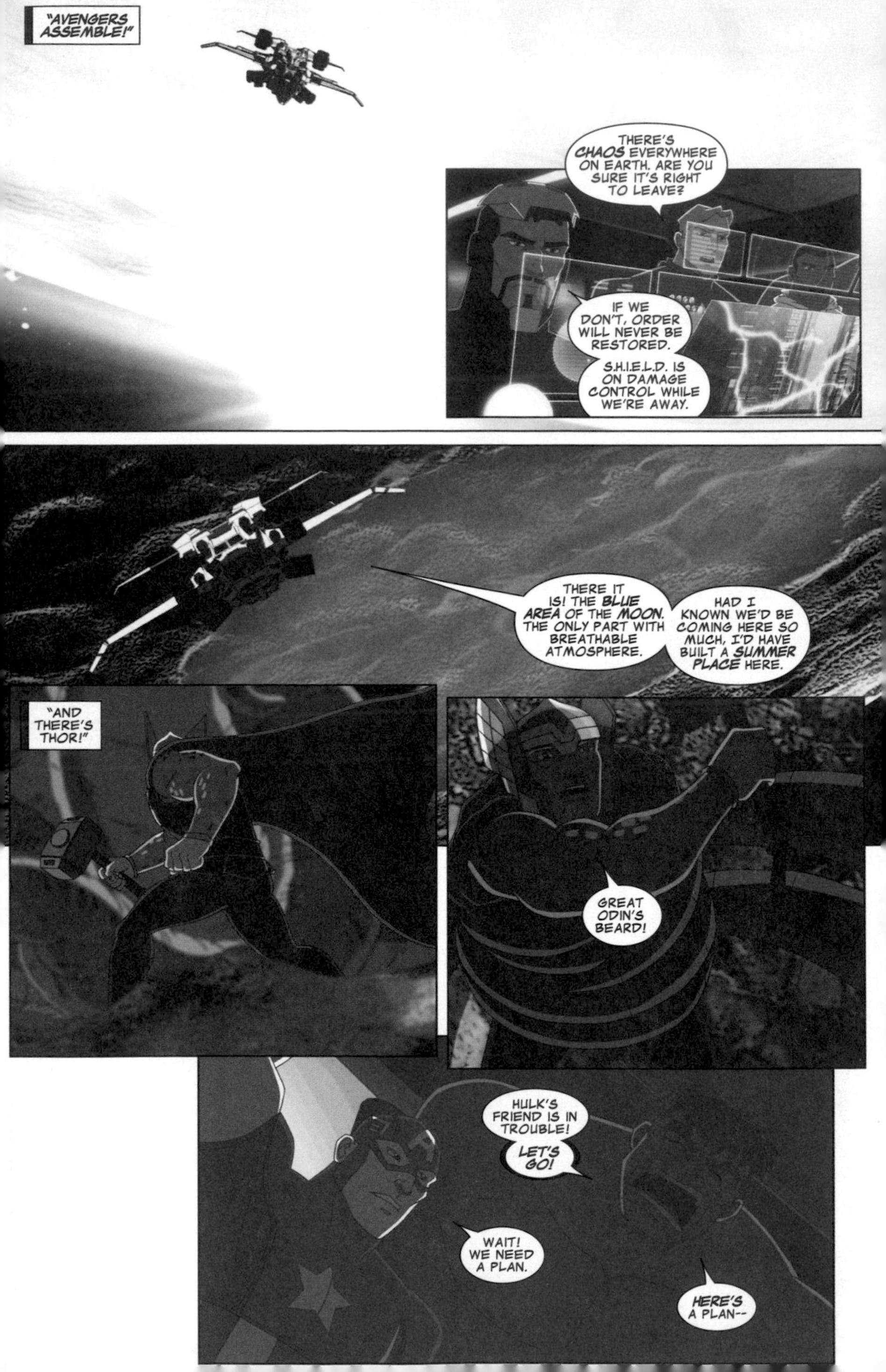
"AVENGERS ASSEMBLE!"
THERE'S CHAOS EVERYWHERE ON EARTH. ARE YOU SURE IT'S RIGHT TO LEAVE?
IF WE DON'T, ORDER WILL NEVER BE RESTORED.
S.H.I.E.L.D. IS ON DAMAGE CONTROL WHILE WE'RE AWAY.
THERE IT IS! THE BLUE AREA OF THE MOON. THE ONLY PART WITH BREATHABLE ATMOSPHERE.
HAD I KNOWN WE'D BE COMING HERE SO MUCH, I'D HAVE BUILT A SUMMER PLACE HERE.
"AND THERE'S THOR!"
GREAT ODIN'S BEARD!
HULK'S FRIEND IS IN TROUBLE!
LET'S GO!
WAIT! WE NEED A PLAN.
HERE'S A PLAN--

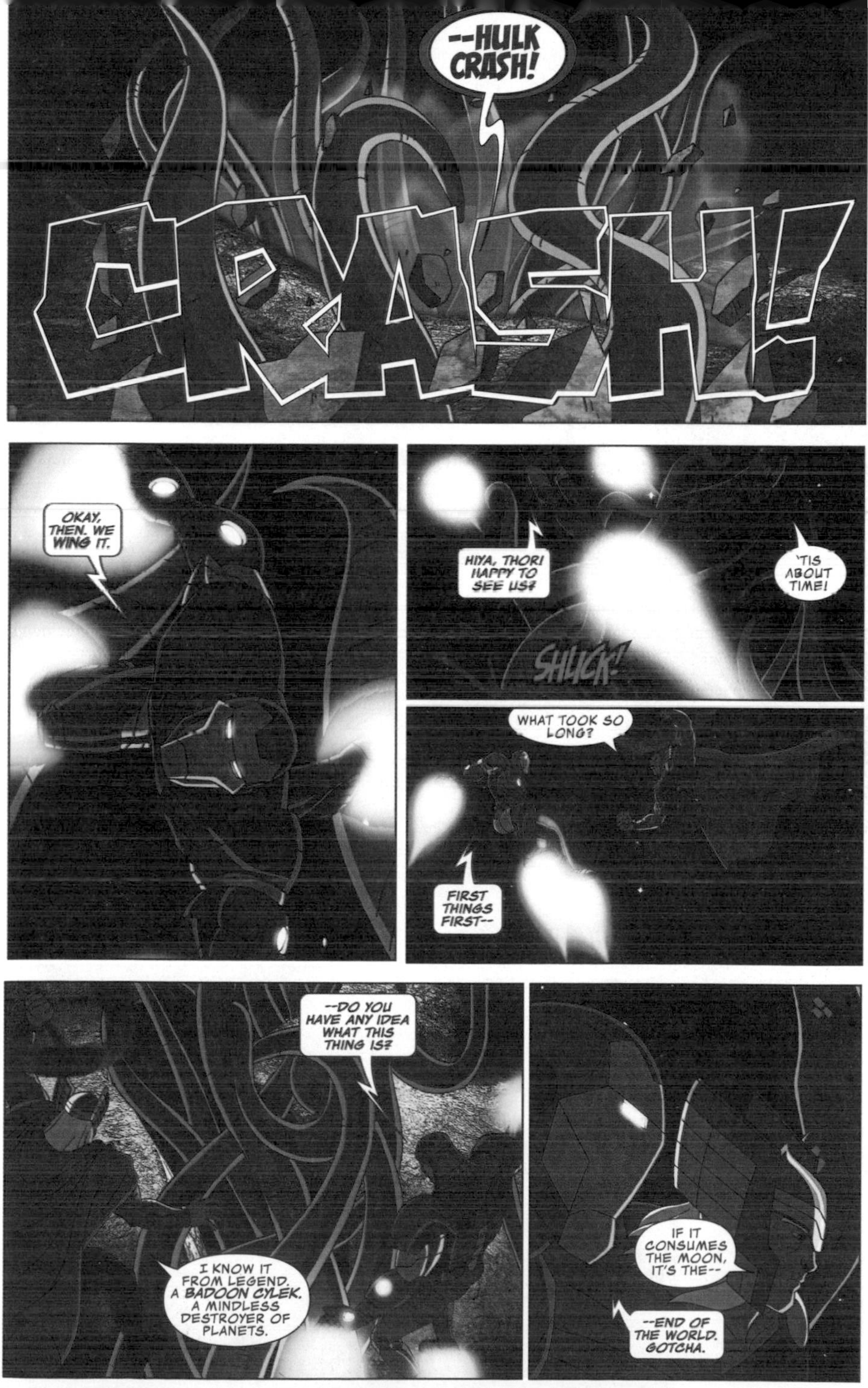
--HULK CRASH!
CRASH!
OKAY, THEN. WE WING IT.
HIYA, THOR! HAPPY TO SEE US?
'TIS ABOUT TIME!
SHUCK!
WHAT TOOK SO LONG?
FIRST THINGS FIRST--
--DO YOU HAVE ANY IDEA WHAT THIS THING IS?
I KNOW IT FROM LEGEND. A BADOON CYLEK. A MINDLESS DESTROYER OF PLANETS.
IF IT CONSUMES THE MOON, IT'S THE--
--END OF THE WORLD. GOTCHA.

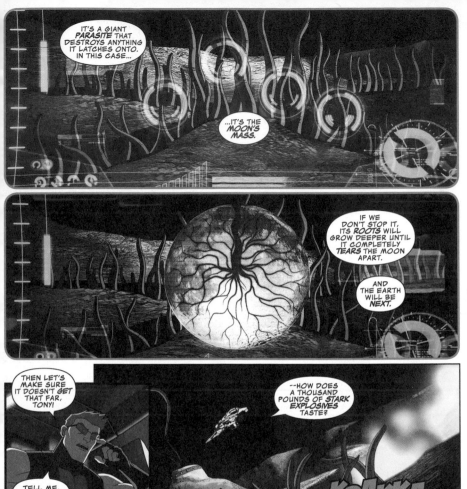

IT'S A GIANT *PARASITE* THAT DESTROYS ANYTHING IT LATCHES ONTO. IN THIS CASE...

...IT'S THE *MOON'S* MASS.

IF WE DON'T STOP IT, ITS *ROOTS* WILL GROW DEEPER UNTIL IT COMPLETELY *TEARS* THE MOON APART.

AND THE EARTH WILL BE *NEXT*.

THEN LET'S MAKE SURE IT DOESN'T *GET* THAT FAR, TONY!

--HOW DOES A THOUSAND POUNDS OF *STARK* EXPLOSIVES TASTE?

TELL ME, TENTACLE MONSTER--

KRAKKA-BAMM!

WHY CAN'T I *REMEMBER* WHAT HAPPENED?

PERHAPS BECAUSE I *HIT* YOU WITH MY HAMMER MJOLNIR.

YOU *DID?!*

YES. IT WAS *YOUR* IDEA!

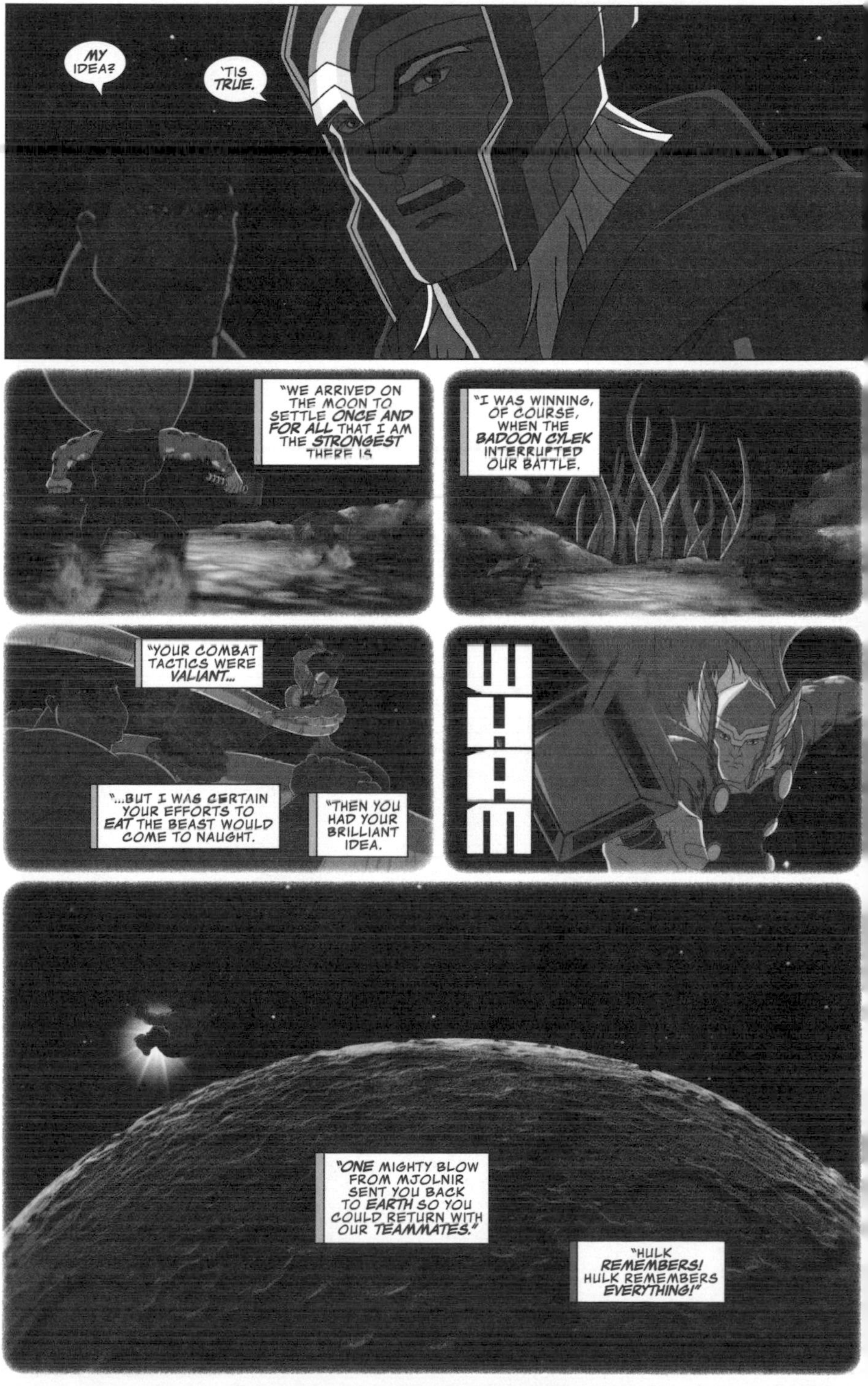

MY IDEA?
'TIS TRUE.
"WE ARRIVED ON THE MOON TO SETTLE ONCE AND FOR ALL THAT I AM THE STRONGEST THERE IS
"I WAS WINNING, OF COURSE, WHEN THE BADOON CYLEK INTERRUPTED OUR BATTLE.
"YOUR COMBAT TACTICS WERE VALIANT...
"...BUT I WAS CERTAIN YOUR EFFORTS TO EAT THE BEAST WOULD COME TO NAUGHT.
"THEN YOU HAD YOUR BRILLIANT IDEA.
WHAM
"ONE MIGHTY BLOW FROM MJOLNIR SENT YOU BACK TO EARTH SO YOU COULD RETURN WITH OUR TEAMMATES."
"HULK REMEMBERS! HULK REMEMBERS EVERYTHING!"

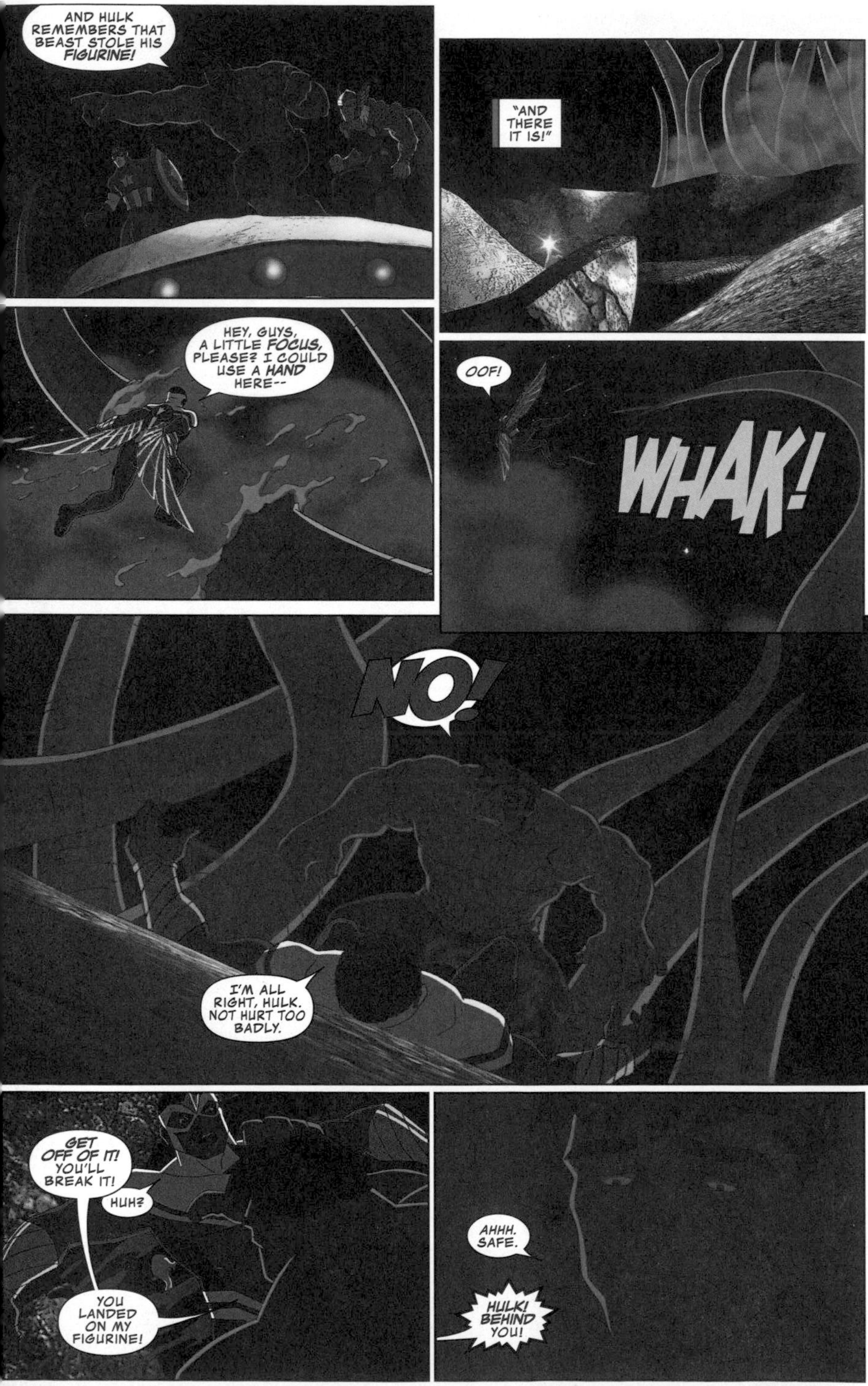
AND HULK REMEMBERS THAT BEAST STOLE HIS FIGURINE!
"AND THERE IT IS!"
HEY, GUYS, A LITTLE FOCUS, PLEASE? I COULD USE A HAND HERE--
OOF!
WHAK!
NO!
I'M ALL RIGHT, HULK. NOT HURT TOO BADLY.
GET OFF OF IT! YOU'LL BREAK IT!
HUH?
YOU LANDED ON MY FIGURINE!
AHHH. SAFE.
HULK! BEHIND YOU!

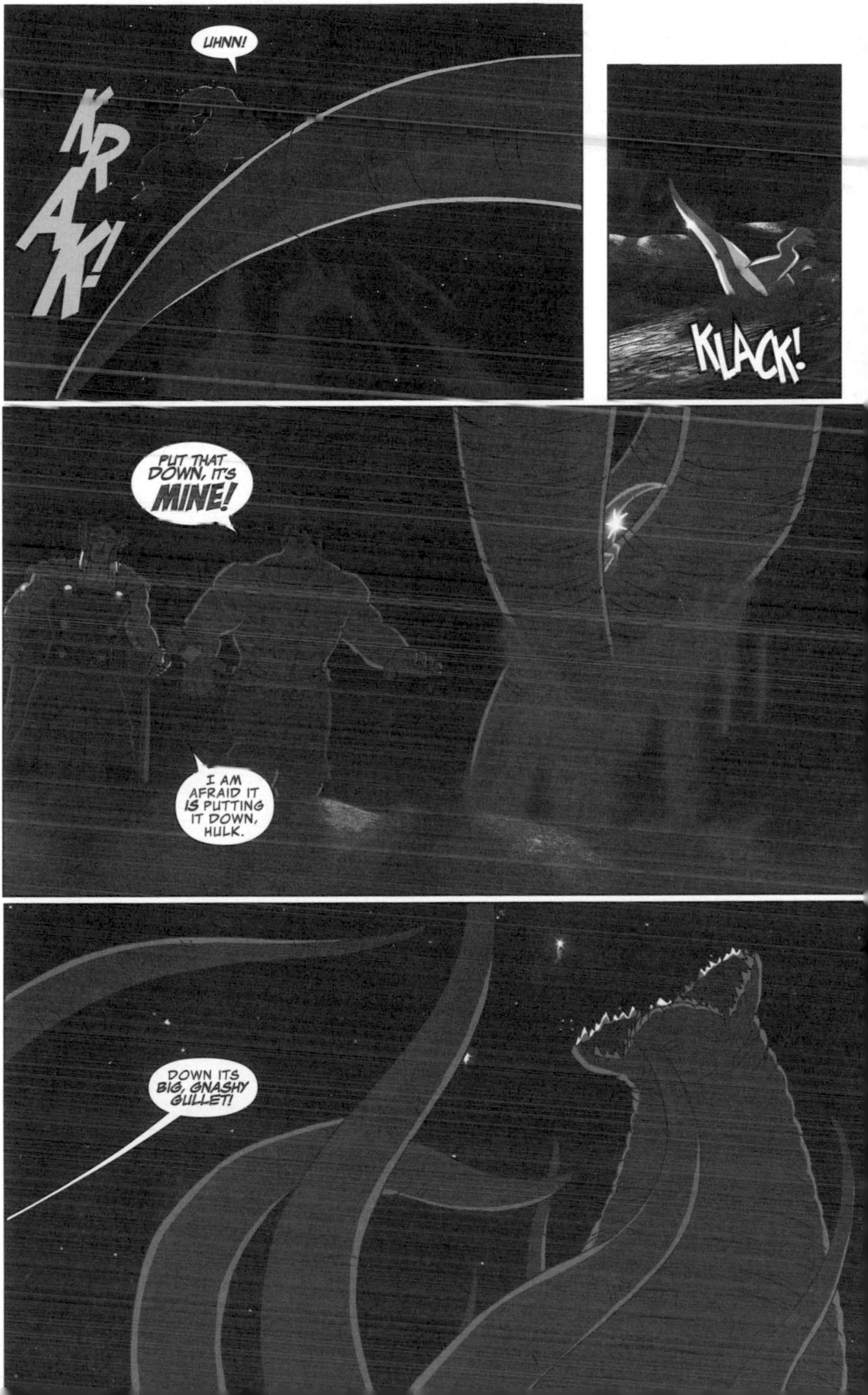
UHNN!
KRAAK!
KLACK!
PUT THAT DOWN, IT'S MINE!
I AM AFRAID IT IS PUTTING IT DOWN, HULK.
DOWN ITS BIG, GNASHY GULLET!

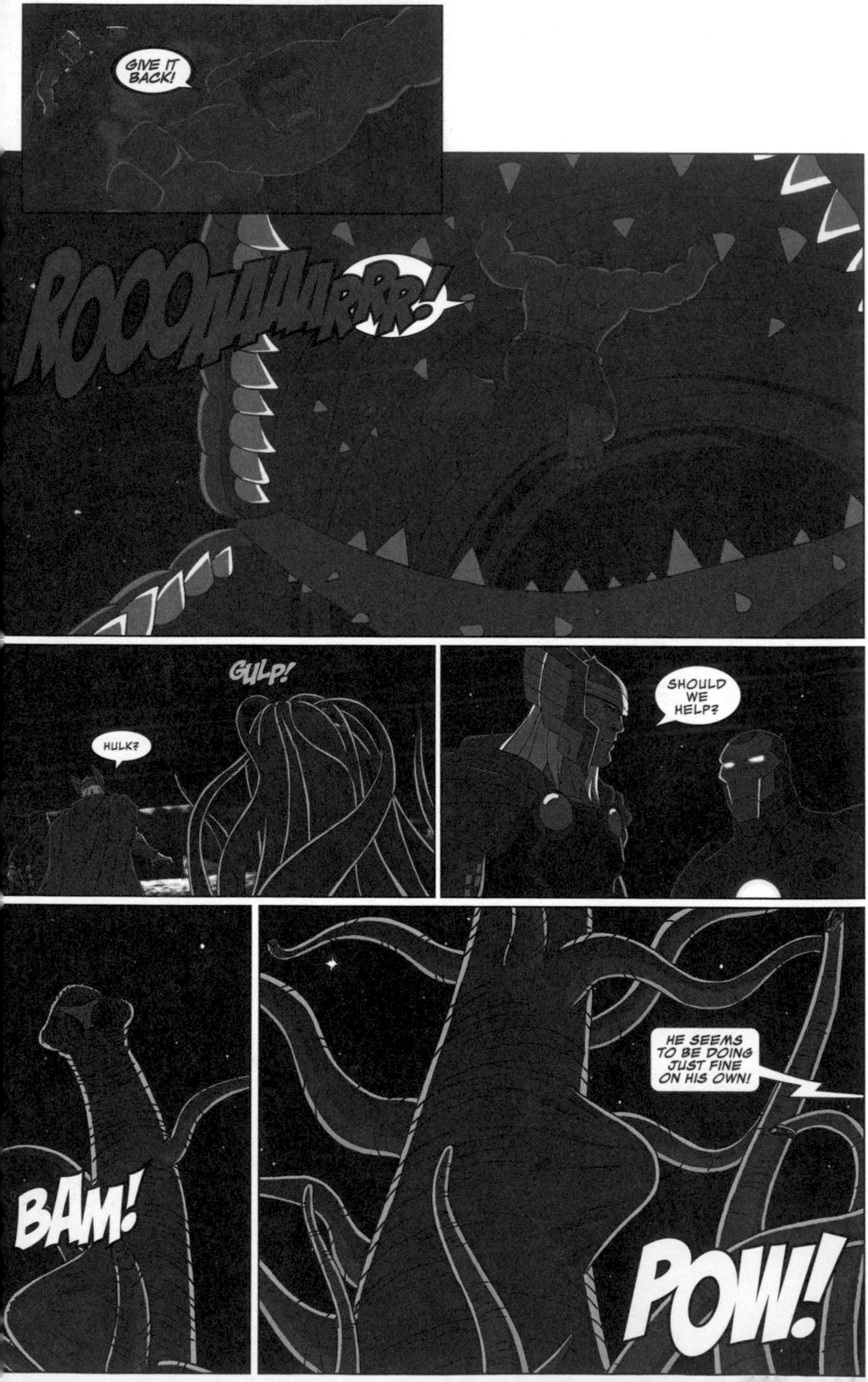
GIVE IT BACK!
ROOOAAAARRRR!
GULP!
HULK?
SHOULD WE HELP?
BAM!
HE SEEMS TO BE DOING JUST FINE ON HIS OWN!
POW!

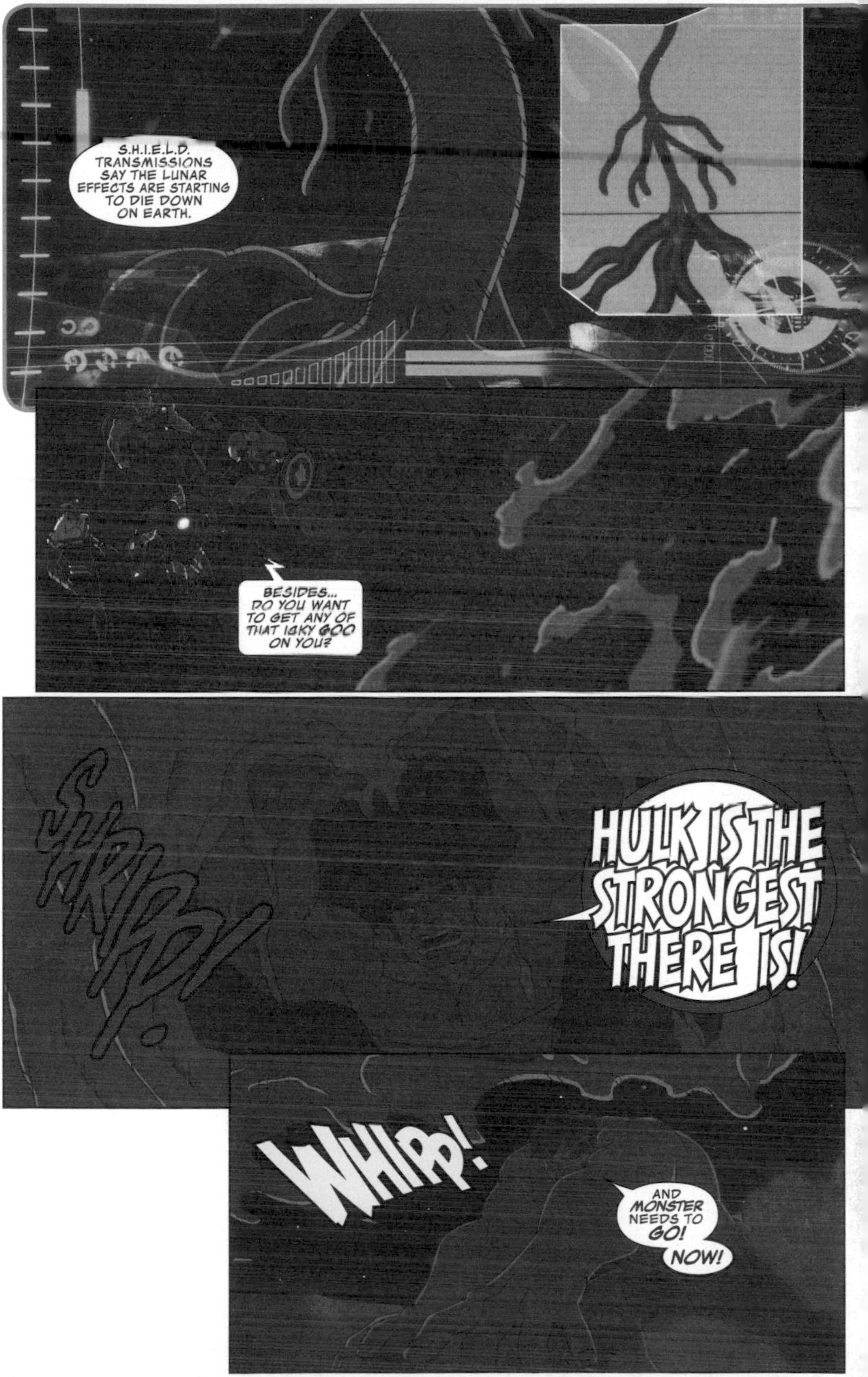
S.H.I.E.L.D. TRANSMISSIONS SAY THE LUNAR EFFECTS ARE STARTING TO DIE DOWN ON EARTH.
BESIDES... DO YOU WANT TO GET ANY OF THAT ICKY GOO ON YOU?
HULK IS THE STRONGEST THERE IS!
WHIPP!
AND MONSTER NEEDS TO GO!
NOW!

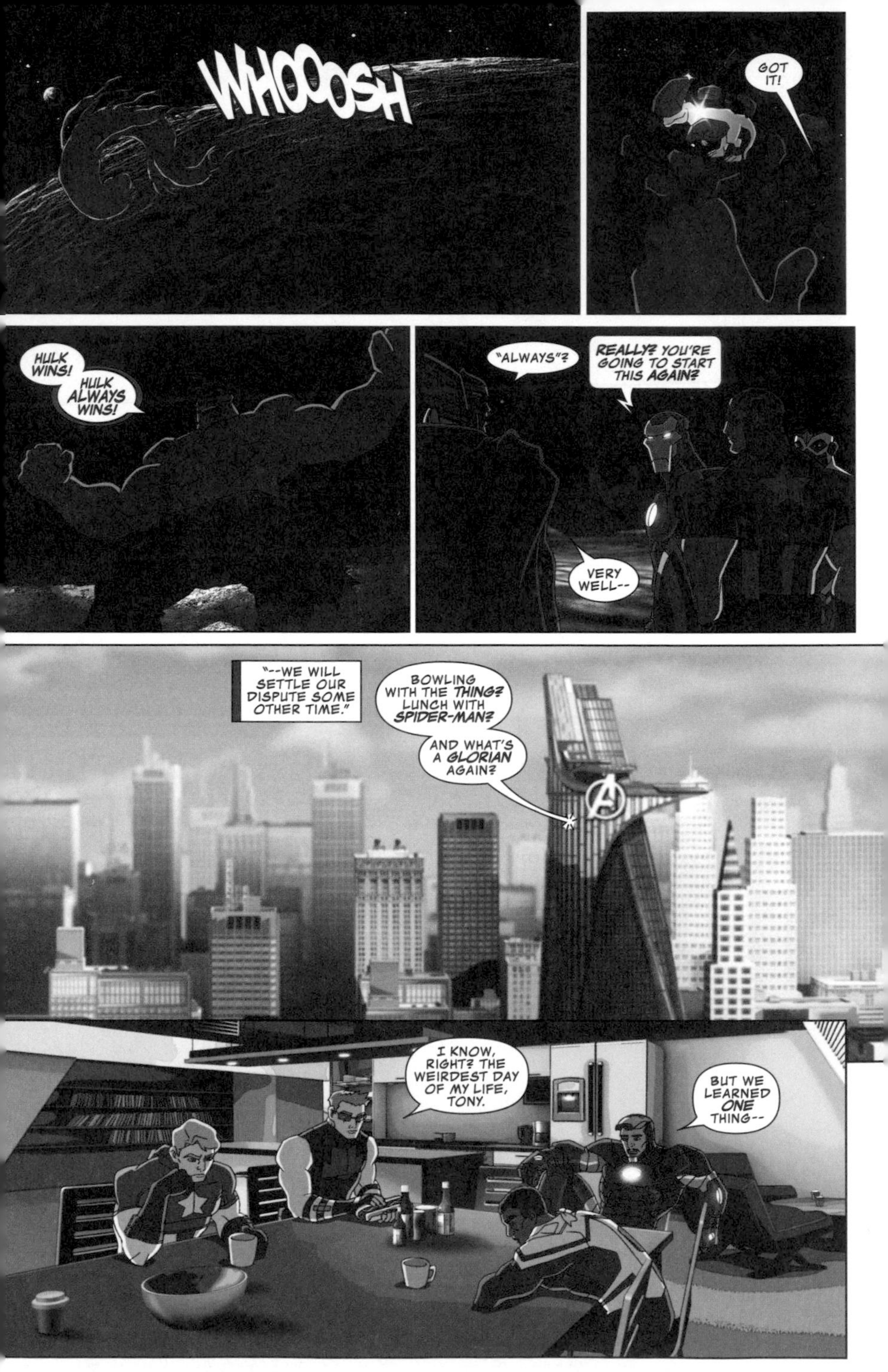
WHOOOSH
GOT IT!
HULK WINS!
HULK ALWAYS WINS!
"ALWAYS"?
REALLY? YOU'RE GOING TO START THIS AGAIN?
VERY WELL--
"--WE WILL SETTLE OUR DISPUTE SOME OTHER TIME."
BOWLING WITH THE THING? LUNCH WITH SPIDER-MAN?
AND WHAT'S A GLORIAN AGAIN?
I KNOW, RIGHT? THE WEIRDEST DAY OF MY LIFE, TONY.
BUT WE LEARNED ONE THING--

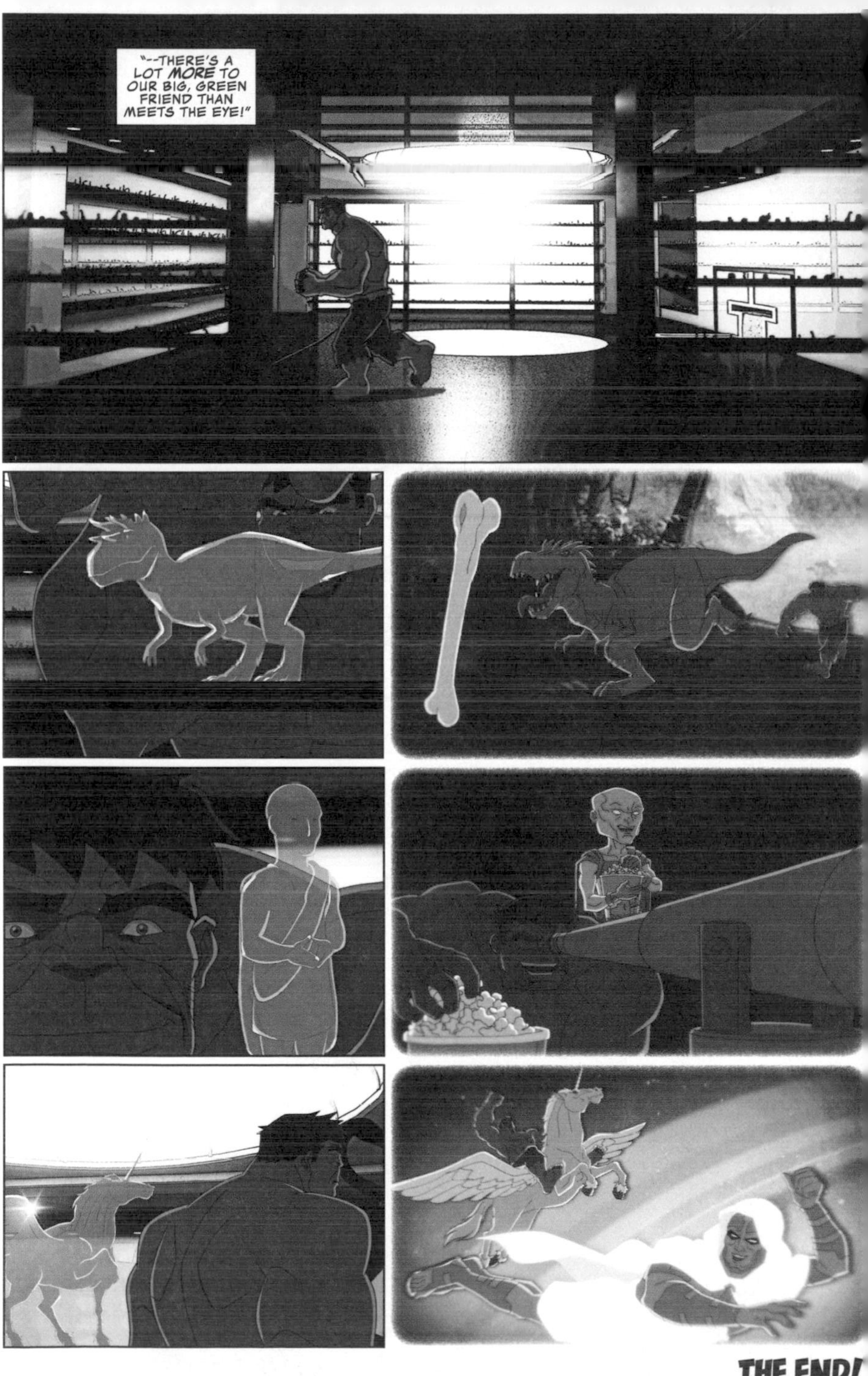
"--THERE'S A LOT MORE TO OUR BIG, GREEN FRIEND THAN MEETS THE EYE!"
THE END!

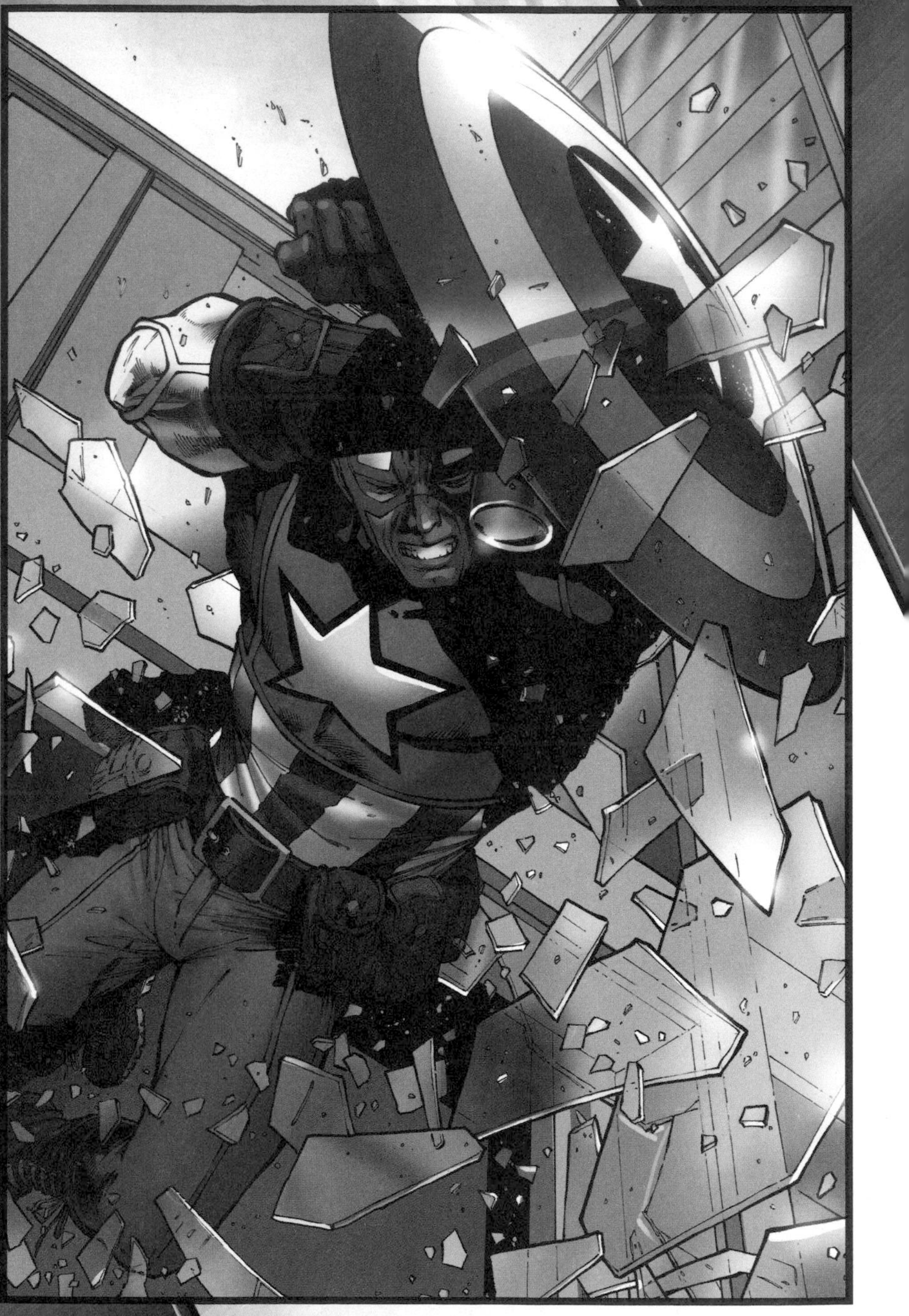

#4 BASED ON "GHOSTS OF THE PAST"

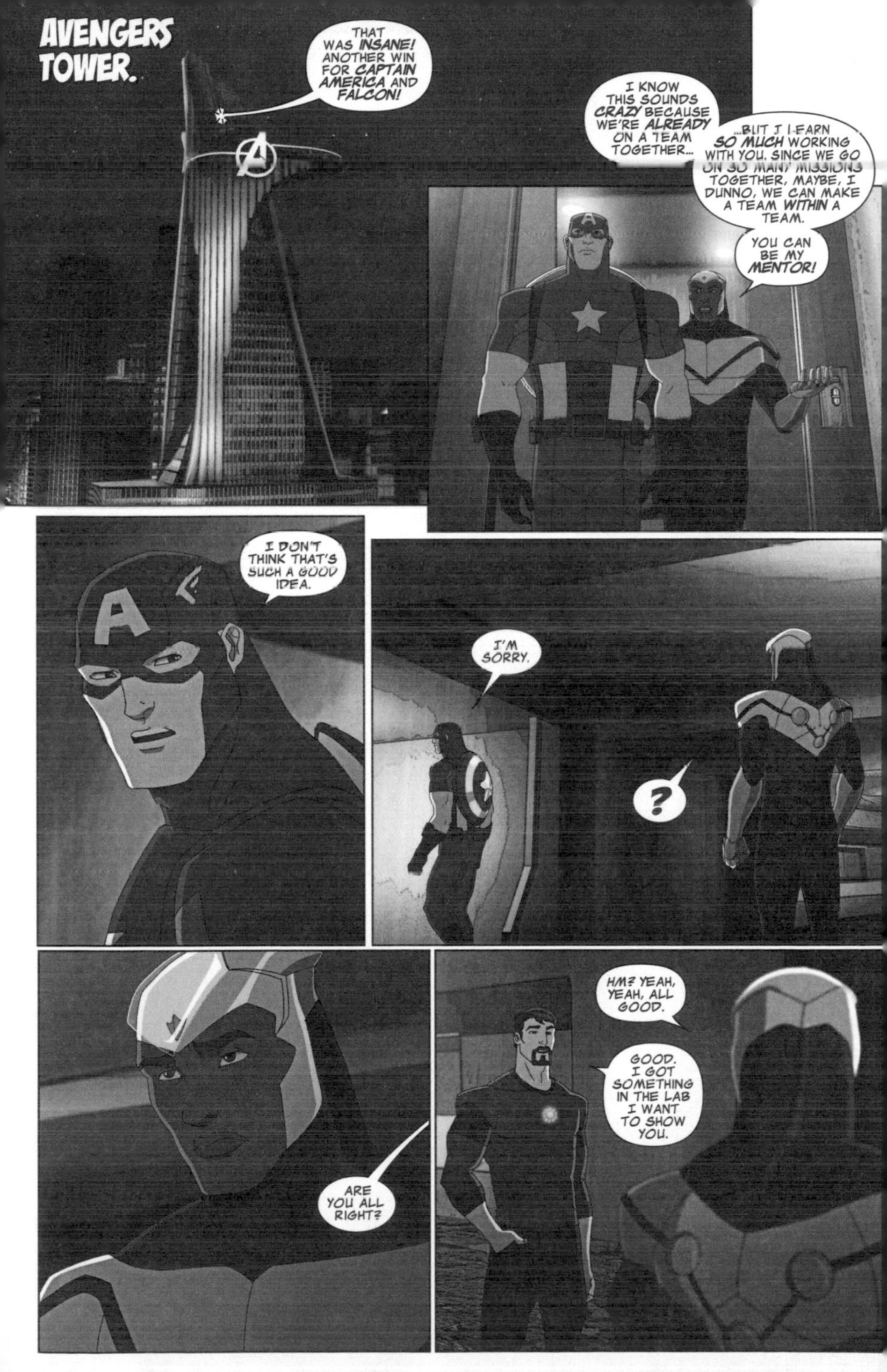
AVENGERS TOWER.
THAT WAS INSANE! ANOTHER WIN FOR CAPTAIN AMERICA AND FALCON!
I KNOW THIS SOUNDS CRAZY BECAUSE WE'RE ALREADY ON A TEAM TOGETHER...
...BUT I LEARN SO MUCH WORKING WITH YOU. SINCE WE GO ON SO MANY MISSIONS TOGETHER, MAYBE, I DUNNO, WE CAN MAKE A TEAM WITHIN A TEAM.
YOU CAN BE MY MENTOR!
I DON'T THINK THAT'S SUCH A GOOD IDEA.
I'M SORRY.
?
ARE YOU ALL RIGHT?
HM? YEAH, YEAH, ALL GOOD.
GOOD. I GOT SOMETHING IN THE LAB I WANT TO SHOW YOU.

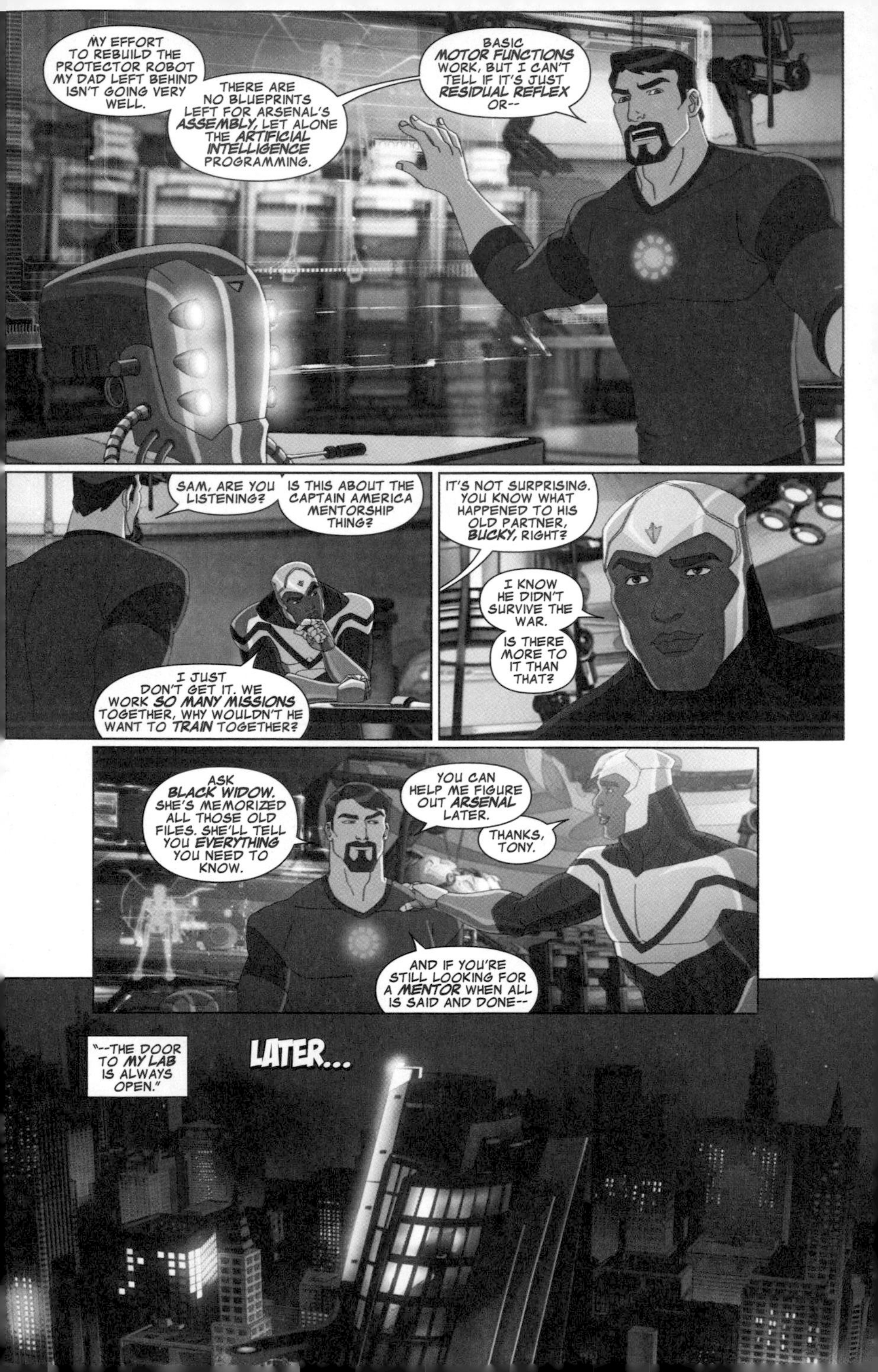
MY EFFORT TO REBUILD THE PROTECTOR ROBOT MY DAD LEFT BEHIND ISN'T GOING VERY WELL.
THERE ARE NO BLUEPRINTS LEFT FOR ARSENAL'S ASSEMBLY, LET ALONE THE ARTIFICIAL INTELLIGENCE PROGRAMMING.
BASIC MOTOR FUNCTIONS WORK, BUT I CAN'T TELL IF IT'S JUST RESIDUAL REFLEX OR--
SAM, ARE YOU LISTENING?
IS THIS ABOUT THE CAPTAIN AMERICA MENTORSHIP THING?
I JUST DON'T GET IT. WE WORK SO MANY MISSIONS TOGETHER, WHY WOULDN'T HE WANT TO TRAIN TOGETHER?
IT'S NOT SURPRISING. YOU KNOW WHAT HAPPENED TO HIS OLD PARTNER, BUCKY, RIGHT?
I KNOW HE DIDN'T SURVIVE THE WAR.
IS THERE MORE TO IT THAN THAT?
ASK BLACK WIDOW. SHE'S MEMORIZED ALL THOSE OLD FILES. SHE'LL TELL YOU EVERYTHING YOU NEED TO KNOW.
YOU CAN HELP ME FIGURE OUT ARSENAL LATER.
THANKS, TONY.
AND IF YOU'RE STILL LOOKING FOR A MENTOR WHEN ALL IS SAID AND DONE--
"--THE DOOR TO MY LAB IS ALWAYS OPEN."
LATER...

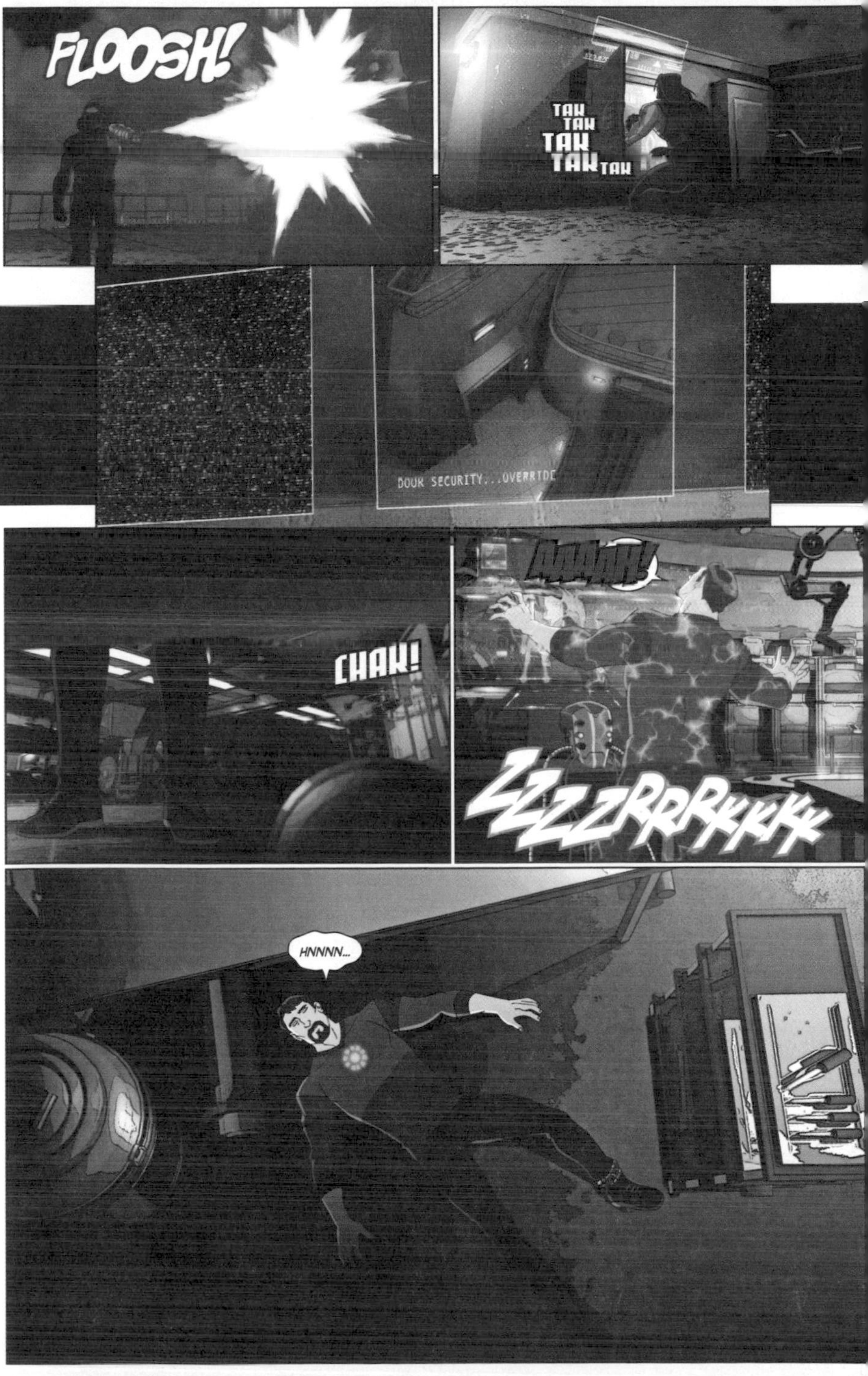
FLOOSH!
TAK TAK TAK TAK TAK
DOUR SECURITY...OVERRIDE
CHAK!
AAAAAH!
ZZZZRRRKKKK
HNNNN...

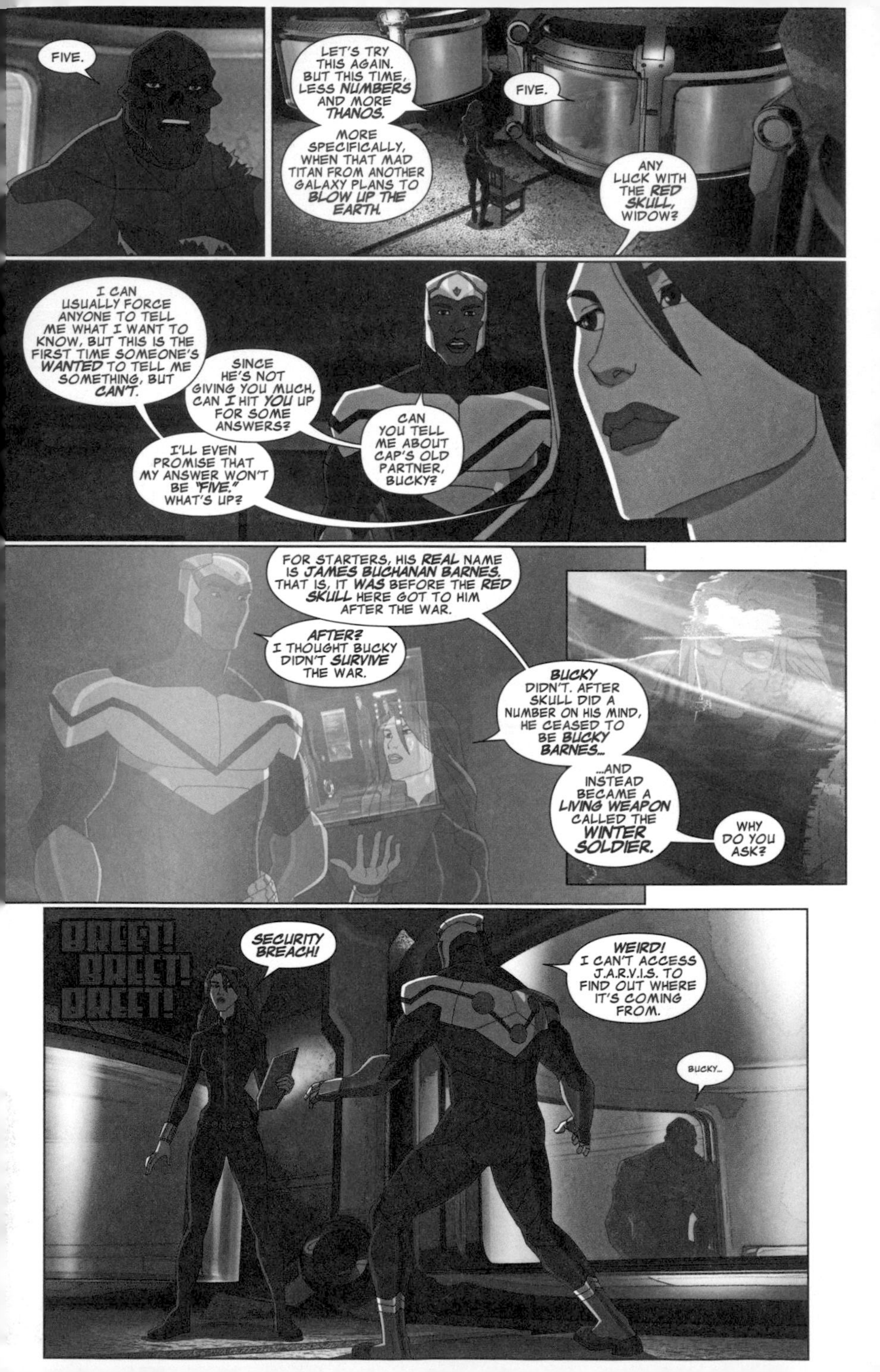
FIVE.
LET'S TRY THIS AGAIN. BUT THIS TIME, LESS NUMBERS AND MORE THANOS.
MORE SPECIFICALLY, WHEN THAT MAD TITAN FROM ANOTHER GALAXY PLANS TO BLOW UP THE EARTH.
FIVE.
ANY LUCK WITH THE RED SKULL, WIDOW?
I CAN USUALLY FORCE ANYONE TO TELL ME WHAT I WANT TO KNOW, BUT THIS IS THE FIRST TIME SOMEONE'S WANTED TO TELL ME SOMETHING, BUT CAN'T.
SINCE HE'S NOT GIVING YOU MUCH, CAN I HIT YOU UP FOR SOME ANSWERS?
CAN YOU TELL ME ABOUT CAP'S OLD PARTNER, BUCKY?
I'LL EVEN PROMISE THAT MY ANSWER WON'T BE "FIVE." WHAT'S UP?
FOR STARTERS, HIS REAL NAME IS JAMES BUCHANAN BARNES. THAT IS, IT WAS BEFORE THE RED SKULL HERE GOT TO HIM AFTER THE WAR.
AFTER? I THOUGHT BUCKY DIDN'T SURVIVE THE WAR.
BUCKY DIDN'T. AFTER SKULL DID A NUMBER ON HIS MIND, HE CEASED TO BE BUCKY BARNES...
...AND INSTEAD BECAME A LIVING WEAPON CALLED THE WINTER SOLDIER.
WHY DO YOU ASK?
BREET! BREET! BREET!
SECURITY BREACH!
WEIRD! I CAN'T ACCESS J.A.R.V.I.S. TO FIND OUT WHERE IT'S COMING FROM.
BUCKY...

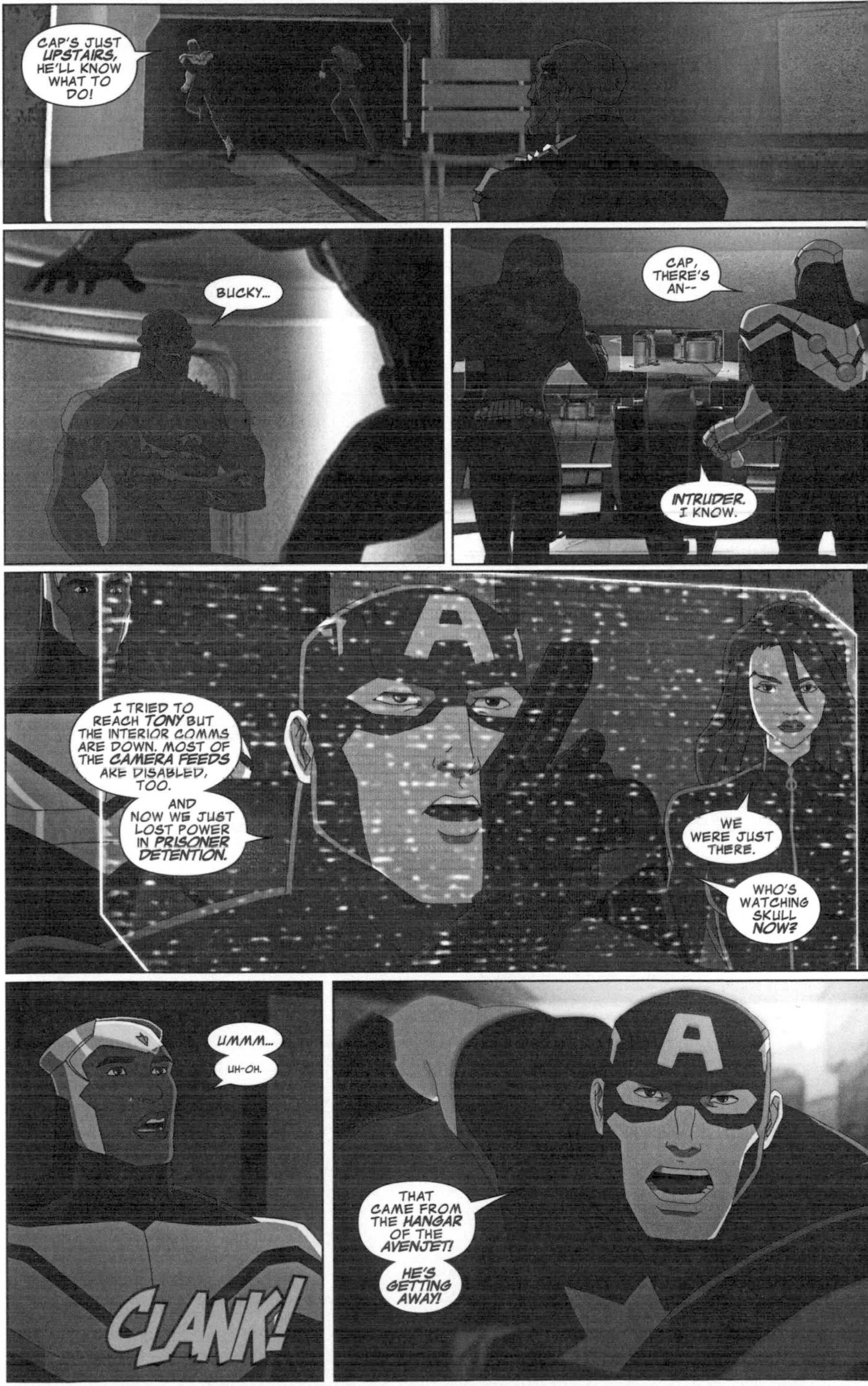
CAP'S JUST UPSTAIRS, HE'LL KNOW WHAT TO DO!
BUCKY...
CAP, THERE'S AN--
INTRUDER. I KNOW.
I TRIED TO REACH TONY BUT THE INTERIOR COMMS ARE DOWN. MOST OF THE CAMERA FEEDS ARE DISABLED, TOO.
AND NOW WE JUST LOST POWER IN PRISONER DETENTION.
WE WERE JUST THERE.
WHO'S WATCHING SKULL NOW?
UMMM...
UH-OH.
CLANK!
THAT CAME FROM THE HANGAR OF THE AVENJET!
HE'S GETTING AWAY!

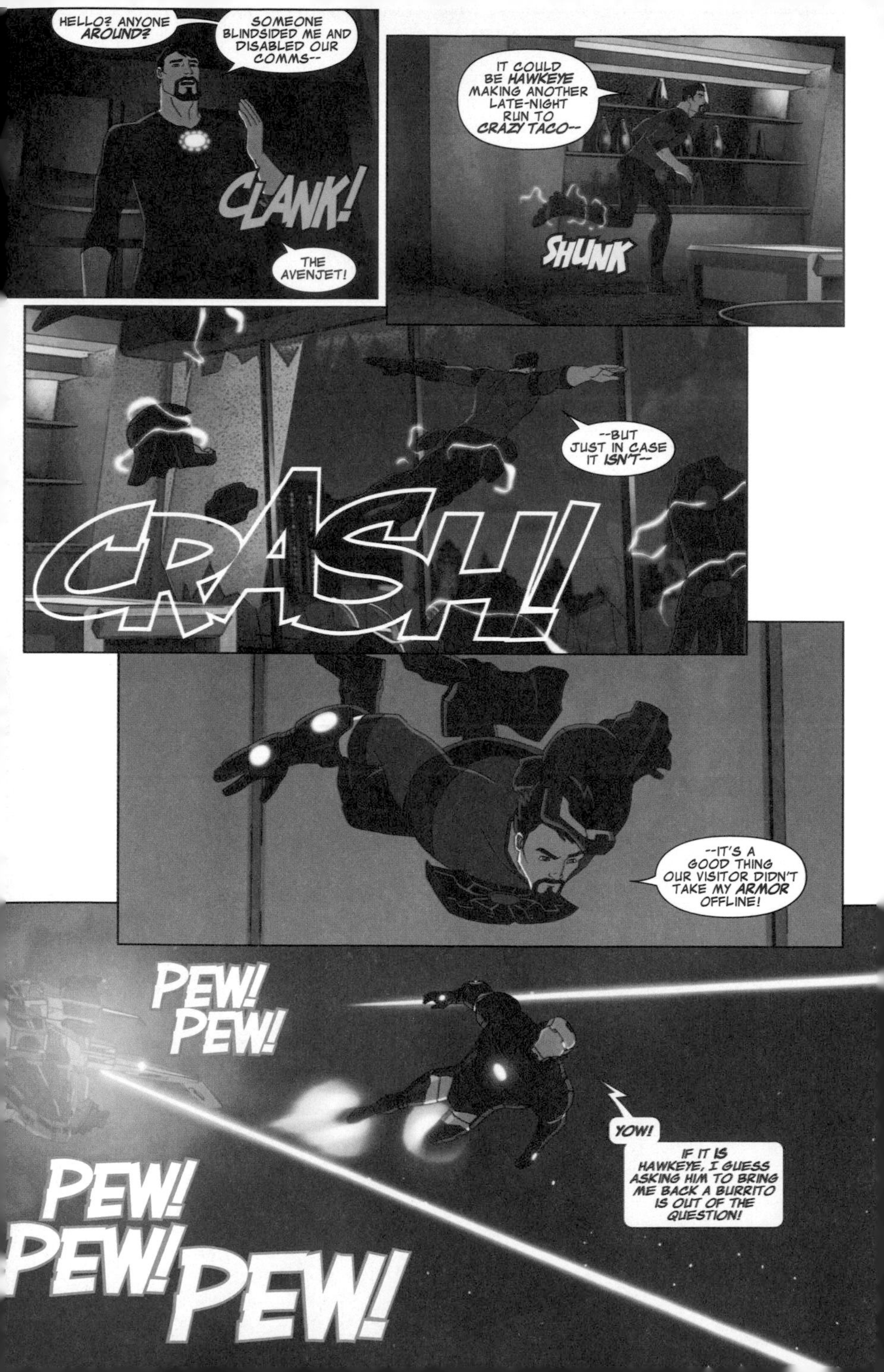
HELLO? ANYONE AROUND?
SOMEONE BLINDSIDED ME AND DISABLED OUR COMMS--
CLANK!
THE AVENJET!
IT COULD BE HAWKEYE MAKING ANOTHER LATE-NIGHT RUN TO CRAZY TACO--
SHUNK
--BUT JUST IN CASE IT ISN'T--
CRASH!
--IT'S A GOOD THING OUR VISITOR DIDN'T TAKE MY ARMOR OFFLINE!
PEW! PEW!
YOW!
IF IT IS HAWKEYE, I GUESS ASKING HIM TO BRING ME BACK A BURRITO IS OUT OF THE QUESTION!
PEW! PEW! PEW!

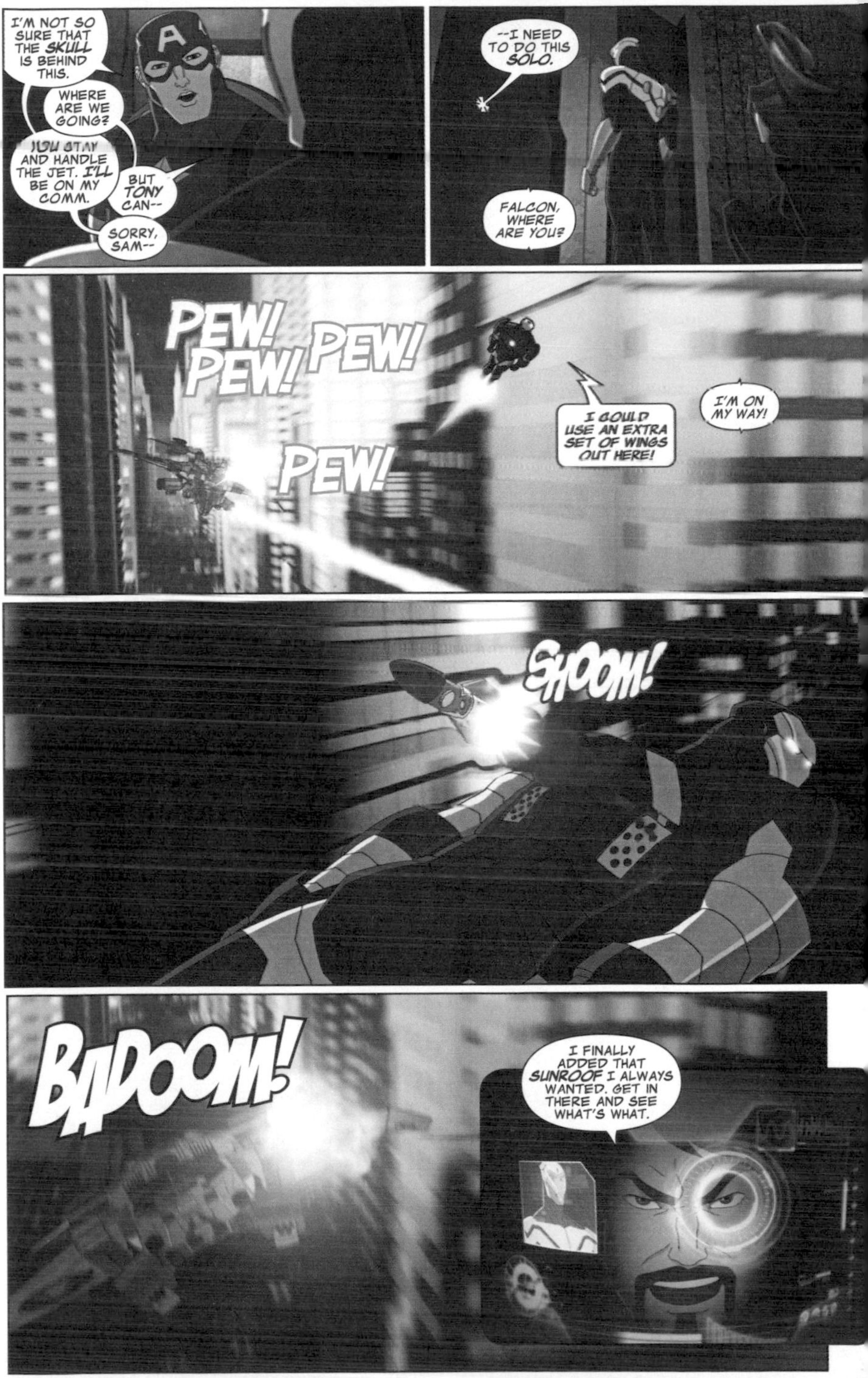
I'M NOT SO SURE THAT THE SKULL IS BEHIND THIS.
WHERE ARE WE GOING?
YOU STAY AND HANDLE THE JET. I'LL BE ON MY COMM.
BUT TONY CAN--
SORRY, SAM--
--I NEED TO DO THIS SOLO.
FALCON, WHERE ARE YOU?
PEW! PEW! PEW!
PEW!
I COULD USE AN EXTRA SET OF WINGS OUT HERE!
I'M ON MY WAY!
SHOOM!
BADOOM!
I FINALLY ADDED THAT SUNROOF I ALWAYS WANTED. GET IN THERE AND SEE WHAT'S WHAT.

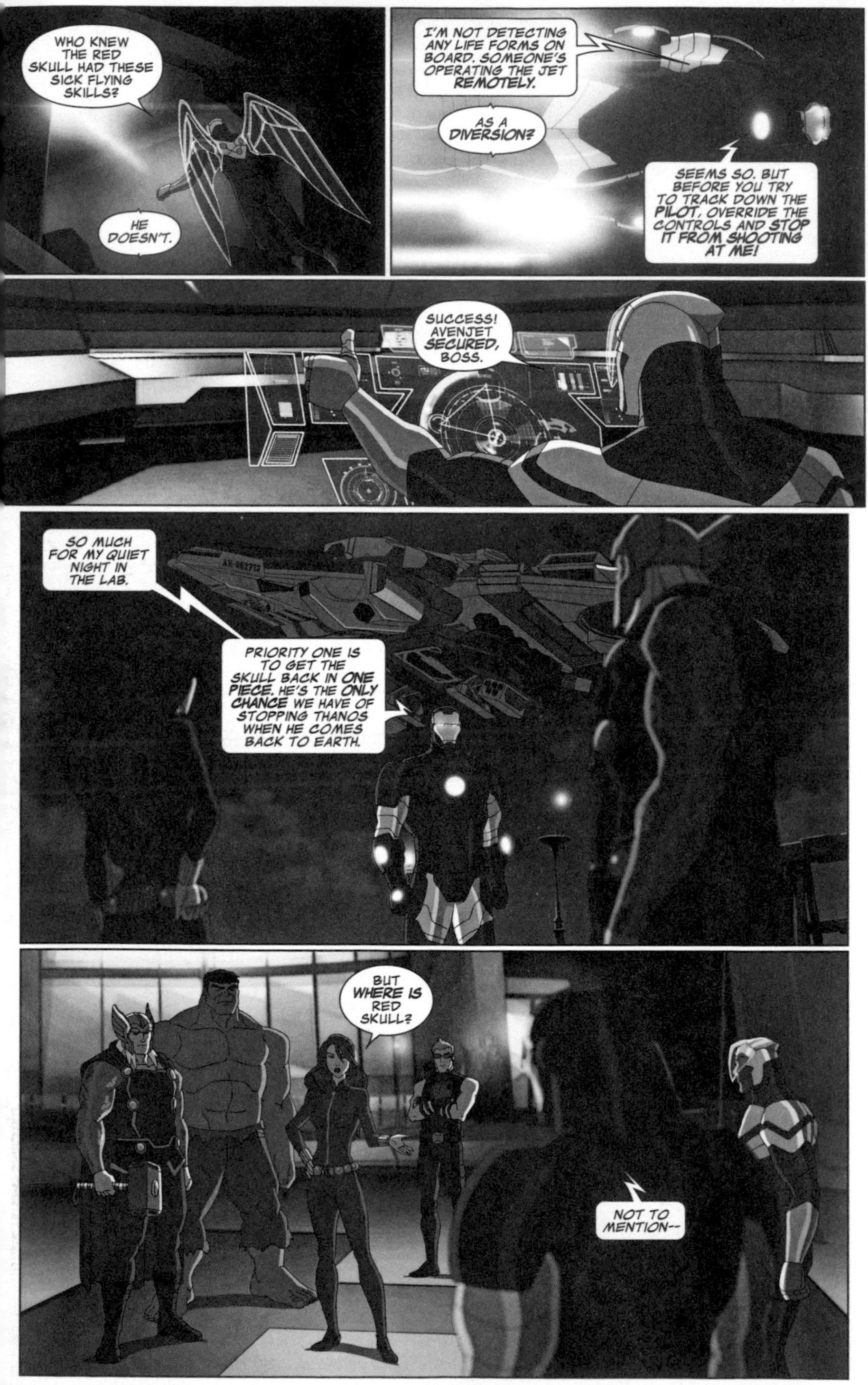
WHO KNEW THE RED SKULL HAD THESE SICK FLYING SKILLS?
HE DOESN'T.
I'M NOT DETECTING ANY LIFE FORMS ON BOARD. SOMEONE'S OPERATING THE JET **REMOTELY.**
AS A **DIVERSION?**
SEEMS SO. BUT BEFORE YOU TRY TO TRACK DOWN THE **PILOT,** OVERRIDE THE CONTROLS AND **STOP** IT FROM **SHOOTING** AT ME!
SUCCESS! AVENJET **SECURED,** BOSS.
SO MUCH FOR MY QUIET NIGHT IN THE LAB.
PRIORITY ONE IS TO GET THE SKULL BACK IN **ONE PIECE.** HE'S THE **ONLY CHANCE** WE HAVE OF STOPPING THANOS WHEN HE COMES BACK TO EARTH.
BUT **WHERE IS** RED SKULL?
NOT TO MENTION--

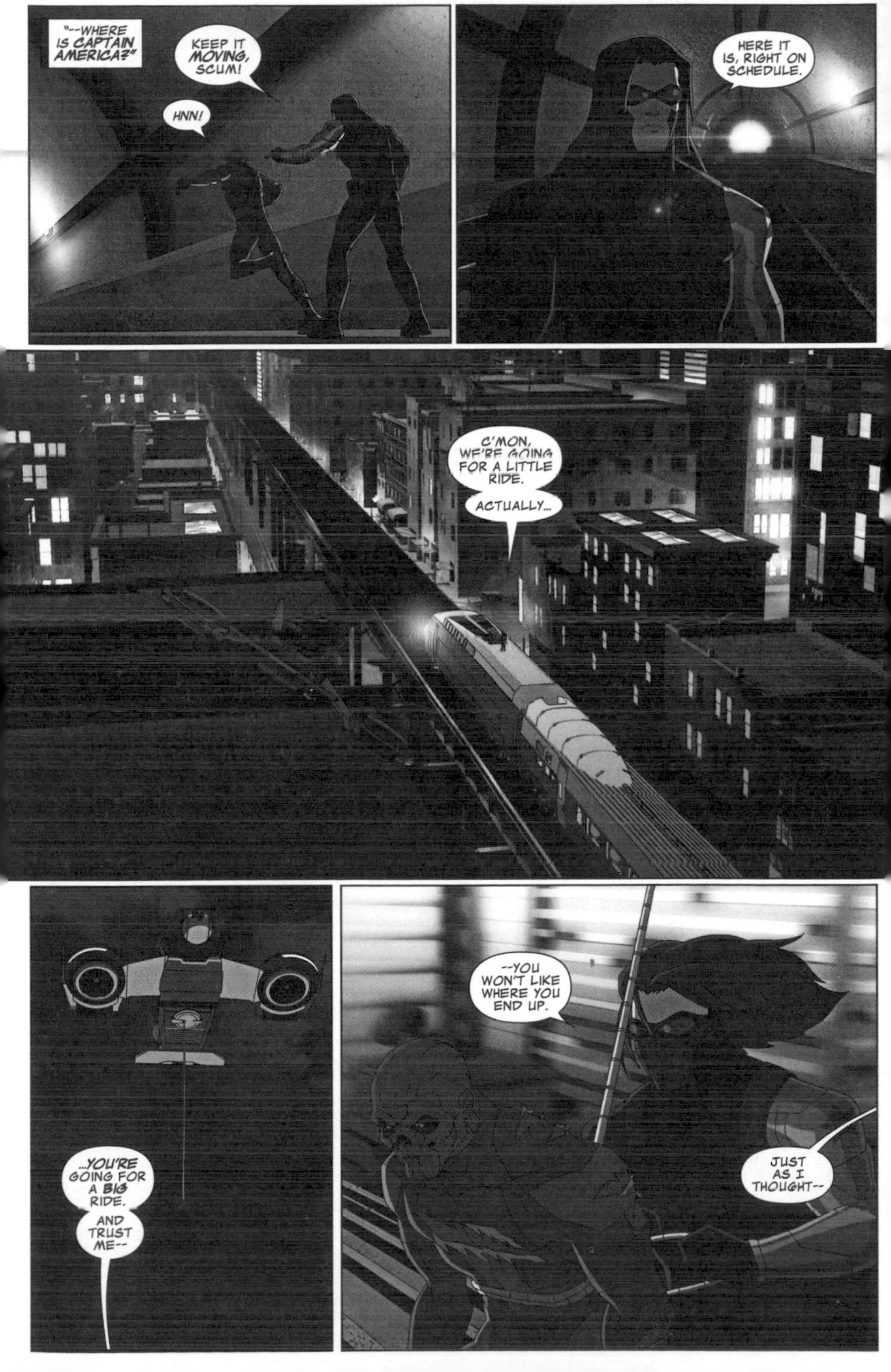
"--WHERE IS CAPTAIN AMERICA?"
KEEP IT MOVING, SCUM!
HNN!
HERE IT IS, RIGHT ON SCHEDULE.
C'MON, WE'RE GOING FOR A LITTLE RIDE.
ACTUALLY...
...YOU'RE GOING FOR A BIG RIDE.
AND TRUST ME--
--YOU WON'T LIKE WHERE YOU END UP.
JUST AS I THOUGHT--

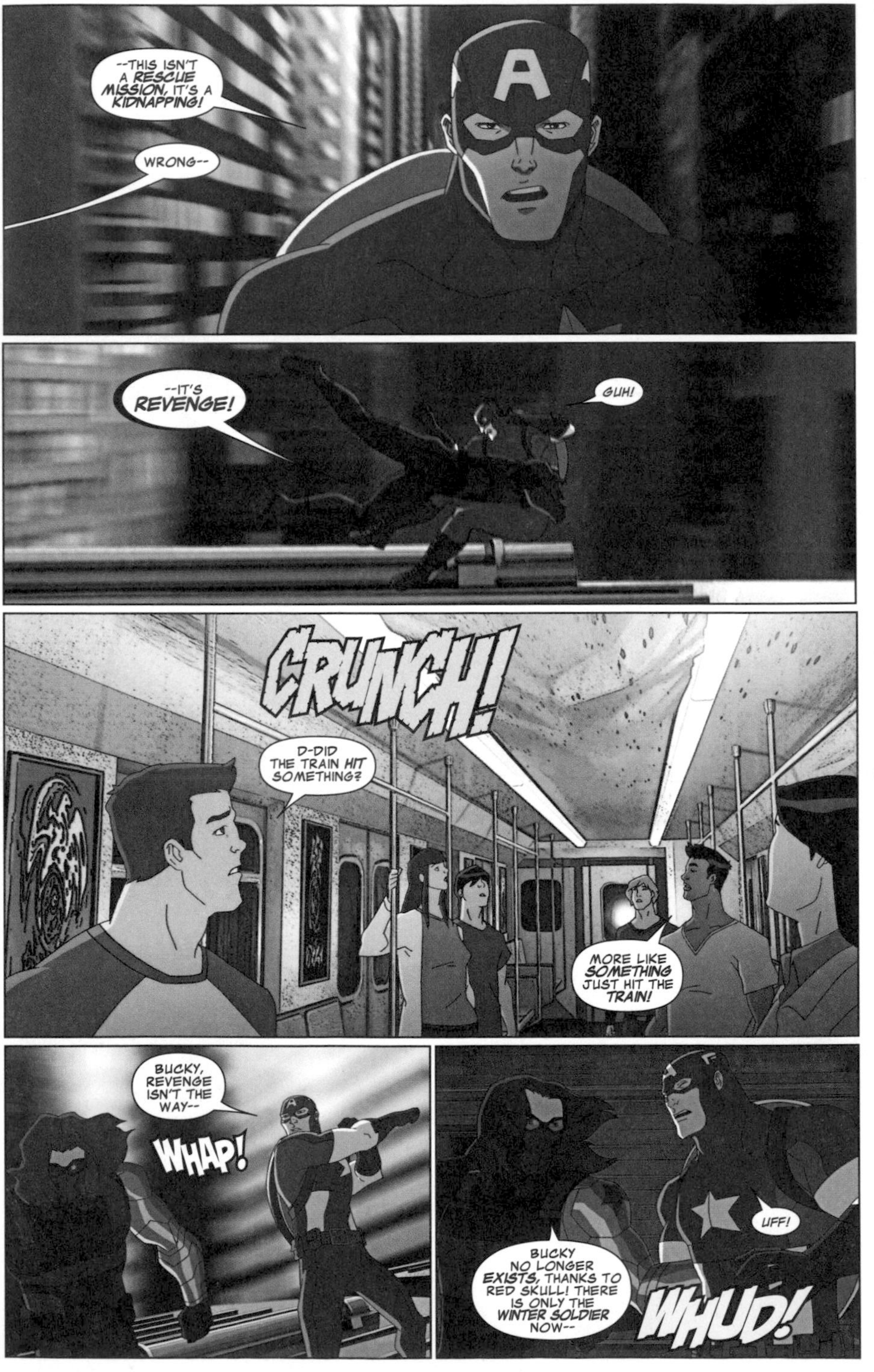
--THIS ISN'T A RESCUE MISSION, IT'S A KIDNAPPING!
WRONG--
--IT'S REVENGE!
GUH!
CRUNCH!
D-DID THE TRAIN HIT SOMETHING?
MORE LIKE SOMETHING JUST HIT THE TRAIN!
BUCKY, REVENGE ISN'T THE WAY--
WHAP!
BUCKY NO LONGER EXISTS, THANKS TO RED SKULL! THERE IS ONLY THE WINTER SOLDIER NOW--
UFF!
WHUD!

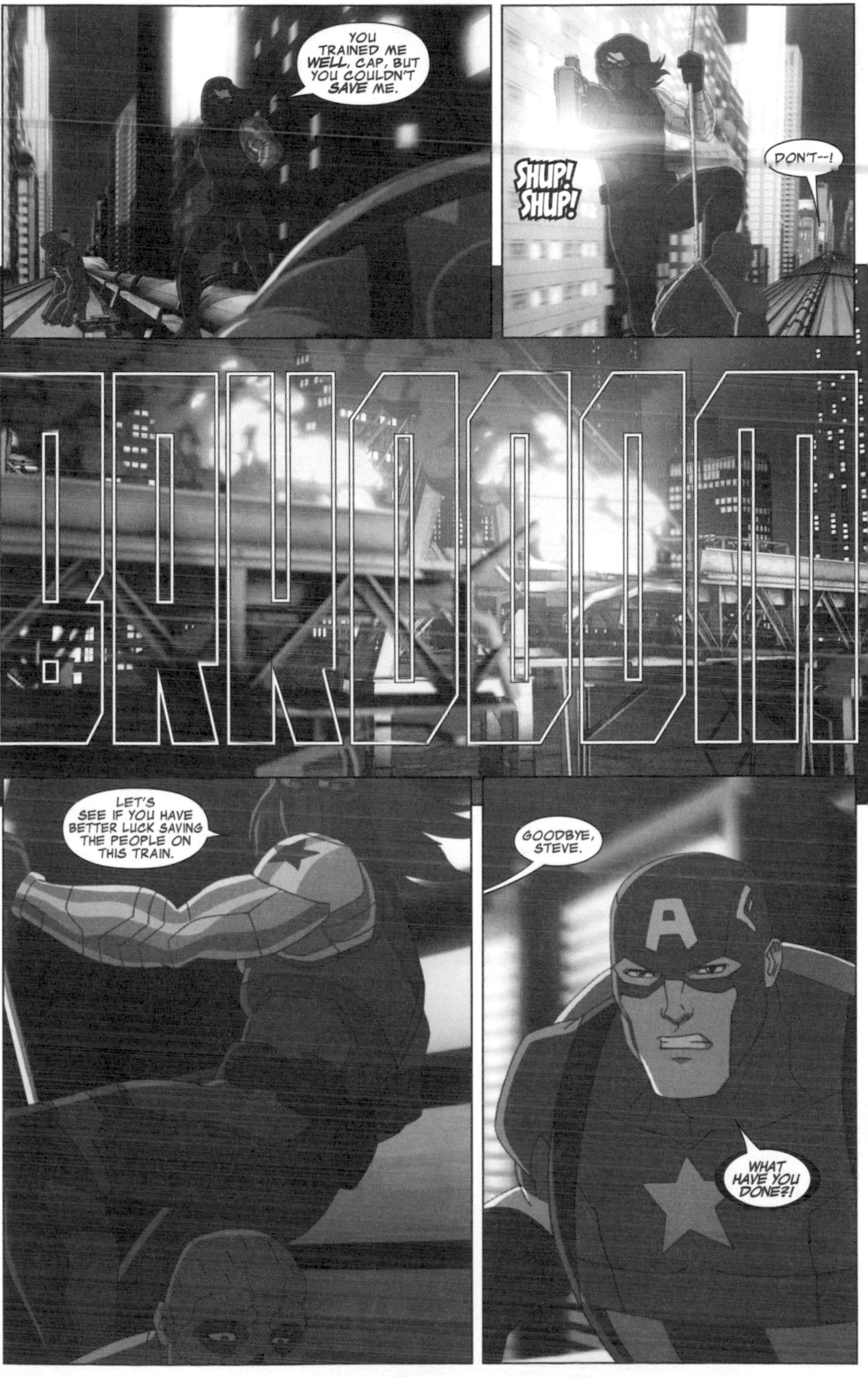
YOU TRAINED ME WELL, CAP, BUT YOU COULDN'T SAVE ME.
SHUP! SHUP!
DON'T--!
BRKOOOM
LET'S SEE IF YOU HAVE BETTER LUCK SAVING THE PEOPLE ON THIS TRAIN.
GOODBYE, STEVE.
WHAT HAVE YOU DONE?!

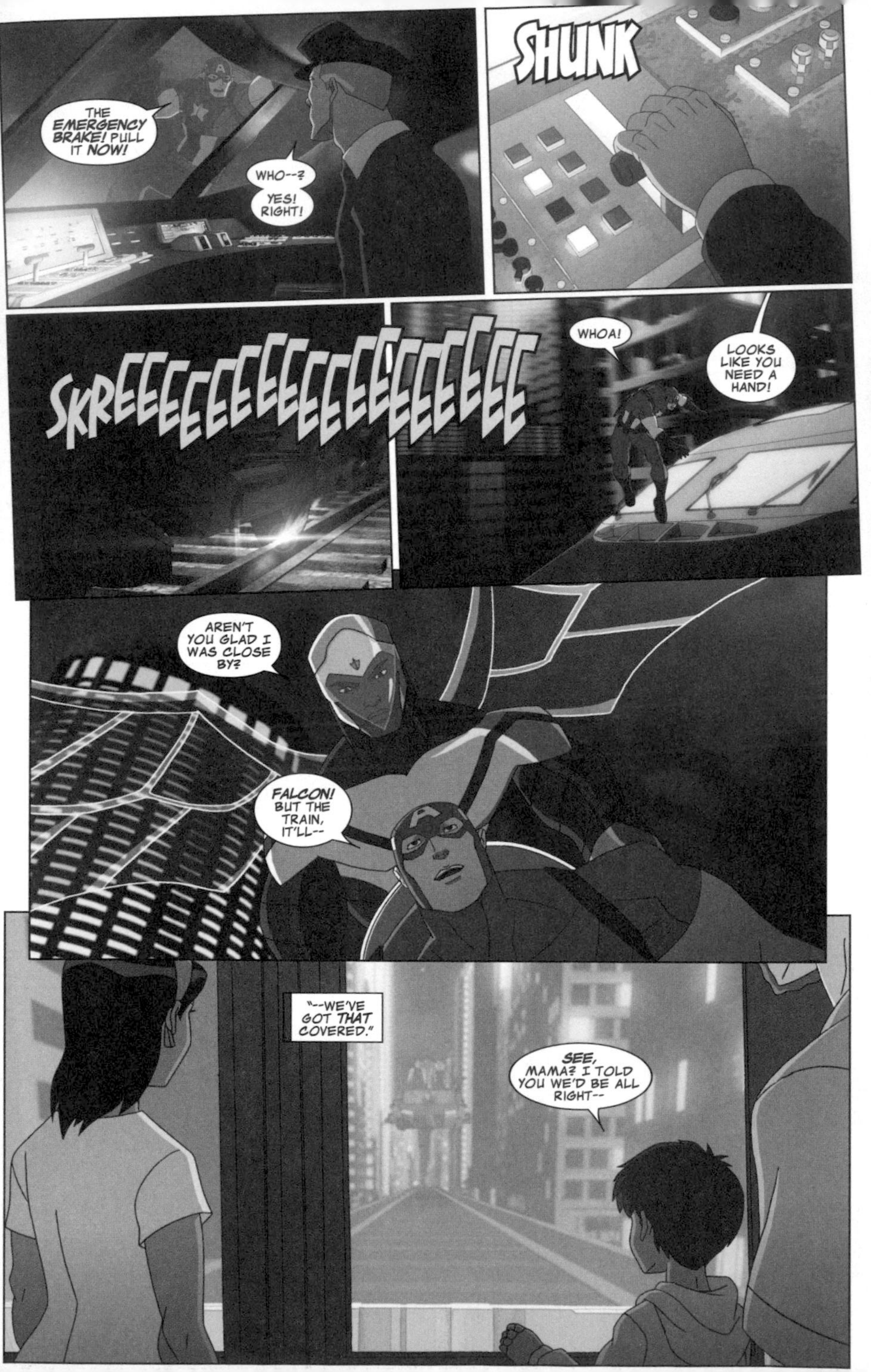

THE EMERGENCY BRAKE! PULL IT NOW!
WHO--? YES! RIGHT!
SHUNK
SKREEEEEEEEEEEEEEEEEEEEEEE
WHOA!
LOOKS LIKE YOU NEED A HAND!
AREN'T YOU GLAD I WAS CLOSE BY?
FALCON! BUT THE TRAIN, IT'LL--
"--WE'VE GOT THAT COVERED."
SEE, MAMA? I TOLD YOU WE'D BE ALL RIGHT--

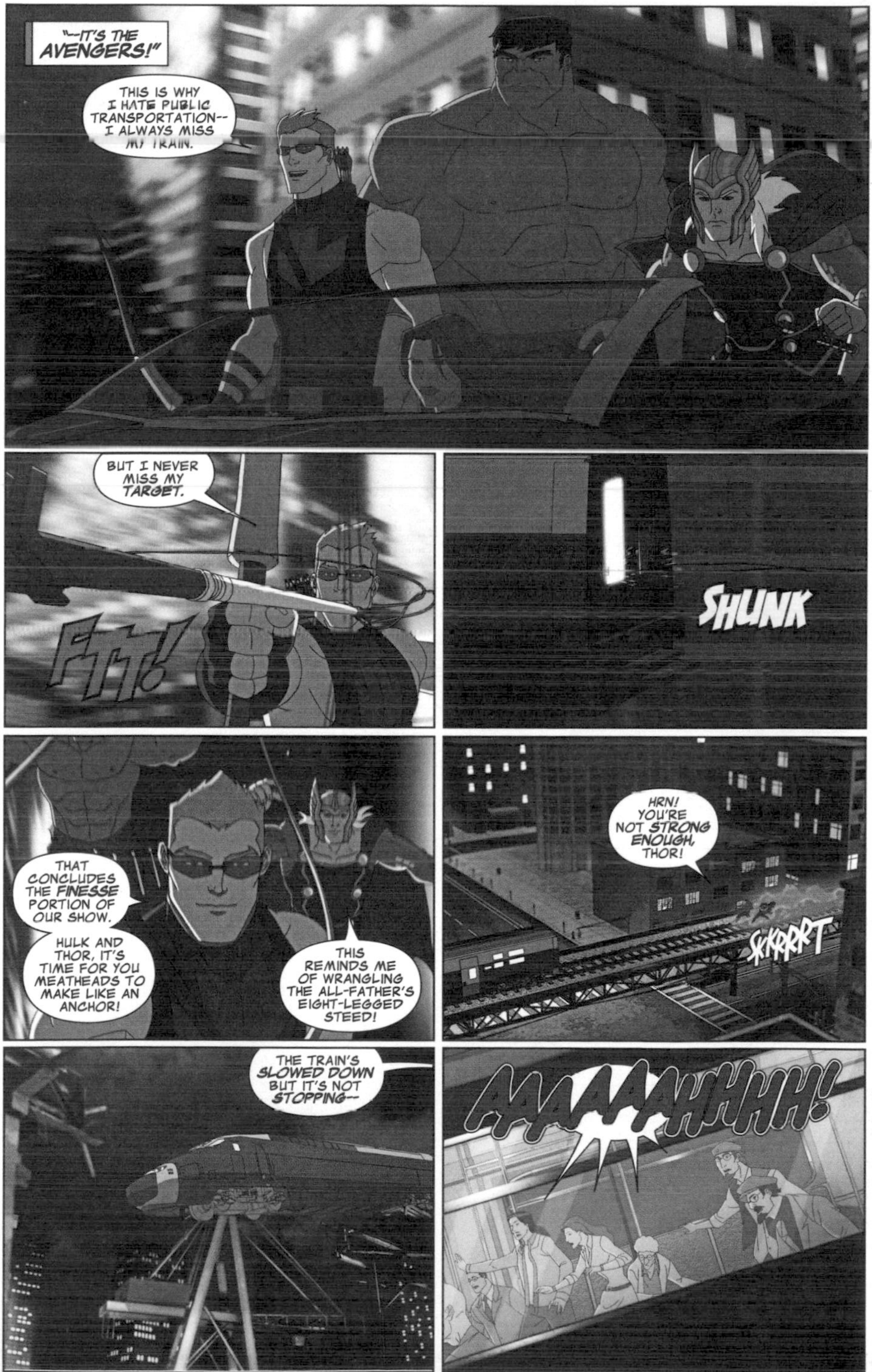
"--IT'S THE AVENGERS!"
THIS IS WHY I HATE PUBLIC TRANSPORTATION-- I ALWAYS MISS MY TRAIN.
BUT I NEVER MISS MY TARGET.
FTT!
SHUNK
THAT CONCLUDES THE FINESSE PORTION OF OUR SHOW.
HULK AND THOR, IT'S TIME FOR YOU MEATHEADS TO MAKE LIKE AN ANCHOR!
THIS REMINDS ME OF WRANGLING THE ALL-FATHER'S EIGHT-LEGGED STEED!
HRN! YOU'RE NOT STRONG ENOUGH, THOR!
SKKRRRT
THE TRAIN'S SLOWED DOWN BUT IT'S NOT STOPPING--
AAAAAAHHHHH!

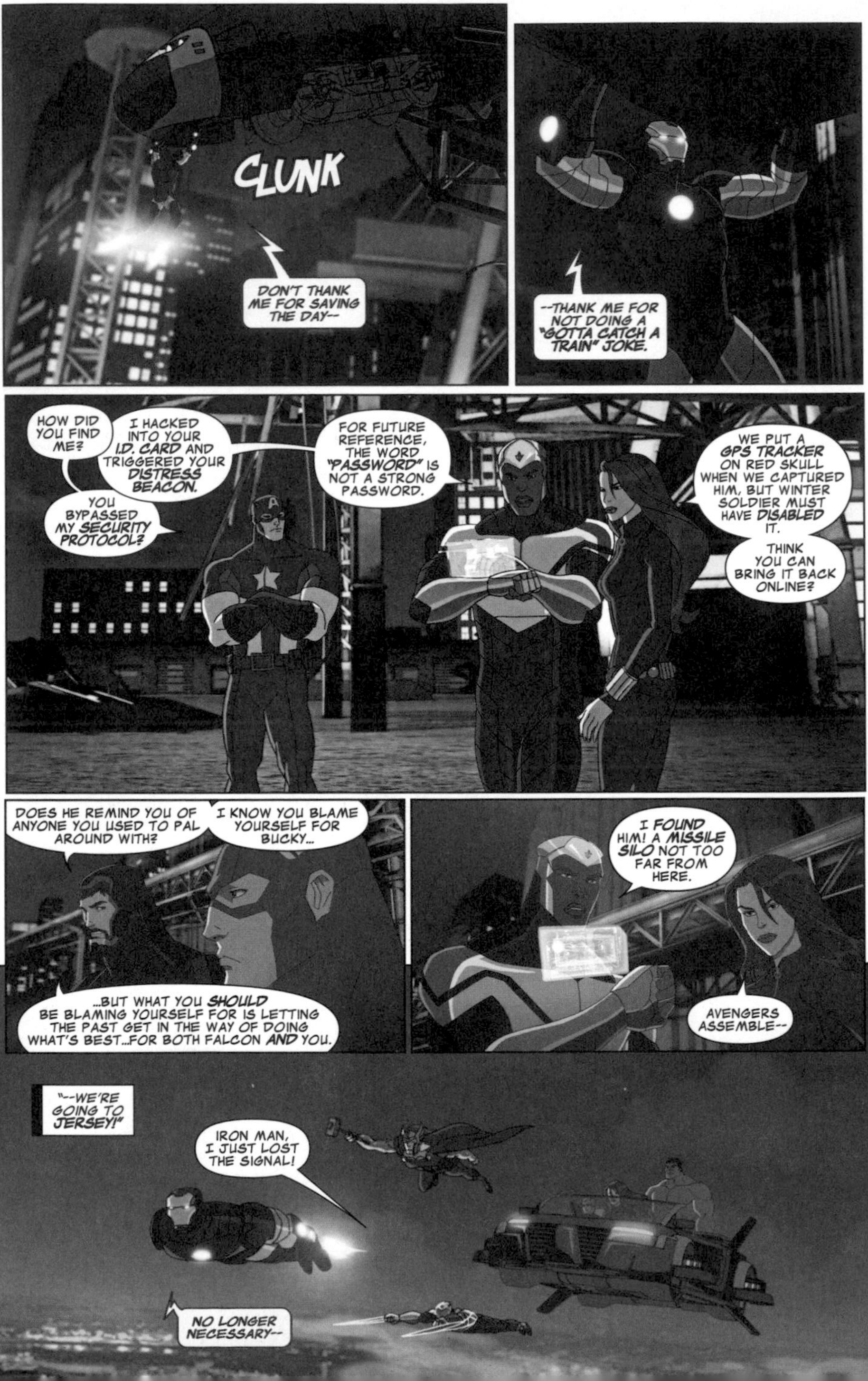
CLUNK
DON'T THANK ME FOR SAVING THE DAY--
--THANK ME FOR NOT DOING A "GOTTA CATCH A TRAIN" JOKE.
HOW DID YOU FIND ME?
I HACKED INTO YOUR I.D. CARD AND TRIGGERED YOUR DISTRESS BEACON.
YOU BYPASSED MY SECURITY PROTOCOL?
FOR FUTURE REFERENCE, THE WORD "PASSWORD" IS NOT A STRONG PASSWORD.
WE PUT A GPS TRACKER ON RED SKULL WHEN WE CAPTURED HIM, BUT WINTER SOLDIER MUST HAVE DISABLED IT.
THINK YOU CAN BRING IT BACK ONLINE?
DOES HE REMIND YOU OF ANYONE YOU USED TO PAL AROUND WITH?
I KNOW YOU BLAME YOURSELF FOR BUCKY...
...BUT WHAT YOU SHOULD BE BLAMING YOURSELF FOR IS LETTING THE PAST GET IN THE WAY OF DOING WHAT'S BEST...FOR BOTH FALCON AND YOU.
I FOUND HIM! A MISSILE SILO NOT TOO FAR FROM HERE.
AVENGERS ASSEMBLE--
"--WE'RE GOING TO JERSEY!"
IRON MAN, I JUST LOST THE SIGNAL!
NO LONGER NECESSARY--

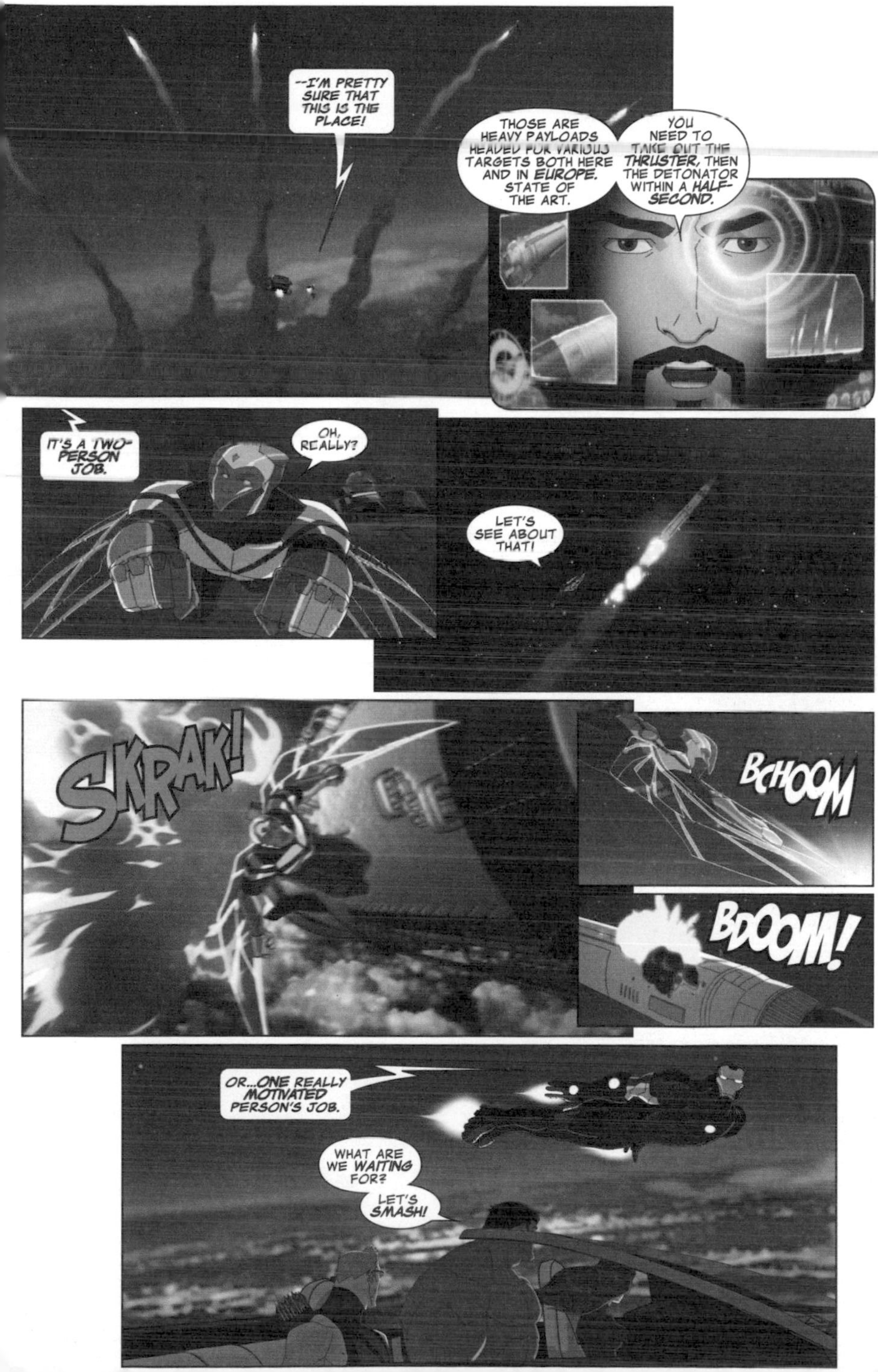
--I'M PRETTY SURE THAT THIS IS THE PLACE!
THOSE ARE HEAVY PAYLOADS HEADED FOR VARIOUS TARGETS BOTH HERE AND IN EUROPE. STATE OF THE ART.
YOU NEED TO TAKE OUT THE THRUSTER, THEN THE DETONATOR WITHIN A HALF-SECOND.
IT'S A TWO-PERSON JOB.
OH, REALLY?
LET'S SEE ABOUT THAT!
SKRAK!
BCHOOM
BDOOM!
OR...ONE REALLY MOTIVATED PERSON'S JOB.
WHAT ARE WE WAITING FOR?
LET'S SMASH!

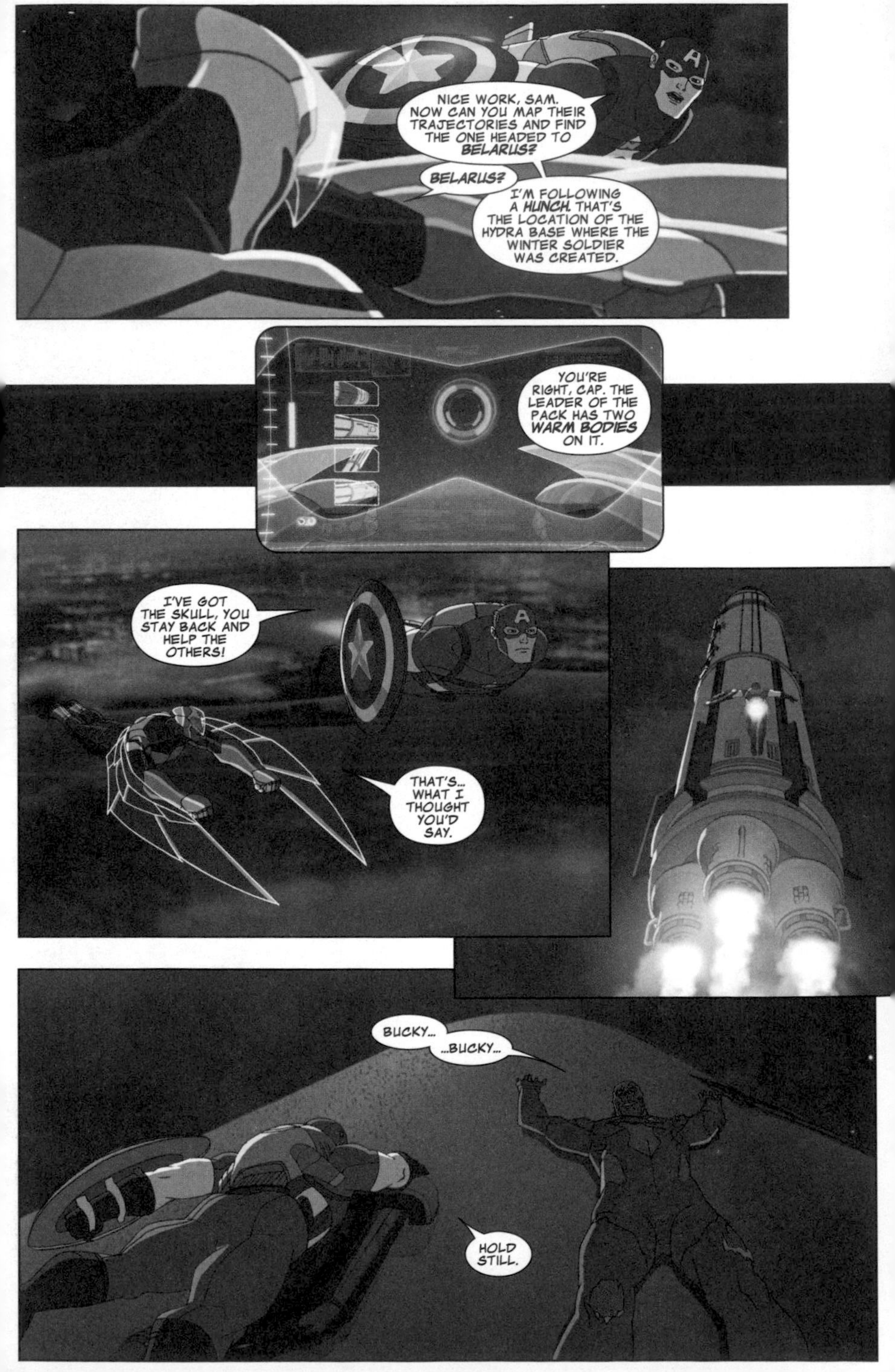
NICE WORK, SAM. NOW CAN YOU MAP THEIR TRAJECTORIES AND FIND THE ONE HEADED TO BELARUS?
BELARUS?
I'M FOLLOWING A HUNCH. THAT'S THE LOCATION OF THE HYDRA BASE WHERE THE WINTER SOLDIER WAS CREATED.
YOU'RE RIGHT, CAP. THE LEADER OF THE PACK HAS TWO WARM BODIES ON IT.
I'VE GOT THE SKULL, YOU STAY BACK AND HELP THE OTHERS!
THAT'S... WHAT I THOUGHT YOU'D SAY.
BUCKY...
...BUCKY...
HOLD STILL.

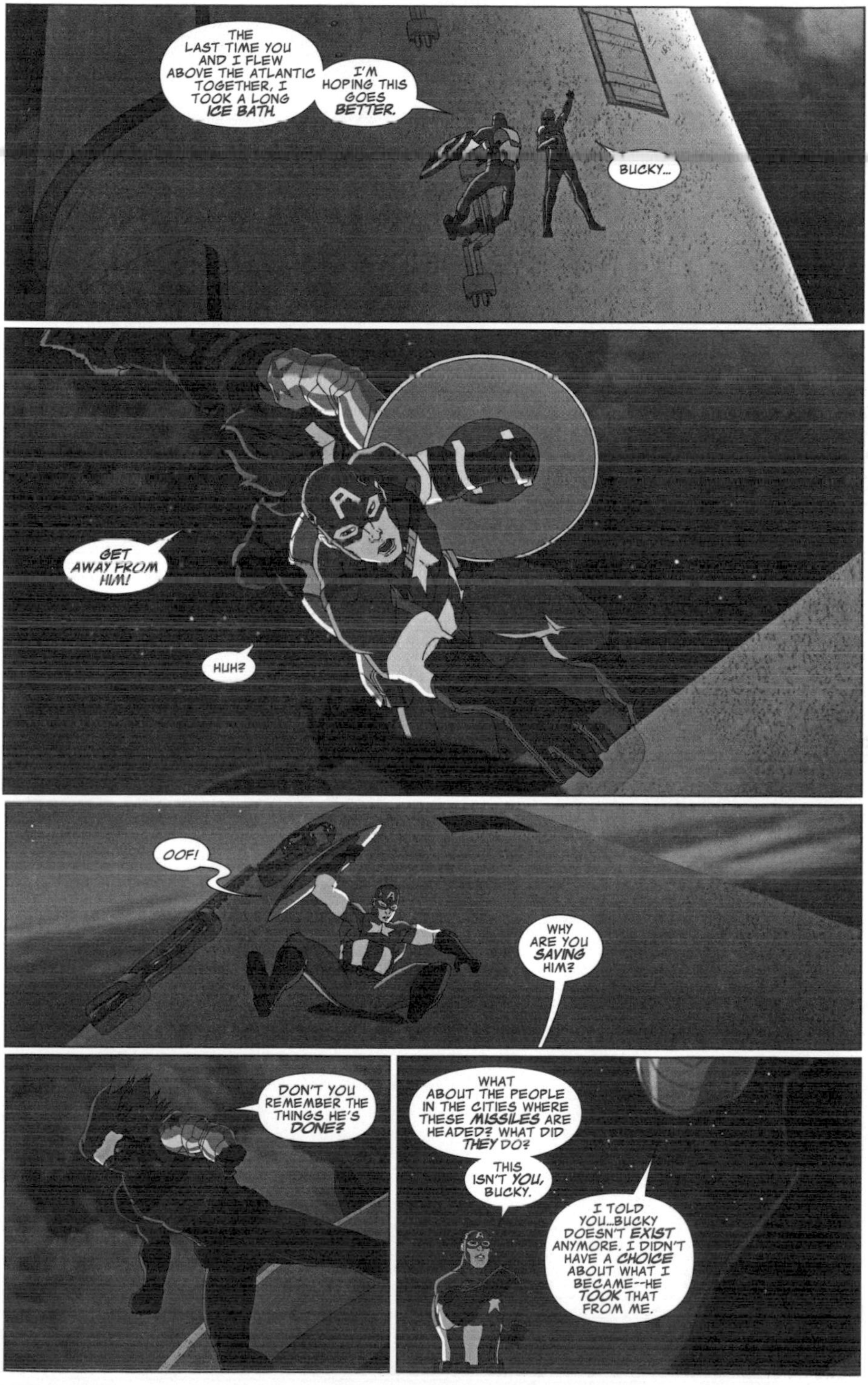
THE LAST TIME YOU AND I FLEW ABOVE THE ATLANTIC TOGETHER, I TOOK A LONG ICE BATH.
I'M HOPING THIS GOES BETTER.
BUCKY...
GET AWAY FROM HIM!
HUH?
OOF!
WHY ARE YOU SAVING HIM?
DON'T YOU REMEMBER THE THINGS HE'S DONE?
WHAT ABOUT THE PEOPLE IN THE CITIES WHERE THESE MISSILES ARE HEADED? WHAT DID THEY DO?
THIS ISN'T YOU, BUCKY.
I TOLD YOU...BUCKY DOESN'T EXIST ANYMORE. I DIDN'T HAVE A CHOICE ABOUT WHAT I BECAME--HE TOOK THAT FROM ME.

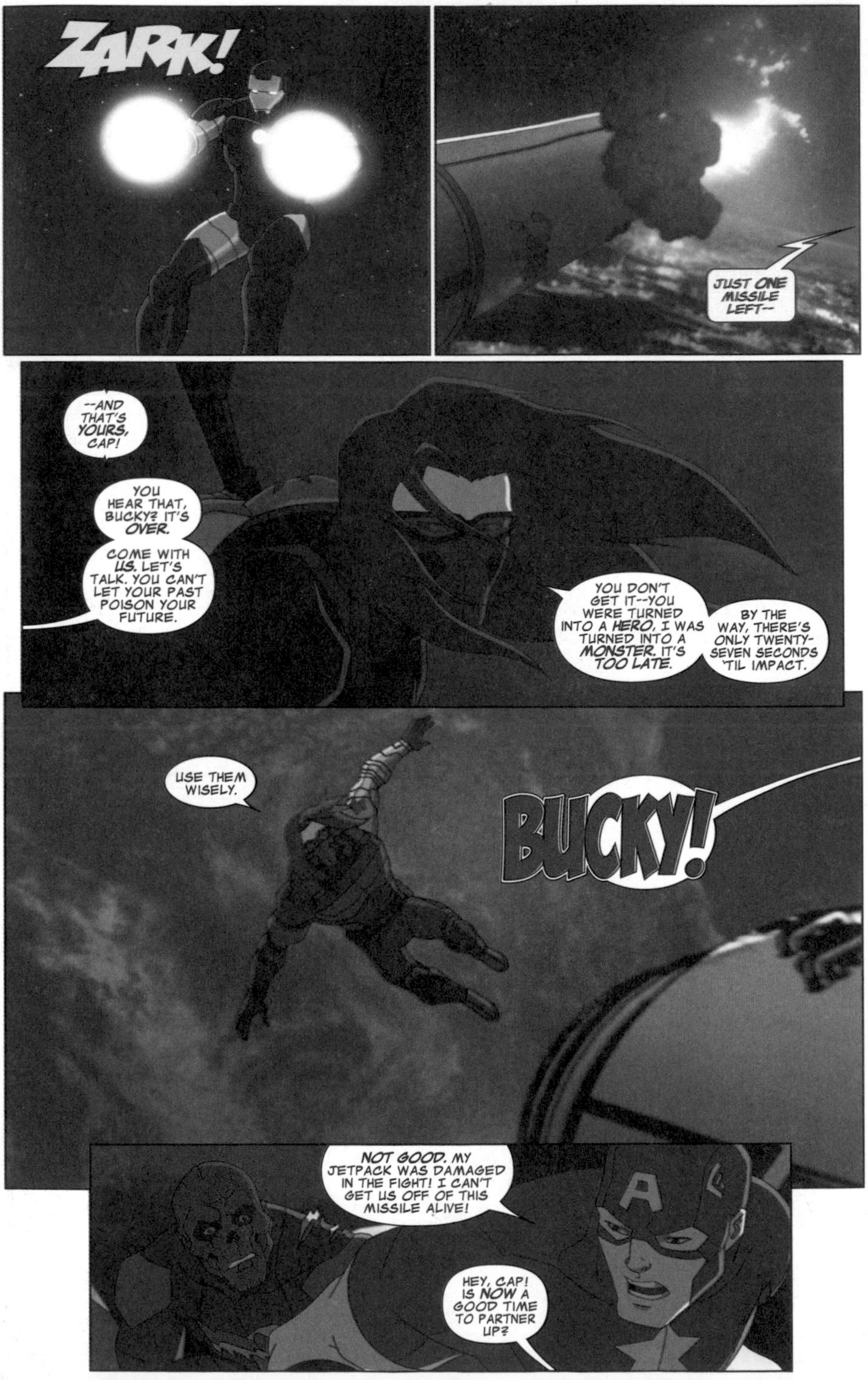
ZARK!
JUST ONE MISSILE LEFT--
--AND THAT'S YOURS, CAP!
YOU HEAR THAT, BUCKY? IT'S OVER.
COME WITH US. LET'S TALK. YOU CAN'T LET YOUR PAST POISON YOUR FUTURE.
YOU DON'T GET IT--YOU WERE TURNED INTO A HERO, I WAS TURNED INTO A MONSTER. IT'S TOO LATE.
BY THE WAY, THERE'S ONLY TWENTY-SEVEN SECONDS 'TIL IMPACT.
USE THEM WISELY.
BUCKY!
NOT GOOD. MY JETPACK WAS DAMAGED IN THE FIGHT! I CAN'T GET US OFF OF THIS MISSILE ALIVE!
HEY, CAP! IS NOW A GOOD TIME TO PARTNER UP?

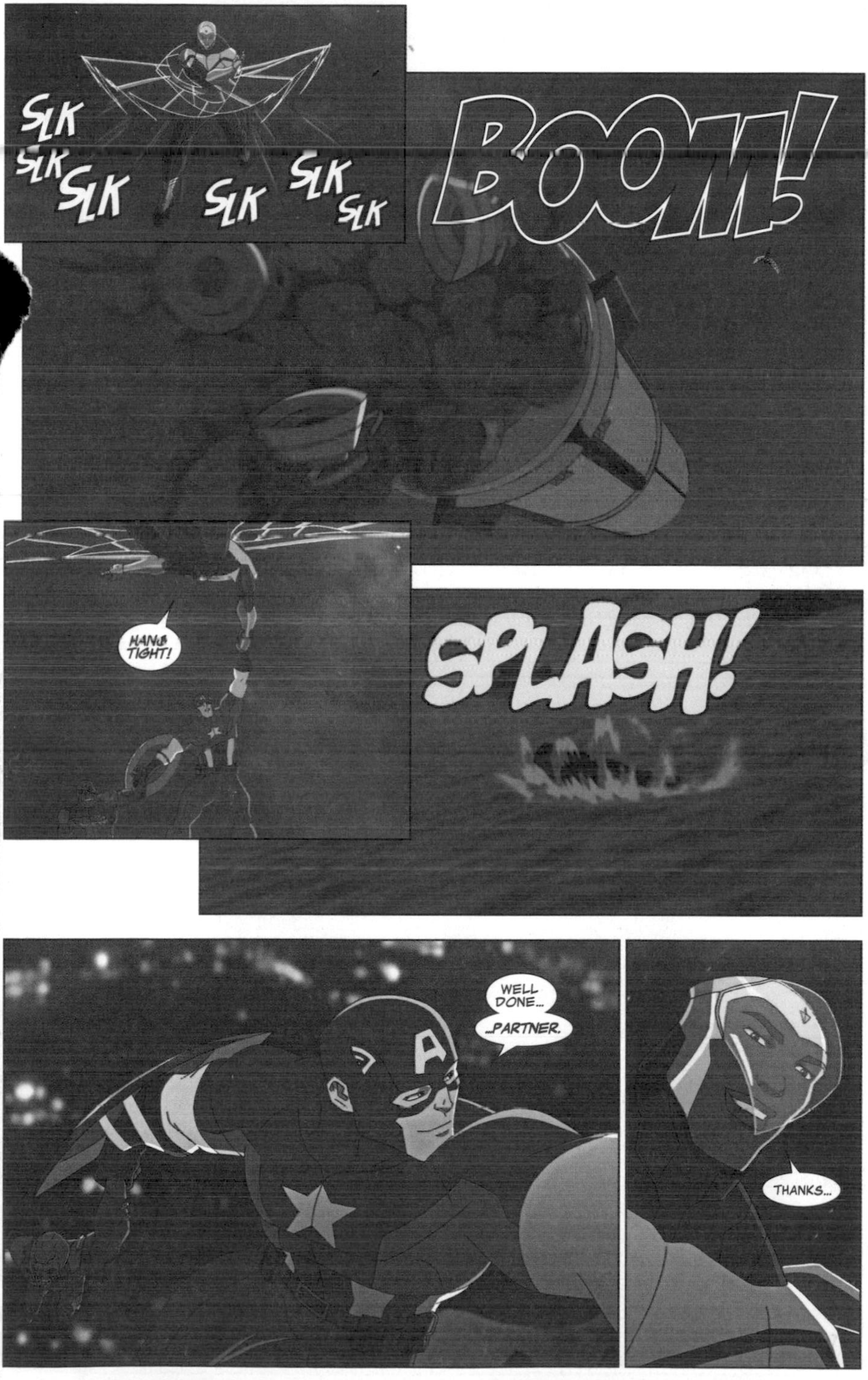
SLK
SLK
SLK
SLK
SLK
SLK
BOOM!
HANG TIGHT!
SPLASH!
WELL DONE...
...PARTNER.
THANKS...

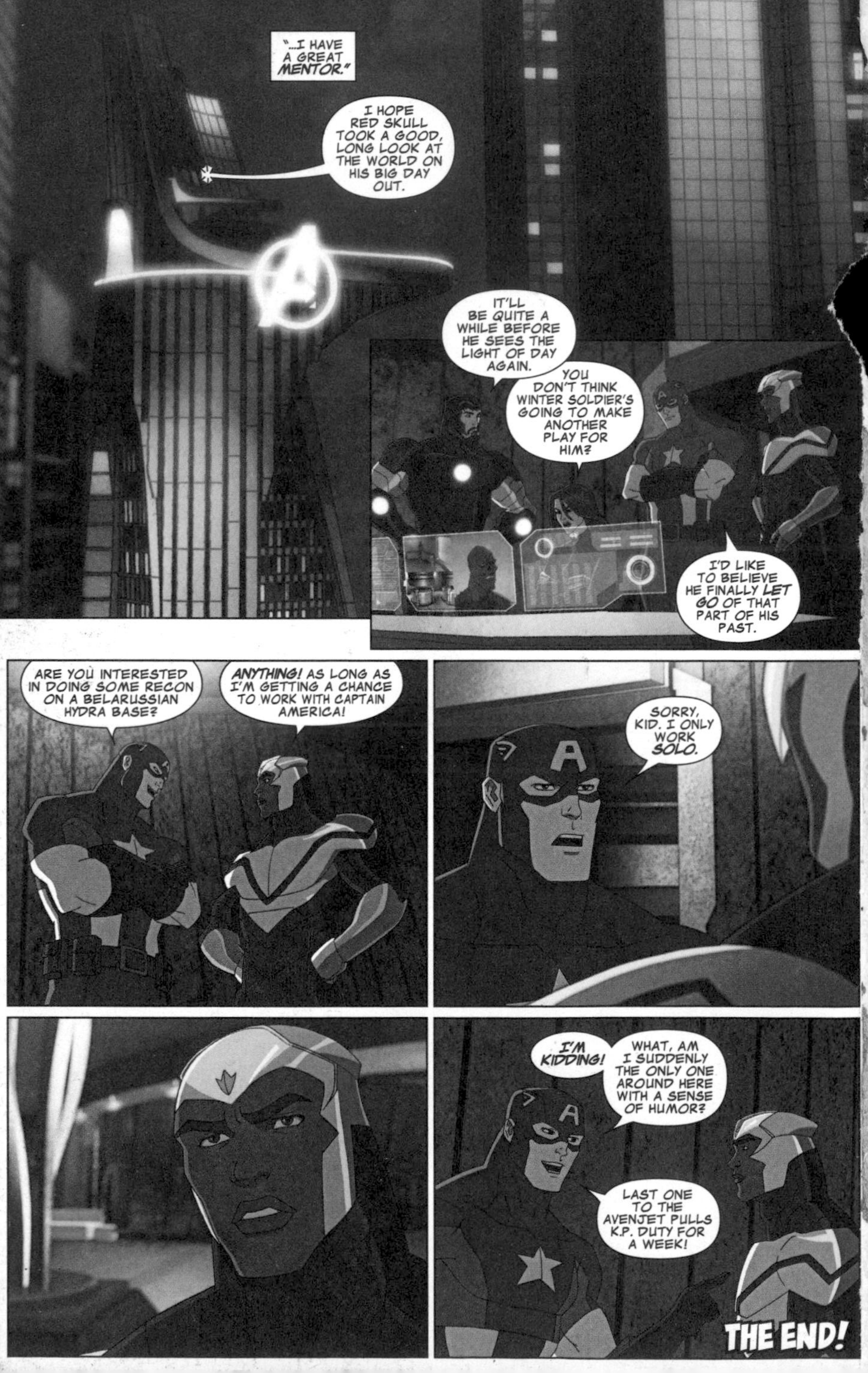
"...I HAVE A GREAT MENTOR."
I HOPE RED SKULL TOOK A GOOD, LONG LOOK AT THE WORLD ON HIS BIG DAY OUT.
IT'LL BE QUITE A WHILE BEFORE HE SEES THE LIGHT OF DAY AGAIN.
YOU DON'T THINK WINTER SOLDIER'S GOING TO MAKE ANOTHER PLAY FOR HIM?
I'D LIKE TO BELIEVE HE FINALLY LET GO OF THAT PART OF HIS PAST.
ARE YOU INTERESTED IN DOING SOME RECON ON A BELARUSSIAN HYDRA BASE?
ANYTHING! AS LONG AS I'M GETTING A CHANCE TO WORK WITH CAPTAIN AMERICA!
SORRY, KID. I ONLY WORK SOLO.
I'M KIDDING!
WHAT, AM I SUDDENLY THE ONLY ONE AROUND HERE WITH A SENSE OF HUMOR?
LAST ONE TO THE AVENJET PULLS K.P. DUTY FOR A WEEK!
THE END!